OVER THE FAERY HILL
MAGICAL MIDLIFE MISADVENTURES BOOK 1

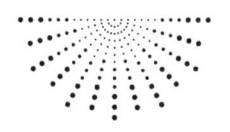

JENNIFER L. HART

ELEMENTS UNLEASHED

Copyright © 2021 by Elements Unleashed All rights reserved.

No part of this book may be reproduced in any form or by any electronic or mechanical means, including information storage and retrieval systems, without written permission from the author, except for the use of brief quotations in a book review.

This is a work of fiction. Names, characters, business, events and incidents are the products of the author's imagination. Any resemblance to actual persons, living or dead, or actual events is purely coincidental.

❦ Created with Vellum

OVER THE FAERY HILL

A MAGICAL MIDLIFE MISADVENTURE

Over the Faery Hill
Hart/ Jennifer L.

1.Women's—Fiction 2. North Carolina—Fiction 3. Paranormal—Fiction 4. Fae—Fiction 5. Time Travel—Fiction 6. Humor—Fiction 7. Small Towns—Fiction 8. Gymnastics—Fiction 9. American Humorous—Fiction 10.Mountain Living —Fiction 11. Divorce— Fiction 12. BBW—Fiction I. Title

ISBN 978-1-951215-50-7

OVER THE FAERY HILL

CHAPTER ONE

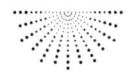

*"If its got tires or testicles, its gonna give you grief.
That's why I always neuter the dogs."
-Notable quotable from Grammy B*

"Joey, you're fired."

I stared over the paper-strewn desk to where my employer—now ex-employer—Rodney Carmichael squatted like a homely little toad. Surely, I had misheard what he just said.

"If this is about the plates that I broke last week, I told you I would pay for them." I pasted a smile on my face and tried to look like the epitome of an excellent waitress. "It was an accident."

Because my bad wrist had locked up at precisely the wrong moment when I had been transferring the stack of plates from the dishwasher to the service line. The crash heard 'round the mountain. As was the nature of small

Southern towns, my mother heard about it before my shift ended.

Rodney removed his glasses and polished them with the tail of his untucked shirt. "It isn't just that. You're always late—"

"My car got impounded. I had to use my mother's and it wouldn't start."

He sighed, effectively shutting off my protests. "And I've had complaints that you were rude to customers."

"They were jerks! They left me a twenty-seven-cent tip on a forty dollar bill!" And one of the boneheads had swatted me on the ass. Twice.

Rodney put his glasses down and just looked at me. Outside birds twittered in the trees, a promise of spring that was still a month and a half away. In the kitchen, I heard Steve say something to Amanda. The scent of homemade chili filled the space. Steve's chili was a local treasure, especially on a brisk winter day. I'd been looking forward to having it for lunch but my stomach had morphed into a ball of ice.

"Can I at least finish my shift?" I needed those flimsy tips if I ever wanted to see my beloved VW bug again.

Rodney shook his head and sighed as though he didn't have a choice and he was the misaligned party. "Greta is coming in to cover for you. Joey, I'm sorry. We gave it a shot. It just didn't work out."

I put up a hand. He could feign sympathy all he liked but that wouldn't change my reality.

That Joey Whitmore had been fired from yet another job.

Rodney handed me an envelope. "I wish you luck."

"Luck, right," I snorted. But I took the envelope. Pride wasn't a luxury I could afford.

Slowly, I rose to my feet and shuffled out of the office and into the hall closet where I'd stashed my purse, coat, and umbrella not even ten minutes ago. The mirror on the door presented me with my reflection. Gray roots showing about two inches long against my dark brown mop of hair because I hadn't had time to grab dye from the pharmacy. Crow's feet around my blue eyes. A big bump on my nose from where it had been broken at the same time as my wrist. A mouth that had forgotten how to smile. Sagging D cups, a midsection that looked like rising bread dough, and stretched the scoop neck t-shirt with the restaurant's logo. I felt a hundred years old, not the smidge past forty that I was.

Could humans age in dog years?

"Look at the bright side," I said then tried to find one. Nothing came to mind. "You can legally drink?"

There. Bright side. Nailed it.

I glanced back toward the kitchen where Amanda and Steve were busy with prep for the lunch rush. The factory across the road would be emptying out in fifteen minutes. All the hungry recycling workers would descend on the diner, which was little more than a greasy spoon for chili cheese dogs and pie to clog their arteries before returning to saving the planet one pickle jar at a time.

Not wanting to see their pity, I decided not to draw out a goodbye. I'd only worked at the place for three weeks. We weren't exactly lifelong chums.

After stuffing the envelope inside my coat pocket, I pushed out of the rear door to the small battered deck and down the three steps that led to the gravel parking lot. I didn't look back at the diner, didn't want to see the patrons eating in the big picture window. Happy people who would head home or back to work, who had lives that were moving steadily forward.

Mine seemed to be on a broken conveyer belt that no one made parts for anymore. Back home to mom's house with the unwelcome news that her divorced and damaged daughter would be crashing with her for another few months.

A chill that had nothing to do with the January mountain wind rolled through me at the thought of that conversation.

I unlocked the driver's side door to mom's ancient Buick, dropped my bag on the passenger's seat, and then inserted the key and turned.

Nothing. Not even any spluttering to indicate that the primeval engine was at least giving it the 'ol college try. I huffed out a breath and then gave it another go. Nada. Zip. Zilch.

I let loose on a string of cuss words that would make a sailor blush and pounded on the steering wheel hard enough to bruise my hand. My bad wrist sang out at the abuse and I slumped forward. Utterly defeated.

My luck. My shitty shitty luck had struck yet again.

Someone rapped on my window and I glanced up, startled.

Bright blue eyes stared down at me from a stranger's face. He wore battered jeans and a black and white checked flannel coat with a heavy lining to combat the winter chill. No hat or gloves. He must be a native. Odd that I had never seen him before. Our mountain town was tiny and I'd lived here all my life.

His expression read as concerned, though there lurked a twinkle of mischief in those eyes. He made a motion to indicate that I should roll down the car window. After a moment's hesitation, I did.

"Are you all right?" He spoke with a distinctly Welsh accent.

I started to laugh. One of those *I'm coming unhinged* sorts of sounds. I could only imagine what I looked like to him.

If I'd been Mr. Blue-eyes, I would have slowly backed away before turning tail and running for the nearest door in case the hysterical Buick driver went full-on looney tunes in the parking lot. But he simply waited for me to simmer down and respond like a human being.

I wiped away the tears along with a good portion of my eyeliner with the sleeve of my coat. "No, actually. I'm having a really terrible day and now my car won't start."

"Do you need me to call a tow truck?" the stranger offered.

I shook my head. "Not yet."

He dug around in his coat. "If you need a phone—"

But I held up a hand and tried to explain. "It isn't that. My ex owns the only tow truck in town."

"Ah, sorry to hear that." He flashed me a dazzling white smile that held a hint of something predatory. "Is there anything I can do to help?"

"You don't have the power to go back in time, do you?" I glowered at my wrist.

Instead of giving me the odd look my comment warranted, he crouched down beside the car. "And what if I did? Where would you go if you could travel through time?"

I leaned my head back against the seat. "October 3, 1996."

He quirked a brow. "That's…oddly specific."

"It's the day that changed my whole life." For the worse.

"Robin?" A twenty-something woman with perfect platinum blonde hair that hung midway down her back called.

I eyeballed the woman and then the guy crouched beside me. "She's a little young for you, isn't she?"

He tilted his head to the side. "You have no idea. But, it's not like that. I'm doing some work for her."

I held up a hand. "Then I *really* don't want to hear about it."

He laughed and then got back up, fished in his back pocket, and handed me a card. *Robin Goodfellow,* it read. That was all, just his name. Huh, why did that sound familiar? I was positive I hadn't seen him before. He was worth remembering.

The corner of his mouth hiked up and he nodded to the card. "That's good for three wishes if we can strike a deal."

I snorted, "You're a comedian."

His grin was infectious. "No, a fae prince. You ever want to bargain, give me a shout."

I watched him back away before my mind could comprehend another question.

He gave me a two-fingered salute and then escorted the blonde into the restaurant.

"What the hell was that?" I grumbled and then dialed the dreaded ex.

❄

When I'd told Robin Goodfellow that my ex drove the only tow truck in town, he probably hadn't pictured the elegantly dressed person sitting beside me.

Red nails tipped with gold sunbursts tapped against the steering wheel. "How have you been, Joey?"

I raised an eyebrow that was nowhere near as sculpted as my companion's. "Fine. And you…Georgia?"

Georgia—who had once been George, the human being who had promised to love, honor, and cherish me 'til death us do part, shrugged easily. As though this situation wasn't awkward as all get-out. "Can't complain. How's your mom?"

"Good. She's taken up sculpting." I didn't mention that all of mom's creations looked like penises. Not intentionally, I was sure. Mom was a dyed-in-the-wool feminist who had recently decided to express her creativity. I wasn't entirely sure that she had much creativity to express, hence the phallus factory. But it still seemed insensitive somehow to bring that up to Georgia.

"Sculpting. Huh. Wouldn't have thought that was her passion." The tow truck turned onto the gravel hill that dead-ended at my mother's Victorian.

"Mostly her passion is reserved for Wine Wednesdays."

"I hear that." Georgia laughed and I had to look away because it was so similar and yet so different from George's husky chuckle.

"I've missed hanging out with you, Joey." Georgia parked and then turned to face me. "Maybe we could get together some time?"

"Sure," I said but didn't mean it. We both knew it, too. I didn't want to hang out with Georgia, mostly because being with her reminded me of George. Who she wasn't. Not anymore. It was weird, like being a widow, even though my ex still lived and breathed and was kind to me and had better eyebrows. Better boobs too, because they would never fall down around her naval. I was happy for Georgia and a little bit in awe of her for fighting so hard to find her happiness.

Even if our marriage was collateral damage.

But all the dreams I had of us living happily ever after had gone up in a puff of smoke. And being with her reminded me how foolishly naive I had been. It was one thing to support transmen and transwomen. Right was right. Yet the part no one talked about was the discarded life that he or she had outgrown and slithered away from like an old snakeskin. That's how I felt when I was with Georgia—dry, brittle, and left on the side of the road to flake away to nothing.

And on that pleasant thought, I decided to make a graceful exit by popping the door and pasting on a faux pleasant smile. "How much do I owe you?"

Georgia waved it off. "No worries, Joey. I've got your back."

My smile turned genuine. "Thanks for that. I'll see you around."

No avoiding it in a mountain town the size of a flea circus. I wish I could afford to move. Then again, where would I go?

Slithering down to the curb, I picked my way past patches of melting snow, only turning to watch the tow truck and my mother's car disappear around the bend in the road. I strode up to the crumbling Victorian which had been my home since birth.

It, like me, had seen better days. The porch was starting to sag, the paint on the white gingerbread trim was peeling and most of the seals had failed in the stained-glass windows. Dented and dinged, it had always been there for me in my hour of need, a constant in a life full of variables.

I picked my way across the cracked and icy concrete and clomped up the steps, dislodging residual snow from my boots. The door was unlocked, which was usual during the days. In summer when the humidity hung in the air the door would be wide open, the battered screen pulled across to let in whatever breeze the mountain saw fit to give us.

After hanging my coat and shoulder bag on the coatrack that stood in a nook by the foot of the curving stairwell, I traipsed down past the living room and kitchen and around the corner to what had once been the conservatory. The door to mom's art studio was closed, the glass blocks long ago painted an opaque crimson. Music spilled from the speakers. Frankie Valli singing about how he couldn't take his eyes off some random broad who was just too good to be true. I shook my head and headed into the kitchen where the coffee pot never actually went off to grab myself a mug of comfort.

My favorite mug from the 1996 Olympic Games in Atlanta was in the dishwasher. I surveyed the other options and then decided that none would suffice. Not when I'd been fired and had to figure out some way to pay for mom's car repair.

Clean mug in hand, I filled the bugger to the tippy top, leaving just enough room for half and half and sugar. A survey of the fridge informed me that there was no half and half. No milk either. Both cartons stuck tauntingly from the trash proving that the house was lactose deficient.

Finally, I added a healthy—or rather unhealthy—dollop of French vanilla ice cream to the mug. About as close as I was going to get to a Starbucks anytime soon.

Coffee-cream in hand, I sat down to consider my financial situation. Maybe I could sell an organ on the black market. My liver was too pickled to be of value. Perhaps a kidney. Could you still drink coffee with only one kidney?

Frankie transitioned into Carol King's "It's Too Late," and then the Beach Boys, "Wouldn't It Be Nice," before the studio door opened and my mother breezed out.

No paint and clay smudged blue jeans for Prudence Whitmore. She wore a blue twinset over charcoal slacks and her shoulder length gray hair was twisted up in an elegant top knot. She sailed into the room and then blinked when she saw me at the table. "Joey? Didn't you have a shift today?"

I let out a sigh. "About that…." The words stuck in my throat.

No words were necessary. She shook her head and moved to the coffee pot. "You're too old for this pity party, Josephine Louise Whitmore."

I wanted to roll my eyes at her use of my full name but was afraid that I would only prove her point. "It's not like I was trying to get fired, Mom."

She put her hands on her narrow hips in her classic lecturing pose. "You know what your problem is?"

I nodded. "Yes, I am a forty-one-year-old divorcee with a bum wrist and no money."

She waved my injury away like it was inconsequential.

"These jobs are beneath you. I keep telling you to go back to school. Get a degree, start your own business."

Like it was that simple. Of course, to her, it was. For forty years, my mother had been the driving force behind the high country's tourism trade. Prudence Whitmore was a force of nature. A people person. A doer. Wherever she went, she made things happen.

"Doing what, Mom? I'm not like you. I don't have any hidden talents or unfulfilled passions. What you see is what you get."

She turned to face the snow-covered back garden. "I don't know where I went wrong with you. You used to have so much self-confidence. You believed in yourself. Didn't I always tell you that you could do anything?"

I pressed my lips together. Really, what was there to say? Here I sat in my mother's kitchen, a giant midlife disappointment.

Turning away from the window, she reached for her mug and belted back the dregs of her coffee like she was doing a tequila shooter. "Well anyway, I need to get going. Paul's taking me to dinner."

This time the eye roll couldn't be avoided. "You can just refer to him as Dad, Mom."

She sniffed. "We don't define ourselves by our relationship to you, Joey. We are autonomous human beings."

It was an old argument. My parents didn't believe in labels. Or marriage. Or living together. Though they still got together three or four times a week to go to dinner— which was also code for sex. I shuddered. No matter how unconventional their relationship, I didn't want to envision my mom and dad making the beast with two backs.

"Anyway, I have a hair appointment. I was going to call Louisa to drive me into town but since you're back, I won't bother. Car's all gassed up I presume?"

I scrunched up my nose, having forgotten about the car. "Yeah, that's the other thing."

Fifteen minutes later, I watched from the octagonal window in my bedroom as Louisa's red pick-up truck putt-putted up to the curb and my mother climbed inside. With her went the heavy cloud of disappointment that her middle-aged daughter couldn't get her act together. I took a deep breath for the first time since walking through the door.

My eyes slid shut and I was tempted to snuggle up on my window seat the way I had as a little girl in desperate need of comfort. The chenille cushions and padded bolster pillows were comfier than anything on my brass bed and the bench was long enough for my five-foot four-inch frame to curl in the fetal position. Instead, I turned away and retrieved my laptop before resettling myself in the window seat, tucking a bolster pillow behind my back for lumbar support. I was determined to find a job before my mother got home. *Any* job. I was past the point in life where I could afford to be picky.

Sadly, the want ads in the *Blue Mountain Times* weren't much more promising than they had been the last time I picked through them. To my dismay, I saw the listing was already up for my waitressing shift at the diner. Rodney the Toad wasn't wasting any time seeking my replacement.

I scrolled down through the listings, many of which were seasonal and wouldn't start back up until spring. All of the nearby ski resorts were full up and things like ziplining and rafting were definitely warm weather-based. Plus, with my bum wrist, it wasn't like I could tackle anything uber physical.

Story of my life.

Irritated, I snapped the laptop shut and stared out the window, massaging the ache in my wrist more out of habit than any real pain. My mother was right. At my age, not knowing what I wanted to be when I grew up was just plain sad.

Maybe because the one thing I had truly wanted to be had been taken away from me at sixteen. My gaze fell on the 1st place ribbons, the trophies and newspaper clippings on the built-in bookcase across the way. Artistic gymnastics, first place. Six years running. A photo of me in midair, doing a back handspring off the balance beam. The headline read —*Local gymnast is heading for Olympic glory.*

It had been more than hope though. It had been my whole life for as long as I could remember. Fate might as well have minced up to me, cracked her gum in my face, and said, "Sorry, Joey. No gold medal for you. How about a lifetime of scraping by instead?" I'd been groping for a purpose ever since.

My cell chirped, alerting me to a new text message. I dug it out of my pocket and looked down at the screen. It was from my bestie, Darcy Abrams. *Call me when you have a sec.*

I hit the green phone icon and held the device to my ear.

"No," Darcy barked in place of a greeting. "Parker Abrams, you take that pincushion out of your mouth this instant."

Darcy was the quintessential stay-at-home-mom with a side hustle. She was a whiz with a sewing machine and had translated her skills into creating custom outfits for dogs themed after book characters. Mr. Darcy for Dachshunds. Gandalf for Great Danes. Sherlock Holmes for Shih Tzus. It seemed like a real niche market to me but her Etsy store was going gang-busters.

The internet was a weird place.

Her home life was something of a disaster though, what with five boys under the age of ten, all of whom were home on a snow day. Between feeding, bathing, and keeping her kids alive and orders that needed to be made and shipped, my friend had a full and boisterous life. Sometimes I filled in watching the rugrats so she could fill her orders promptly.

"Joey, aren't you supposed to be at work?" Darcy asked when she finally refocused on the phone.

"Rodney let me go."

She made a sympathetic sound. "Margarita Monday?"

"Can you get away?" I asked as something on her end crashed.

"My mother-in-law is staying with us through next week," Darcy said through clenched teeth. "Mike owes me and I plan to take it out of him in girl-time."

"Sounds like a plan. Mom's going out. I've got the salt and limes if you bring the tequila."

"Can't wait. I need to get out of this zoo for a spell before I lose my ever-loving mind. No, Dylan! Take that back into the kitchen this minute!"

There was another crash and then Darcy sighed, "Joey, I've got to go. See you at seven."

"Looking forward to it," I said and then hung up.

Damn it, if Darcy could deal with that circus and make a buck there had to be some job that I could swing. I was a free agent and could come and go as I pleased.

With my resolve back in place, I opened the laptop and continued reading the want ads. I paused on an unusual one that I must have overlooked at first glance.

Assistant wanted immediately. Reliable person needed to help out with life coaching. Some nights and weekends. No experience necessary.

Life coaching. Huh. Didn't think that was something that would be lucrative around these parts. Then again, some weekenders and tourists might require such a thing. Last year we'd gotten our first Starbucks. They'd fired me already. So, I would probably be fetching coffee and sending emails for the life coach specialist.

I frowned at my bum wrist. Hopefully, there wouldn't be too much typing. I could handle a few emails and social media, but day-long typing wouldn't work.

After one more quick search through the listings, I decided that the assistant to the life coach was my best bet and dialed the number listed.

An automated message answered. *Hello. If you are interested in the assistant job, please come to 676 Firefly Lane to apply in person. Thank you.*

I raised a brow. Firefly Lane was a dirt road in the middle of nowhere. This job was sounding stranger and stranger.

What the hell. Even if the job didn't pan out, at least it was still Margarita Monday.

CHAPTER TWO

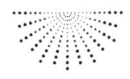

"Never a borrower or a lender be. Why? Because keeping track of stuff is a pain in the rump."
-Notable quotable from Grammy B

"Grammy?" I called as I walked into the front door of my grandmother's cottage that was two streets back from our own. "Are you here?"

Grammy B appeared wearing a powder blue tracksuit with white piping and pink fuzzy bedroom slippers. "Joey! What a nice surprise. And don't you look all gussied up?"

"Thanks." I had taken a hot bath and put on my best outfit. Tailored black slacks and a matching jacket topped a deep blue shell that matched my eyes. I'd even re-applied my make-up. Mascara and eye shadow made my eyes itch like the devil and peri-menopause hot flashes caused me to sweat foundation off, but anything to take a few years off my face. I had scrounged in my bathroom drawers and found a tinted lip balm to give my winter pale face a bit of color. My dark brown hair was still threaded with gray because I didn't have time or money to deal with it. I had spent a few moments pulling it back up into a French twist. Even though it was treacherous in the winter, I had dusted off my black heels, though I carried them. My feet were currently shod in my standard hiking boots and thick socks.

"So, what brings you here?" Grammy settled herself in her scuffed Lay-Z-Boy recliner and kicked up her feet, clad in socks that said, "Fuck off, I'm reading." Grammy didn't believe in beating around the bush.

"I was wondering if I could borrow Earl." Earl was my grandmother's ancient truck. It got about three miles to the gallon but it ran and I was out of options. "I know you don't like to loan him out, but I have a job interview and no other way to get there."

Grammy moved her dentures around as she considered my offer. "How about a trade? You make me some of those fancy apple oatmeal cookies of yours and I'll let you drive Earl as long as you want."

"Grammy," I sighed. "You know the doctor said you're supposed to cut back on sugar."

She waved me off. "Doctors, what do they know?"

"Um, a lot. Because they went to school for like a decade to become doctors."

"You know what your grandpappy used to say. You can send a monkey to college but all you get back is an educated monkey."

It was no use arguing with her. Grammy B was ninety-three years old and feisty as the day was long. She had a bit of country wisdom for every occasion and was more stubborn than any one person had a right to be. There was no changing her. She'd said once that the main benefit of aging was that you could speak your mind and not give a damn about who took offense. I was still waiting to crest that particular peak.

"One batch of cookies," I said, feeling like a bad granddaughter. Maybe I could call the doctor's office and ask about sugar alternatives.

She folded her hands, looking like the cat who'd gotten into the cream. "Keys are in the silver dish on the counter. And bring me my crossword. And a cup of tea."

"Thank you." I got up and headed into the kitchen.

The counters were all wiped down and the sink stood empty of dishes.

I raised my voice to make sure she heard me. "Grammy, did you eat today?"

A grunt was my only reply. I put the kettle on and then checked in the fridge to make sure that her milk hadn't gone bad and that she had plenty of meal options. Mom and I took turns cooking for Grammy and cleaning her house. It would have been easier to move her into the Victorian, but Grammy had set her foot down. She would live in her house until the undertaker carted her lifeless carcass away. Her words.

The kettle started to sing and I pulled out the mug she always used, plopped in a teabag, and filled it up to the three quarter mark. Letting it steep, I pulled a sugar-free banana nut muffin out of the freezer and popped it in the microwave to defrost. I added milk and then set the tea and warm muffin on a plate along with her crossword puzzle book and the glasses she was forever misplacing and carted the haul out to her.

"No butter?" Grammy frowned at the offered muffin.

I heaved out a sigh. "You need to cut back."

She *tisked* at me but removed the wrapper.

I kissed her wrinkled cheek. "Mom will be by after her date. Call if you need anything."

"More sugar in this tea," she hollered an instant before I scooted out the door.

I held the handrail and descended the steps that headed into the carport where Earl, the ugly old rust-bucket diesel, sat dripping oil on the concrete.

Grammy had a few containers of oil in the cabinet. I grabbed one, and then popped the hood, careful to stand far enough back so that my suit wouldn't get smudged. After adding the oil, I secured the hood, then snagged an extra container to take with me. I tossed it on the floor and then set my heels and shoulder bag on the seat beside me and cranked the old boy up.

Which sounds dirtier than it was.

The ancient engine rumbled to life like Frankenstein's monster. Within a minute, I backed Earl out of the driveway and headed for the hills.

"Okay, Joey Whitmore, why do you want to be an assistant to a life coach?" I asked myself as I navigated the twisty roads that led away from the center of town. I'd experienced enough job interviews to know that sincerity was more effective than lies that could trip me up.

"Well, I am a people person looking to expand out of her comfort zone," I said in my best interview voice.

"What would you say are your greatest skills?" faux interviewer Joey asked.

I took a moment for a deliberate pause to make the response sound less rehearsed. "I'm punctual,"— unless I was having car trouble— "organized, and a fast learner." All of that was true, if not the whole truth.

"Why did you leave your last position?" I asked in my detached interviewer tone.

The best technique for this loaded question. A classic serpentine followed by a bob and weave. "Foodservice isn't something I am passionate about. I'm looking for a place to shine."

My gaze cut to the rearview mirror and I nodded at the professional me. Nailed the sucker.

"Do you have any children?" I asked myself and, even knowing it was coming, couldn't stifle the flinch.

Damn it. That particular question popped up often. I needed to come up with a good way to answer it. To prospective employers, my single status meant my day wouldn't be interrupted by phone calls from schools or requests to leave early for dance recitals or soccer practice. To me, it always felt like admitting failure. I'd intended to have kids. And a husband. And a gold medal. Those things just weren't in the cards I'd been dealt though. What I had instead was crap luck. A bum wrist, an ex who probably looked better in a thong than I did, and a penchant for being fired. If you looked up "underachiever" in a dictionary, there would be a duck-faced selfie of me.

The pity party was getting ugly. Time to focus on the road ahead. Literally. Firefly Lane was a couple hundred feet up on the left.

Earl's left blinker was broken so I rolled the driver's side window down and stuck my arm out into the chill mountain air. Unnecessary as no one was coming, but the way my luck ran, if I didn't signal, that would be the moment a cop crested the hill.

The terrain turned steep almost immediately. Earl's diesel engine rumbled like a locomotive as we chugged ever so slowly uphill. The road narrowed to a single lane which Earl ate up like nobody's business. I hunched over the wheel, trying to see past the low hanging fir branches that hung even lower with heavy wet snow. The road was pitted with potholes and partially washed out. No signs of utility poles or chimney smoke. As far as I knew, no one lived this far from town. Strange spot for a life coach to set up shop. I hoped he or she wasn't some kind of hippy woo woo tree hugger that lived in a yurt. Frostbite wouldn't make for a pleasant working environment.

Then again, the views were incredible. I chanced a glance to my right. Through a gap in the trees there sat a jaw-dropping meadow. Slanted sunlight kissing rolling hills. A waterfall crested downward into an ice-encrusted pool. I couldn't hear the roar, not over Earl's grumbling engine, but I could feel the power of it—nature. Raw, untamed, wild. Having lived in the mountains all my life, I'd grown accustomed to breathtaking vistas as just part of the landscape but this was something special.

The trees swallowed the view and I could see the incline crested up ahead. The trees had thinned as well. There was the occasional pop of gravel. I saw two deer darting through the trees and they gave the truck a curious look. No sign of humanity or my potential job interview.

An unexpected bump in the road lifted my ass off the seat. I banged my head on the roof hard enough that I saw stars. Then Earl just…stopped. Like he had been caught in a great big butterfly net. The engine chugged once, twice, and then sputtered its last.

"Are you freaking *kidding* me?" I yelled. I'm not sure to who, maybe the universe. Earl was a behemoth, a beast. His engine was Hulk-smash strong.

And yet it had given up the ghost in the middle of nowhere.

My rotten luck had struck yet again.

Grammy B was going to kick my butt halfway down the mountain.

❄

MY SUIT WAS RUINED. Possibly my fingernails too as I'd been digging around in Earl's innards, trying to look for the reason why the big engine would have just died like that. No torn hoses, or leaks. No weird steam billowing out. The oil level was fine according to the dipstick. Plenty of gas. Of course, I wasn't a mechanic but I was putting off the inevitable—calling for a tow for the second time in a day.

Could Georgia's truck even make it up those series of switchbacks? Only one way to find out.

Not bothering to lower the hood, I used one of my grandpappy's handkerchiefs that Grammy kept in the glove box to root through my bag and extract my cell.

The face of it was blank. Weird, I didn't turn it off, did I? I depressed the power bar on the side and waited for the face to light up with a picture of me and Darcy, Margaritas in hand on her last birthday party. Nothing.

"Oh no," I breathed. "No no *no* no NO!"

But like Earl's engine, the battery was kaput. My heart thumped against my chest in a frantic tattoo and for a second, I wondered if I was gonna have a heart attack. That would be just my luck, wouldn't it? Fired, stranded at the ass-end of nowhere and cardiac arrest? Maybe my luck was trying to do me in.

I gripped the door of the truck and tried to focus on my breathing. "Okay, Joey. Don't panic. Analyze the situation from a place of reason. Consider your options."

I could hike back down the hill to the county road and flag down help. People knew me around town. Someone would stop and pick me up. My teeth chattered as I imagined that long, slow, slippery slog. The sun was already going down. No way I could make it before dark.

I could stay inside Earl. He blocked the wind at least. But the temperature was dropping. More snow had been predicted in the overnight forecast. Without heat, I would freeze.

My gaze lifted to the crest of the hill, about a hundred feet ahead. I'd come up the mountain for a job interview. That meant there must be someone up there. A person who presumably had a working vehicle and a functioning phone. Not that my current state was the best first impression for a potential employer. But compared with my other options, there really wasn't much of a choice.

I abandoned my heels but retrieved my purse and then closed Earl's hood and turned to tackle the hill. My grimy suit wasn't the best at cutting the winter gusts or for allowing freedom of movement but at least I had on good hiking boots. The wind tugged hair out of my twist. I swiped a hand over my face to get it out of my eyes, only after which I realized I had just probably smeared grease all over my cheek and forehead. Fan-frigging-tastic.

My breath puffed out in little white clouds as I slogged up the hill. Shouldn't have had that ice cream in my coffee. Or the second helping of Shepard's pie the night before. Or the big glass of red wine that I'd had with it.

Holy crap, was I ever out of shape.

"Diet. Starts. First. Thing. Tomorrow," I huffed as I slogged ever upwards. My Olympic hopeful self would have kicked my middle aged-kiester if she could see my sorry state. I was breathing so hard that I didn't notice the point when I crested the hill. I did however notice when the road came to an abrupt halt by dead-ending at a massive oak. I paused and took in my surroundings.

"Hello? Is anyone here?" I scanned frantically for any signs of human habitation but nothing. No vehicle, no cute little cottage, or newly finished mansion. At that point, I would have given my left boob for the dreaded yurt.

Was that want ad some sort of joke? If so, it might prove to be deadly.

"What sort of sick bastard—?"

"Hey, what's all the shrieking about?" A male voice said from above me.

I craned my neck and locked gazes with a pair of brilliant blue eyes for the second time that day. "Robin Goodfellow?"

"In the flesh." He smirked as though it was some sort of joke. He stood on a platform that jutted out from the trunk of the tree about thirty feet above my head and was leaning over the railing, peering down at me.

"Joey Whitmore, right? The woman who wants to change October 3rd, 1996. What are you doing here?"

Odd that he remembered the date. Then again, meeting me was probably the strangest part of his day. "My"–behemoth gas guzzler—"car died."

"I recall." The lines around his eyes crinkled with amusement. "You look cold. Hold on a sec, I'll be right down."

"Okay," I said because really, what else was I going to say?

The sound of footsteps came from *inside* the tree. And then a door shaped like an upside-down acorn that I hadn't even realized was there swung inward. He appeared, silhouetted by an amber glow. "Come on in."

Something was unsettling about Robin Goodfellow. He seemed amused like there was a private joke and he was the only one in on it. Deep-seated instinct warned that I would be an idiot to trust him.

"Where's your client from earlier? Is she here?" Maybe I wouldn't be alone with him.

He shook his head and his golden locks tussled in the breeze. "Nah, she had some stuff to work out at her place."

So much for that hope. "You said you were doing some work for her. Like, life-coaching work?"

A slow smile spread across his lips in a secretive grin. "In a manner of speaking."

I swallowed. If I had known that *he* was the life coach, I wouldn't have come. Good looking men unnerved me ever since high school....

I slammed the door on that train of thought.

But my situation was dire. I hadn't told anyone where I was going. Grammy knew I had Earl. Darcy would be looking for me for Margarita Monday. My mother might see my laptop was open and check to see what I had been looking at. They might piece my location together. With a dead cell phone, would they get the sheriff to track me before I froze into a human popsicle?

Then again, if Robin Goodfellow was some sort of weirdo serial killer that lived in a tree, they probably couldn't help me before he started making his woman-skin suit out of my hide.

A gust of icy wind from the north cut through my clothes and made the decision for me.

Feeling like the dumb broad in every horror movie I had ever seen, I crossed the threshold into the handsome stranger's treehouse.

As soon as the door shut, I felt immediately warmer. The cozy golden light spilled down from some unseen source. Before us sat a spiral staircase that seemed to be carved out of the tree itself. Like the inside of a lighthouse but made completely out of wood.

"Coffee? Tea?" Robin asked and turned toward the stairs.

"Anything hot." After a moment's hesitation, I followed him. In for a penny in for a pound.

He smirked at me over his shoulder as he trudged ever upward. "You know some males would make a lewd comment after a beautiful woman asked for anything hot."

"Some guys would get kicked in the balls for aforementioned lewd comment." I glared at him even as my heart pounded. Had he really called me beautiful?

No one ever had, except for my grandfather.

Robin laughed out loud. "Oh yes, I believe you'll do nicely."

All the hairs on my arms rose at that moment. "Do for what? The life coach assistant position?"

He didn't answer, just held back a curtain that appeared to be formed from strands of twinkling lights and freshly fallen autumn leaves to reveal the room beyond.

And woah baby, what a room.

Everything was made from wood. A live oak table with matching chairs. The couch and counters. The open shelving in the kitchen held wooden plates and mugs. Even the mantlepiece over the stone fireplace. No sign of a fridge or a stove or dishwasher. Perhaps they were hidden behind the glorious cabinets.

I spun in a slow circle, trying to take it all in. "This is incredible. The detail work. It looks as though someone carved all of this out of the tree. And it was so well camouflaged."

He shrugged. "It's home. Go stand by the fire and warm up while I fetch your something hot." He put a gentle hand on my back and urged me toward the massive fireplace. I jumped at the touch, startled at the heat that seemed to seep from him, through my clothes and into my skin.

Without any hesitation, I went, holding out my hands and soaking in the warmth and wondered about the house. Why had I never heard about the construction of this place? It seemed like something that the town would have been talking about for months, if not years. Every detail was flawless.

Still no sign of the light source. No television or tablet sat on the wood table. Another of those leaf and light curtains covered an opening on the far side of the room. His bedroom perhaps?

And you have no business thinking about his bedroom. I firmly told my lusty hormones.

"Here you go." Robin handed me a wooden mug and gestured toward the chair that looked as though it had been dug out with a massive sweep gouge by a giant-sized whittler. "Have a seat. And let's talk terms."

I hadn't heard a kettle whistle or the ding of a microwave. Yet the heat from the steaming mug seeped into my palms. I settled on the whittled chair, which was surprisingly comfortable for such a hard surface. It was almost as if it had been carved exactly for my body. "Terms for employment do you mean? I came because of the want-ad for the assistant to the life coach."

Robin lowered himself onto the couch and raised both eyebrows. "And do you feel like you are in a position to help others because your life is going the way you want it to?"

I set the mug down on a low side table and straightened my shoulders. Stick to the truth. "Is my life perfect? No. But I get up every day and I try harder than I did the day before."

"Do you though?" Those blue eyes seemed to sparkle like polished sapphires. "Do you embrace every moment?"

I opened my mouth, then closed it again. No lying. "No, I don't suppose I do."

He leaned forward his expression intent. "And what would you trade for the chance to redo it all?"

I frowned. "I'm not sure what you're getting at."

His fingers steepled together and he said, "I'm not looking for an assistant. The position is one of great opportunity."

Was this the part where he asked for money? Figured, the whole beautiful compliment was just his way of buttering me up. "Look, I'm not doing one of those pyramid scheme things—"

He held up a hand, effectively cutting me off. "Nothing like that. What I need from you, Joey, is a favor. You make a commitment for one open-ended favor to me. Anything I require in the future within your ability to give it. And in return, I'll grant you the chance to change your life."

"Or my money back?" I raised a brow.

He waved it away. "No money will change hands in this bargain. I have no use for it."

"Yeah, right." I rolled my eyes. Who didn't need money? What about food? Electricity? Taxes, for crying out loud. "So, this isn't an actual job."

"It's an *opportunity*. To alter the course of your life and reshape the person you are today."

He was a hell of a salesman. I had to give it to him. "How?"

"You'll become your own faery godmother."

I blinked. "Excuse me?"

"You, Joey Whitmore, will go back in time. Imagine it. A shot to change the course of your destiny. You already named one date in your past that you want to change. I'm sure there are others."

He was insane. All that much scarier because he looked as though he believed the crazy words coming out of his mouth.

My tongue darted out and I licked my lips nervously. "I should probably be going." I rose, eager to get away from the handsome and mentally unstable person.

He stood and blocked my path. A jolt of apprehension went through me but he didn't touch me, just held my gaze. "Ask me how I made the tea."

"Did you put something in it?" Thank God I hadn't drunk any of it.

"Just water and tea leaves. But ask me how I heated the water."

I huffed out a breath, "I don't see how that matters but I'll bite. How did you make the tea, Robin?"

"With magic." He held out his hand. I stared as the same amber light that illuminated the house filtered from his palm. There were flecks of gold and a yellow so pale it was almost white. It looked like something out of the movies. Except it was happening right before my eyes sans the special effects department.

My lips parted and with a shaking hand, I reached forward. "How…?"

"You said your car died. How about your cell phone? Smartwatch?"

I shook my head, my gaze glued to his hand. "No smartwatch. But yeah, my phone crapped out."

"That's because human technology can't function in the presence of true magic. Magic shorts it out."

"Like an EMP?"

The corner of his mouth kicked up and his brilliant sapphire eyes reflected the glowing amber light in his palm. "Sort of."

I sank back down onto the chair. "But magic isn't real."

"Oh, it's very real, Joey." He closed his palm and the magic winked out. "People don't want to believe magic is real because most of them will never be able to control it. And control matters to people. But magic is real and I can teach you how to use it."

I shook my head. There had to be an explanation for all this. Maybe I'd hit my head harder than I thought. Maybe I'd knocked myself unconscious and it was all some elaborate dream brought on by too much ice cream in my coffee.

"Don't you want that chance?" Robin raised an eyebrow. "To save yourself the pain? To teach yourself how to be better?"

"In exchange for some open-ended favor," I snipped.

"Don't think about the favor. Think about how you could make a difference. Not just in your own life but in the lives of those you love. Friends. Family. The sky's the limit." He crouched down so we were once again eye to eye. "Magic is the key to all of it, Joey. And I am offering you the chance of a lifetime. No more regrets."

He put his hand on my knee. I jumped at the touch, the heat of his palm. It was an oddly intimate touch. Then again this was the strangest interview that wasn't an interview but an opportunity for personal growth I had ever been on. My heart thudded against my ribs. I felt strange, almost giddy.

"I need to go." I blinked, shaking off my stupor.

"Think about it," he said. "I'll be in touch with you soon."

He rose and I missed the feel of his hand. Then shook myself. Magic was real. And I was almost sure he had put a spell on me.

"Joey?"

"I feel strange," I muttered. The room started to spin. My vision tunneled to a pinprick and the last thing I heard was the sound of his laughter.

CHAPTER THREE

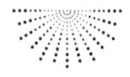

*"Never trust a wolf in sheep's clothing. Or a wolf in wolf's clothing.
A predator's a predator no matter what covers his backside."*
-Notable quotable from Grammy B.

"Joey? Hey! Let me in. It's colder than a pair of witch's britches out here!" Darcy's frantic knocking pulled me back to consciousness. I blinked and then pushed myself up off the fainting couch in the parlor and stumbled to the front door.

"Well, don't you just look like something the cat dragged in?" She thrust a full bottle of Jose Cuervo into my arms and then proceeded to unwind her scarf. "Rough day?"

I put out a hand to steady myself because, for some odd reason, the room was spinning. "Let's put it this way, getting fired was the high point."

"Yowch." Darcy hung her parka and scarf on the antique hall tree, toed off her outdoor boots, and then slipped on her ballet flats before retrieving the bottle of booze. "Well, just

FYI, the whole damn town is talking about you. Merna Fleming was in line in front of me at the grocery store and I heard her tell Doris Leech that she saw you leave the café before the lunch rush. And then I ran into Brandie Rutgers at the post office and she said Rodney Carmichael called the paper and put out a help wanted ad online. Want me to mince on down there and give him a knee to the old bait and tackle?"

She'd do it, too. Darcy was one of those short, blonde feisty types that got things done. No one ever saw her as a threat. Between her diminutive stature and preference for wearing pastels, she was the quintessential killer bunny rabbit. Maybe her way of busting balls first and taking no prisoners was not always the most diplomatic way possible, but I appreciated her loyalty.

Slowly, so as not to exacerbate the dull ache in my temples, I shook my head. "I don't want to have to bake a cake with a nail file in it when you get yourself locked up for assault and battery."

"So, are we gonna just fart around all night or are we gonna get our drink on?" Darcy didn't wait for me to respond. She knew where we kept the goods and headed down the hallway to the kitchen. "Although from the looks of you, I'm guessing maybe you started without me?"

"What are you talking a—?" My reflection in the hall mirror stole the rest of the question directly out of my mind. It was a ghastly sight. Hair disheveled, grease smeared across my forehead and down my nose. Pants cuffs covered in mud almost up to my knees.

Wait, why was I wearing my interview suit?

It came back to me in a rush. Looking for a job online, borrowing Earl, getting stranded on Firefly Lane. The truck dying and my cell being dead.

How much of it had been real? I studied my ruined suit.

So okay, I had obviously gone up to Firefly Lane and Earl had pooped out. And then…?

Magic. A house carved out of a tree. Robin Goodfellow—where did I know that name from—offering me a chance to be my own faery godmother.

But how had I gotten home?

The whirr of the blender pulled me out of my recollections and I stumbled into the kitchen.

Darcy paused the blender. "Salt?"

I pointed to the cabinet above the stove. Had it all been a dream? That would explain the magic and the fact that I had woken up on the couch. But not the suit. Or the mud.

Then it hit me. "Earl!"

"Who's Earl?" Darcy made a hop and missed the salt by three inches. "Damn it all, people were my height when they built this house and I still can't reach the top shelf. Little help?"

I moved to the stove and retrieved the salt. "Earl is Grammy B's diesel truck. I drove him to what I thought was a job interview."

And Earl's location would let me know if my trip to Firefly Lane had been real or just a figment of my imagination.

I reached for the phone and dialed Grammy B.

"Hello?" She croaked into the receiver.

"Grammy, it's Joey. Listen, did you see me drive Earl back to your house?"

"Sure did and I thought it was mighty strange that you didn't stop in to tell me how your interview went." She sounded hurt.

I gripped the phone until my knuckles turned white. I had no memory between drifting off at Robin Goodfellow's house and waking up on the couch. But Grammy had seen me.

Grammy cleared her throat. "Joey gal? You all right?"

"Sorry, Grammy. Yeah, I'm fine. Interview was…odd. I'll be by with cookies first thing tomorrow."

"What was that all about?" Darcy had moved on to rimming the margarita glasses with lime juice. "You had an interview already? Oh, tell me it's not for the Waffle Hut. You know they were shut down by the sanitation department again."

I shook my head. "No, not the Hut. And you really need to stop eating there."

"It's the only place that serves food all my kids will eat. Mike says what doesn't kill them will make them stronger." Turning the prepped margarita glass upside down, she swirled the edge into the salt and then handed it to me. "Okay, so you were saying you had a job interview and you borrowed Grammy B's truck to get there. What was the job for anyway?"

I took the green slush-filled blender and filled my glass with margarita and then topped off the one she held out to me. "Assistant life coach."

Darcy had just lifted her margarita to her lips but she lowered it again. "You're damn lucky that I hadn't drunk any of this down yet or there would have been a big old comical spit-take. Which is less funny as an adult and you know how much a fifth of this stuff goes for. What on Earth would compel you to think you could be a life coach?"

I narrowed my eyes on her. "I could totally be a life coach."

"Yeah, okay." Darcy shook her head and sipped her drink.

"Well, not without training obviously, but I mean, that's why I wanted to be the assistant to the life coach. To get trained."

"Joey, how long have we been friends?" Darcy set her margarita down so I knew she meant business.

"Since the first day of tumbling camp before Kindergarten." We'd both taken to the mat with unbridled enthusiasm. Me, because I loved the act of bending and moving my body in all sorts of ways. Darcy because she liked rolling into other kids and knocking them down.

She shut one eye and held her drink up to me. "Right. I was there when you got your first rip from overworking on the uneven bars. I was there when you did your all-around routine. I was there when your period started and you freaked out because your mama's version of the birds and the bees talk was too focused on female empowerment and less on the nuts and bolts of how to handle yourself. I was there when you wanted to date that awful jackass Bill Tucker in high school and he didn't know you existed. I was there when you got married and I was there when you signed divorce papers and when your grandfather died. So, for argument's sake, let's call me an expert on Joey Whitmore."

I huffed out a breath. "Fine, you're the expert. You really should have been a lawyer."

She perched on a barstool and crossed her legs. "We're on you right now. And as an expert on Joey Whitmore, I know that the idea of working with a life coach was not one that organically entered your brain. Something sent you careening towards it."

I raised a brow. "You mean something other than the lack of decent jobs in this town?"

She waved that away as though my objection was irrelevant. "You could work with me."

I sighed. "Baby-sitting your kids on snow days does not constitute full-time employment."

Darcy took another sip of her margarita. "This have something to do with seeing Georgia?"

No use asking how she knew. If she had been to the supermarket and the post office, someone would have told her that Georgia had been towing my mother's car out of the parking lot. "It's just…I envy her. George knew what he wanted and went after it no matter how strange it sounded to the people around here. And then my mother came home and was on a tear about me finding direction and when I saw that want ad, I just thought…." I trailed off, unwilling to admit the truth.

"Thought what?" Darcy prompted.

I drew my finger through the condensation on the outside of the glass. "Thought that maybe if I did something a little off-beat it would help me reignite my spark."

Darcy's thin blond brows pulled together. "When you say your spark…?"

Frustrated, I threw my hands up in the air. "You know, that something special feeling. A zest for life. I can't remember the last time I had that."

We sat in silence for a moment.

Then Darcy reached for the pitcher and refilled both our glasses. "You know all you need is a really good vibrator."

I rolled my eyes. "Seriously? I tell you I have no zest for life and you tell me to get a sex toy?"

"Well, I'd tell you to get a man but you never have been good with the catch and release thing. Next thing you'd be cooking his meals and washing his skid-marked skivvies right alongside Grammy B's."

A laugh bubbled out of me. "Grammy B does her own laundry and I doubt she has skid marks."

"Right, because that's apparently a Y chromosome thing." Darcy shuddered. "I have six guys in my family and the proof is in the bacon strip."

Tears were starting to form. "You know these are things I can't unhear."

Darcy snapped her fingers. "Hey, I know how we can find out for sure. Let's ask Georgia."

"Ask Georgia what?"

"That should be proof if it's in the chromosomes or not. Because she was a man and is now a woman. We could answer the age-old question."

My mouth fell open. "You seriously want to call my ex and find out if she still has skid marks?"

"What? Is that taboo?" Darcy shrugged. "Okay forget I mentioned it."

"I will be struggling to do just that for the rest of my natural life," I vowed.

"Or until the next time I'm full of tequila and sage advice." Darcy held up her margarita and we clinked glasses.

※

I HAD to call Darcy's husband Mike to come to pick her up. As Margarita Monday was a regular occasion, he was expecting the call and made it in record time.

"He doesn't want to be alone with his mother any more than I do." Darcy hiccupped as I helped bundle her into her coat. "That and tequila makes my clothes fall off."

"It's definitely one of those. Good night, you crazy lush. Have some good sex for all of us who aren't getting any."

She threw off a jaunty salute. "Aye aye. It's a dirty job but someone has to do it."

I hugged her and then watched her pick her way down the steps. The buzz was still with me but without Darcy's overwhelming presence the big Victorian felt empty.

Chilled, I headed upstairs and into my bathroom. It was a study in black and white old-world elegance. Black tile, white toilet, and pedestal sink that was shaped like a scallop. A massive white claw-footed tub. I had a little wooden bath tray that my grandfather had carved for me that held a book, a candle, and a container of bath salts.

Looking at it made me think about Robin Goodfellow's hewn treehouse. I turned my back on it and filled the tub and then stripped off my mud-stained clothes. After pouring in a generous dollop of bubble bath, I stepped into the tub and then closed my eyes, letting my mind drift along with the white noise from the water flowing from the tap.

When the water reached the tippy top, I used a toe to shut it off and then leaned back with a contented sigh.

"Thinking about me?" A male voice purred.

I jumped and water sloshed over the edge of the tub and onto the white fur bathmat. Instinct propelled me to cover my breasts from his intense blue gaze, but the movement was unnecessary as the bubbles preserved my modesty. Still, I wasn't used to an audience while bathing.

"What the hell are you doing here?" I barked.

Perched on the edge of the tub like he had done so a thousand times before, sat Robin Goodfellow. "Waiting for you to come back to your senses. But then your friend showed up and your conversation with her was too delicious. As is this margarita. Anything special you use?" He held up one of the abandoned glasses, once more filled to the brim.

"Extra lime and a little bit of agave," I said, unnerved that he was in my space while I was naked. "What did you mean when you said you'd been here all along? I didn't see you."

"Ah, it's one of my little tricks. I can change my form, and even shrink down to the size of a pinhead if I want. Though some things stay proportional, no matter what size I am, if you get my meaning." He waggled his eyebrows suggestively.

My face blazed with heat. "That was a very private and personal conversation you eavesdropped on."

"I *know*." He grinned, completely unashamed. "I like your friend. She has some interesting ideas."

Suddenly his voice changed into Darcy's high-pitched Southern drawl. "And why the hell has no one invented a

Bluetooth vibrator yet? There's a command function that would get used constantly. Alexa, get me off and take the scenic route." He chuckled and his voice returned to his normal deep drawl. "I can't say she's wrong."

My body was so flushed with heat I was worried I might spontaneously combust. I pointed to the door. "Out. Get out."

"Not until we talk, lamb. Have you given any further thought to my offer?"

"No. I thought you were a figment of my imagination until you popped in here." Which reminded me. "Did you drug me with something? Why can't I remember anything after being at your house?"

His expression sobered. "I swear to you it was not drugs. You were under a thrall."

"Thrall?" I asked. "What's that?"

"When a mortal slips under a trance from being in the presence of a faery too long, it's called a thrall. Most mortals have a much higher tolerance for enthrallment. Odd that yours is so low." He raised a brow as though he had asked some sort of question.

I stared at him. He'd said something about being a fae prince. At the time I thought it had been an odd joke but now…. "A faery. You're telling me you're a faery."

He threw up a hand and said in a tone that echoed off the tile, "What fools these mortals be!"

My response was a blank stare.

His hand dropped to the side. "Shakespeare? A Midsummer Night's Dream? *Puck?*"

My head went back and forth. "Is that supposed to mean something?"

He huffed out an impatient sigh. "Yes, Joey. I am a faery. Which is why I have magic and my soul essence can enthrall any mortal with enough exposure."

Mortification was being quickly displaced by anger. "In

my book, that doesn't sound much different than being drugged, pal."

"It's unintentional. A defense mechanism to keep me from being permanently ensnared by mortals. Normally it takes days or even weeks for a mortal to fall under my thrall. As I said before, your tolerance is remarkably low."

"Gee, thanks." I squirmed, uncomfortable with only semi-transparent bath water between my body and his intense gaze and wondered why on earth I was offended by a man who thought he was a faery telling me I was a magical lightweight.

"Of course, I take care of my thralls. I made sure you and your conveyance returned to your places of origin, didn't I?"

He had. "So, you can enthrall me any time you want?"

He shook his head. "I've given you full immunity from my particular thrall. Which means I have no true defense against you. If you wanted to ensnare me the way mortals have captured the fae for millennia, I have no true way to stop you."

My lips parted. If what he was saying was true…. "Why would you give me immunity then?"

His eyes glittered like emeralds. "Because I want to bargain with you. I have traveled the world searching for a true trader, someone who has just as much to gain as I do from our trade. You are that trader."

I glared at him. "Are you saying I'm desperate? Look pal, I know there's a stigma about women of a certain age—"

He leaned forward and placed his index finger over my lips, effectively cutting off my words. "I'm saying you're unfulfilled. Just as you told your charming friend."

Again his voice changed, this time into mine. "You know that something special feeling. A zest for life. I can't remember the last time I had that."

"That's some talent you have," I whispered.

He dropped back to his own lilting Welsh voice. "My point is that your life is literally passing you by. But I can help you change that. If only you're brave enough to take the leap. Are you?"

Outside the bathroom window, I heard the slam of a car door. My mother, home from her boink fest.

"What say you?" He leaned back and waited.

"Joey!" The slam of the front door. "Josephine Whitmore!"

My heart pounded against my ribcage. Adrenaline surged through my system in a way it hadn't in years. The spark of life. Fear filled me and I shook my head. "I don't believe you."

My mother's tread and the creak of the stairs.

"You have to leave," I said to the faery in my bathroom. "Quick, before my mother sees you."

He drew back. "Twice I have offered. Only thrice will I offer. When I next approach you, Joey Whitmore, it will be for the last time."

With a snap of his fingers, he vanished.

A sharp rap sounded on my bedroom door. "Joey!"

"In the bath." There was something stuck in my throat. "I'll be right out."

I checked all the dark corners of the bathroom but saw no sign of Robin Goodfellow. Warily, I stood up, one hand covering my boobs, the other between my legs. Of course, he had seen me strip earlier. But I hadn't known he was there. If he wanted an eyeful, he would have gotten one already.

Plus, my mother was waiting, rather impatiently, right outside the door.

I climbed from the tub and reached for a towel and wrapped it around myself. Then I stepped over the side and, bent down to let the water out.

"Hurry," my mother snapped from the other side of the door. "I haven't got all night."

"Jeez, Mom. Where's the fire?" Hastily, I dried off before

OVER THE FAERY HILL

slipping into my bathrobe and padding toward the door, turned the lock, and, with one last cautious glance around the bathroom, opened the door.

My mother stood there, her hair and nails were freshly done, looking elegant and excited. For a moment I worried that someone had told her they had seen me riding around town with a strange man. But her vibe was all wrong. She seemed energized, not upset.

"What's up?" I tried to sound casual, not at all like I had just been schmoozing with a faery.

"I found a job opportunity for you," she said. "It's perfect."

My eyebrows drew together. The last time my mother had found me a job opportunity, I had spent the better part of the summer sweating my ass off in an unairconditioned mobile unit outside a construction zone. "Where?"

In typical mom fashion, she couldn't just answer the question. Instead, she had to drag it out into a movie of the week length production. "So we were driving to dinner and I spotted your former coach, Alina Muller. You remember Alina, don't you?"

"Of course." Alina was a robust Romanian woman who had been the toughest gymnastics coach on the face of the planet. She'd been the one training me to become an elite gymnast, before the accident.

"Well, I saw her standing in one of the vacant storefronts downtown so I insisted we stop in to say hello."

"Of course you did." And my dad, as always, would have acquiesced without complaint.

Mom ignored my tone. "You'll never believe it. She's renting out the space to start a new gym right here in town. And she's looking for an assistant. Isn't that wonderful?"

Wonderful wouldn't have been my first choice of words. I tilted my head to the side. "So, naturally, you thought I, who haven't been on a mat in years, would be a perfect fit?"

41

She frowned at me. "Why aren't you more excited about this?"

I held up my bad wrist and pointed to it. "Um, maybe because of this.? I can barely carry a stack of plates, Mom. How am I supposed to help people with gymnastics?"

Her eyebrows scrunched together, forming little lines at the bridge of her nose. "You have been blaming that wrist for everything for over two decades. Maybe if you had done the exercises the physical therapist told you to do instead of sulking, you would have recovered a little better."

There she was, the judgmental harpy that lived inside my mother's skin. "I'd lost my shot to transition to an elite, to make the Olympic team. Rehabbing my wrist wasn't going to fix that."

She shook her head. "Fine. Well, if you are determined to waste the rest of your life, then go on and do it. I thought you would like to know. I'm going to bed."

I leaned my head back against the wall and *thunked* it hard. It felt better than standing there and feeling like a big, fat forty-plus failure so I did it twice more before heading into my darkened bedroom.

The radiator was whistling and I stood in front of it while I pulled on my flannel pajamas and then slid into the brass bed. The moonlight glinted off the ribbons and trophies scattered around the space. How would my life have turned out if I had become an elite? Made it to Nationals? Gone to World. If I had qualified for the team and made it to the 2000 Olympics?

Somehow, I doubted that I would still be sleeping in my childhood bedroom with nothing to show for the first half of my life but a mountain of regret. That just wasn't the story of a winner.

CHAPTER FOUR

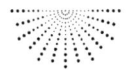

"You can go broke buying into other people's BS."
-Notable quotable from Grammy B

I was up before the sun rose. After dressing in yoga pants, a loose cranberry-colored sweater, and thick socks I headed down into the kitchen to make the apple-filled oatmeal cookies that Grammy B had requested. I doubled up on the apple and reduced the sugar to assuage my guilt over feeding her contraband and baking helped me keep my mind off of yesterday and the strangeness that had gone on.

Could I really change my past? Prevent the accident that had pulverized my wrist and change the future? It seemed insane. Yet I'd seen Robin Goodfellow do magic. He'd disappeared right before my eyes.

I'd brought my laptop down to the kitchen and fired it up while I waited for the cookies to bake. I typed Robin Goodfellow into a search engine and scrolled through the mishmash of hits. The first result that caught my eye was the play he had mentioned the night before, Shakespeare's *A Midsummer Night's Dream*. I read a quick plot description. It seemed the Puck character had caused nothing but trouble for a pair of mortal lovers and the faery court as well.

I returned to the results and read a few pages until the timer went off. I extracted the cookies from the oven and left the sheet on the stovetop to cool. The sun was just coming up over the mountain and my muscles felt stiff and achy. I slipped into my boots and parka and headed out for a breath of air to clear my head.

My feet carried me across the street to the small hiking trail that led to the top of the hill. The snow from the day before had mostly melted and I dug in, needing to move and burn off some of my uncertainty.

Shakespeare hadn't created the Puck character on a whim. In fact, according to the internet, a puck referred to a race of magical domestic creatures that appeared in rural areas. They were also known as hobs or hobgoblins. Different cultures had reported various divergences in appearance and a few online scholars had argued that a puck was another form of demon. It was said a puck could mislead people who wandered in the dark and evoke night terrors in old women.

It wasn't all bad though. In fact, many accounts claimed a puck was neither good nor evil, but instead a spirit of chaos. He would do favors for people who offered him small gifts and he was believed to be an inherently lonely creature often searching for companionship.

But all the sources agreed on a few key points. He could change forms as he had claimed. He was an offshoot of the fae. And wherever he appeared, mischief ensued.

Somehow, I had caught the attention of an agent of chaos.

A magical being that offered me a way to fix my past and the things that went wrong.

The trail grew steeper and I was out of breath by the time I crested the hill. Huffing in a great lungful of air, I stared out at the red-gold hues of the rising sun as it sparkled on the snow and thought about his final words before he vanished. *Twice I have offered. Only thrice will I offer. When I next approach you, Joey Whitmore, it will be for the last time.*

Something rustled in the bushes to my left. I jolted and whirled. It was too early in the season for bears and whatever was there was much too small anyway. Maybe a raccoon. Or a coyote?

I was about to run when a tabby cat with a crooked ear made her way out of the underbrush.

"Hey there," I said and crouched down offering my hand. "Here kitty kitty kitty."

The cat butted her head up against first my knuckles and then my yoga pants before twining herself through my legs. She was skinny, half starved and I didn't see any sign of a collar. A stray maybe? Judging from the bent ear, she wasn't fairing too well by herself.

I knew better than to try and pick her up. With my luck, she would scratch the hell out of me. So I petted her for a few minutes, crooning nonsense. She purred, demonstrating her appreciation.

Grammy B had had a cat up until a few months ago. Maybe she still had some food. I could bring it up here later and leave it for my new friend. And make some inquiries to see if anyone in town was missing a cat.

"I better get on with my day, kitty. I'll try and bring you something to eat, later." I stood up, stretched my back, and headed down the hill.

"Meow."

I turned back and saw that the cat was following me.

"Okay then. I guess I can box up the cookies and head over to Grammy's to see about the food."

"Meow."

Weird. It almost sounded like the cat was answering me. "Can you understand what I'm saying?"

"Meow."

"You are a girl cat, right?" Robin had said he could change shape. But gender?

Then again, George had. And he had done so with science, not magic.

"Robin?" I asked hesitantly. "Is that you?"

The cat glared, giving me the disdain that only a cat could manage. I shook my head. All that reading about hobgoblins and pucks had obviously messed with my head. It was a cat. Just a plain old mackerel tabby. Nothing more.

Still, as the sun rose, I could swear the green eyes were glittering like emeralds.

Mom was in the kitchen when I returned and she scowled at my companion. "Where did that cat come from?"

"She was at the top of the hill." I turned to the sink and washed my hands. "I'm going to take these cookies over to Grammy and see if she has any food left from when she had Tiger."

"One of us needs to grocery shop." Mom sipped her black coffee pointedly.

No sense mentioning the ice cream trick. Mom would be horrified. Hopefully, there would still be room on my credit card for a few essentials. "I'll go later today. You need anything?"

Mom shook her head. "Did you think about the job I mentioned, with Alina?"

She wasn't going to let it go. Her determination was the lone trait she had inherited from Grammy B. "Yes, mother. And I promise I will stop by today."

"In that?" She gestured to my yoga pants that were currently smattered with cat hair.

"I'll change." Though my suit was wrecked from yesterday's mishap, there were other things I could wear.

Mom nodded crisply. "Good. Oh, and I meant to tell you. Your cousin Diedre will be staying with us for a while. She's coming by bus from Baltimore this afternoon."

"Um, okay. Why?" Diedre was mom's younger sister Hannah's only daughter. She was still in high school. The middle of winter seemed like an odd time for an extended visit.

"Hannah needs to go out of town. You know she works for the UN."

"You may have mentioned it a time or two." Another chronic overachiever in the family.

Mom ignored my sarcasm. "Well anyhow, Diedre's been somewhat troublesome lately. Running with a bad crowd, skipping school. Hannah can't afford any distractions while she's working. So, I offered to take Diedre in so she could finish high school here, away from all the influences that are disrupting her."

I thumped down hard in the chair. "Mom! You can't just take in a troubled teen on a whim. It's a huge commitment."

She cast me a pithy look. "Honestly, Josephine. You act as though I don't have a clue what it takes to raise a teenage girl when I raised you. And believe me, you were no picnic." She breezed out of the room, having had her say.

The cat jumped into my lap and I stroked her absently.

"And look how well that turned out," I muttered.

"Meow."

※

Grammy B did indeed have cat food, a metric ton of it. The ingredients displayed on the side of it were better quality than what I typically ate.

"Holy, hoarders, Grammy," I grunted as I hefted the box down from the shelf in the carport. "Where did you get all this?"

Grammy had picked up the cat and was stroking her easily. "Your mother bought it on sale before poor Tiger stopped eating. I was gonna donate it to the animal shelter but I forgot all about it until you asked. Glad it won't go to waste."

With me humping the box and her carrying the cat we headed back into her kitchen. I opened a can and dumped it into Tiger's old ceramic bowl. Grammy set the cat down and then we watched as she stalked toward the bowl. She sniffed delicately and then looked back at me.

"It's okay." Just to be sure, I picked up the can and checked the date. Grammy had been known to keep canned items decades past expiration. The woman was the embodiment of the word thrift. "Yup, all good."

The cat crouched down with her feet tucked beneath her body, tail wrapped around her backside, and dug in.

"I think she has ear mites." Grammy gestured to the flat ear. "Possibly fleas as well from living wild. If you want, I can call the vet, set up an appointment for you to bring her in."

The vet. The one business in town where I'd never applied for a job. I flashed hot and then cold again as I imagined it. Stupid middle-aged hormones.

But bugs…. Ick. I hadn't thought of that. "It's probably a good idea if I can get her into Tiger's old cat carrier. She might be chipped and the vet could find out who she belongs to."

Grammy patted my hand. "You're a good girl, Joey. You always have been." She reached for the cookies.

"Um, Grammy. Don't you think you ought to wash your hands first? Or wait until after lunch to eat cookies?"

"What's the point of being a grown-up if I can't eat cookies whenever I want?" She did get up to wash her hands though. Small victories. I dialed the number and then squeezed my eyes shut.

Luckily, it was the answering service who picked up. I exhaled and closed my eyes. Putting off the inevitable. I gave my cell number and explained that I had found a stray and wanted to get her cleaned up and checked out.

Five minutes later, I got a call back from the vet's assistant, my personal nemesis, Ursula. We had been in gymnastics together for years. Had been friends when we were younger but as it became clear that I was being pushed to reach for elite status, Ursula had resented my success. Even after my accident, her frosty attitude hadn't thawed one bit.

Haltingly, I explained the situation with the cat.

"I suppose Pete could squeeze you and your stray in around two." She sounded like it was a huge imposition.

Two. That didn't give me much time to go home and change into a mom-approved ensemble, get to the grocery store, and interview with Alina. I covered the receiver and turned to face my grandmother. "Grammy, would it be all right if I left the cat here for a little while?"

Grammy wiped her mouth, dislodging a cookie crumb. "Sure."

"Two is fine. Thanks, Ursula."

She hung up without acknowledging me at all.

I sighed and set the phone down. Grammy asked, "What are you going to call her?"

"She's not my cat. It doesn't seem right to saddle her with a name for just a little while."

Grammy waved me off and the cat, having finished her

vittles, hopped back up on Grammy's lap. "Still, you should call her something."

The cat's green eyes met mine as though she were waiting for a verdict. I thought about the internet search and the information I had been stewing over that had sent me out on that hike. It probably wouldn't matter in the long run. She must have an owner somewhere.

"How about Puck?" I asked.

Grammy harrumphed. "Sounds like a boy's name. Course, girls can do anything boys can do better so Puck it is."

"Anything except pee standing up. Thanks, Grammy. You're the best." I pushed away from the table.

"That was one of Grandpappy's favorite sayings." Grammy smiled wistfully.

My grandparents had been married for sixty-two years before my grandfather's passing. My marriage to George hadn't even lasted two. Was a forever kind of love like they had shared even possible for someone like me?

It occurred to me that if I accepted Robin Goodfellow's deal, I would get to see my grandfather again. See me the way I'd been before my accident. A trip back in time. I'd only need one to right the ship. Just prevent the accident that had shattered my wrist. But maybe there were other tweaks I could make.

"Grammy, if you could travel back in time and fix something, what would you fix?"

Grammy actually considered the question instead of dismissing it as a whimsical flight of fancy. "There was this hairstyle I wore in the sixties that I absolutely hated. I'd undo the 'do."

I stared at her a moment. "That's it? That's what you'd change? A hairstyle?"

She worked her dentures around for a bit before nodding.

"Yeah, I burned all the pictures of me from those years and now there's a gap in my albums."

If I ever reached my grandmother's age, I hoped I would be half as content with my life as she was with hers.

"Try to keep her in the kitchen." I gave Puck one final scratch behind the non-dented ear and made a mental note to scrub Grammy's kitchen from top to bottom if Puck did in fact have fleas. I just hoped my grandmother wouldn't end up covered in bites.

After washing my own hands again, I headed back up the street to our house. Mom's car had been repaired and was sitting in the driveway. Mom was in her studio listening to Aretha Franklin. I hurried up the stairs and pulled on a plain gray straight wool skirt, a black V-neck sweater, and black boots. I pulled my hair up into a tight ponytail and then stuck diamond studs in my ears. After a glance in the mirror, I added a swipe of raspberry lip balm to help combat my pasty pallor. Not as snazzy as my interview clothes, but Alina already knew me. More importantly, I knew her and what mattered to her. Alina wasn't a woman who was impressed by flashy clothes. She would want someone who had knowledge and skill, and she knew that once upon a time, I had both.

I printed up another copy of my resume and stuffed it in a folder for my shoulder bag. Blood rushed through my ears and it took a moment for me to realize that I was actually looking forward to seeing my hard ass coach again. But what would she think of me?

I stuck my head into Mom's studio. "So, the car's fixed? What was wrong with it?"

"Yes, it's fixed. Bad spark plug or something." She waved it off.

"A bad spark plug, hmmm?" I raised an eyebrow. "Did your boyfriend Randy tell you that?"

Mom got huffy the same way that she did whenever the head mechanic was mentioned. "He is not my boyfriend."

I smiled to myself. Randy, the head mechanic at the garage had a terrible crush on my mother and had since they were in high school. My father's face turned puce whenever the other man was mentioned, though mom remained oblivious.

"May I borrow the car for my interview?"

She studied me from head to foot and then nodded in what I could only assume was approval. "Keys are in the little dish in the hall. Good luck."

"Thanks," I said and then sauntered to the hall to retrieve the keys and my purse, don my boots, and then headed out to the vehicle.

"Please work, car," I muttered under my breath as I unlocked the vehicle and slid behind the wheel. "Please, please, *please* work."

I inserted the key and with a final prayer, turned. The engine turned over. I sagged in relief, buckled my seat belt, and headed into town.

Perhaps my luck was finally changing.

❋

"You got fat." Alina glared at me from where she stood behind the reception desk.

I stared down at the outfit which I had foolishly believed to be so slimming. Then again, Alina hadn't seen me in over two decades.

"Yes, well, middle age, you know." Professional gymnasts usually put on weight after they retired. Less exercise, more indulgences, but, in my case, the weight gain was extreme. What could I say? I liked food and booze.

"That is just an excuse. I run ten miles every day. I do one hundred sit-ups in the morning and another one hundred sit-ups at night. I eat a special diet that works with my body type, high in protein so I do not lose muscle tone. I never consume dairy, sugar, or a drop of alcohol. My body is a temple." Her thick Romanian accent was pious as she boasted about her severe regime.

"And it shows." She wore a long-sleeved polo shirt that showcased bulging muscles. If I had to eat and drink the way Alina did, I wouldn't want to get out of bed in the morning.

"Lifestyle habits do show." Alina scowled at me again. "What happened to you, Josephine?"

"Um, the car accident when I damaged my wrist?" I was surprised that she would have forgotten.

"That was one event. But you have made choices that lead you farther away from who you were destined to be. You let yourself go." Alina shook her head as though my body mass index was the greatest travesty the world would ever know.

The interview wasn't going at all the way I had imagined. Mostly because Alina didn't know it *was* an interview. I hadn't gotten my resume out of the folder. She had greeted me with, "You got fat" and from there it swirled the bowl.

"The place looks great." To take the focus off my plus-sized self, I looked around the space. Even in its raw form, I could tell the studio was going to be amazing. There were skylights in the ceiling and mirrors along the two side walls reflecting the brilliant natural light as well as the recessed lighting. The oak floors had been newly finished and awaited the thick mats and equipment.

It was a good space. Almost as good as the gym where I had spent endless hours training with Alina in my formative years. It had been in a much larger town that was a solid forty minutes away.

"It will suffice." Alina surveyed the room with the same critical eye she'd had as my coach.

"What sort of classes will you be instructing?" I asked.

"Gymnastics," she announced

"And?" I prompted.

"Gymnastics." She really was a one-trick pony.

"I see. Well, it might be a little more lucrative if you thought about adding other types of classes?" I smiled. "Like maybe yoga or Pilates for the women. Or kickboxing?"

She sniffed indignantly. "I have no interest in teaching fat old women to do yoga. I train champions."

My smile grew tight. "Alina, this is a small town. A champion comes along only once in a while. You need to cater to some of the normal people, too, if you want to stay in business."

She turned away. "I will run my business how I choose. I understand success."

She did too. Alina had her own Olympic bronze medal in the All-around and gold on the balance beam. And really, what could I say to that?

I stuffed my disappointment down deep, to the vault where all emotions were supposed to go whenever I was in Alina's presence. I could still hear her words from my first session so long ago. *What you bring onto the mat shows on the mat. You bring what you want them to see.*

At the moment I wanted Alina to see me as someone not about to cry. "It was good seeing you." I lied and then scurried out of the store as fast as my fat feet would take me.

I headed down the street, tucked in against the wind as the misery doubled and then quadrupled like a mushroom cloud erupting in my chest. Damn it, why had I let my mother talk me into that? How humiliating.

I had forgotten how much I hated Alina. Mostly because she didn't pull any punches. Even though my head was down I wasn't truly tracking my footfalls. The toe on my right boot hit a patch of ice and I went down hard, ass first, into a slushy puddle.

Cold wetness seeped into my backside through the wool skirt. I scrambled up, frantically looking for a place to hide and safely lose my shit.

There. I ducked into an alley before my emotions ran amok. I hid in the shadows like some misshapen swamp creature and let the tears flow.

Two minutes. That was all it had taken Alina to get inside my head. And the worst part was, she was right about everything.

"I am fat," I sobbed. "A big, fat quitter."

"Joey? Sweetheart, what are you doing back here?" My father appeared at the mouth of the alley.

I turned my head away. "Nothing." Where did I decide to humiliate myself? Across the street from my father's office.

My shitty luck had struck again.

He moved closer. His hands held up in front of him like a man who didn't want to startle a wild animal. "I saw you through the window. It looked like a bad fall. Are you hurt?"

I let out a sigh. "Only my pride."

His smile was gentle. "Well, come on inside and get cleaned up."

Ever the hero, my father removed his suit jacket and wrapped it around me. Even if it did only leave him in thin shirtsleeves to combat the bitter mountain air as we made our way across the street to the real estate attorney's office.

The receptionist, Edith, was asleep at her desk, her reading glasses hanging from a chain around her neck, chin against her chest. Her hair was shock white and curled up in a big poof, though there was a flat spot on top which Edith either couldn't see or couldn't reach. She looked like nothing more than a pigeon, cooing in her nest. Dad shook his head at her, but he smiled.

He kept his voice low as he moved through the front room and gestured toward his little kitchen in the back which was nothing more than a mini-fridge, a sink, and a coffee pot. "Poor thing is dozing off more and more during the day. I've taken to keeping an eye out whenever we're expecting someone for a closing."

Which is why he had spied my mishap with the puddle.

"Are you expecting someone?" I asked.

He shook his head. "No. Winter is slower than usual. Come on upstairs."

He gestured for me to climb the stairs that led to his two-bedroom apartment. I waited in the living room while he rummaged around in his bedroom and came back with a set of sweats and a big fluffy towel.

"Go ahead and get changed. I'll make us some tea."

I slipped into the small bathroom. My butt and the back of my legs were freezing from the puddle. After shucking the soggy wool and drying off, I hung my skirt up to dry over the shower door and then pulled my father's too long sweatpants up over my frozen rump.

I studied my dad as he moved around his kitchen. Paul Blackthorn was a tall man. His salt and pepper hair was always neatly trimmed bi-weekly and his hands were the hands of a man who had spent his life lifting books, not bricks.

His apartment was tidy. The only decorations were ones I had given him. Black and white shots of nature scenes around North Carolina. From the Cape Hatteras Lighthouse to a view of Grandfather Mountain. There was one color picture of me on his lone end table, almost hidden behind a stack of paperback science fiction novels. I smiled as I picked it up.

My father came over and handed me the steaming mug.

"Regional finals for the Southeast. I think you were about thirteen."

A lump had formed in my throat. "I remember."

He sighed. "I loved those competitions of yours. Not just watching your routines, though they were great. But the togetherness, you know?"

I knew exactly what he meant. The three of us in a hotel room, going out to meals like a real family. It was a big change from the way we typically lived, with Dad consigned to an outer orbit around my mother and me.

"Dad, why didn't you ever push her on the marriage thing. I know you wanted it."

He shook his head. "It takes two to tango, Joey."

"I know but…you stayed here. In this town. For her." My father had been a Yankee born and bred but had fallen in love with Prudence Whitmore and had shifted from studying criminal law to the more locally lucrative mountain real estate. It wasn't exciting. He had made a hell of a sacrifice to be with my mother and she never even seemed to acknowledge it.

"Joey, something you need to understand about your mother is that I love her *because* of her independence. I don't want to change a thing about her or ask her to compromise who she is. Marriage is anathema to her."

"It makes no sense." No matter how many times my parents had explained their situation to me, I had never understood. All I knew is that my family didn't live the way other families did. And my mother called all the shots.

"Prudence is the only woman I want to be with. And if this is the only way she will accept me into her life…well, it's better than not being with her at all."

"Didn't you ever just want to find someone else? Someone who wanted the same things you did?"

He shook his head. "I only ever wanted her."

It wasn't unrequited love. It was a holding pattern that had gone on for over four decades. My poor, devoted dad.

His expression shifted, turning wistful. Whatever he was looking at wasn't in the room with us. "There was a time, years ago, when I thought that she might be softening about the whole subject. That maybe we could at least live together. We were spending so much time as a family. You were about sixteen and training so hard. You were hardly ever home. I think that even though she was happy for you she was lonely too. But then—"

He stopped abruptly and looked away.

"But then I had my accident and broke my wrist." It felt like a punch to the gut.

"It's not your fault, Joey." My father said. "There were other times too, like when you were married. But she was set in her ways by then."

If only I had flown the nest sooner.

"Dad," I whispered. "If there was one thing in your life that you had a chance to do over, what would it be?"

"That's easy. I wouldn't have put you in public high school. Where you met that boy and got in the car with him…."

I closed my eyes and nodded. "I need to go. I have things to do."

We both stood and I wrapped my arms around him. My hero.

He escorted me downstairs, past the sleeping Edith, and I handed him his suit jacket back.

"How about we have dinner tomorrow night?" he whispered. "I would love to hear about what's going on with you."

No, you wouldn't. I thought but nodded. "Sounds great. *Gianni's* at eight?"

My father adored Italian food. His smile was genuine. "Sounds wonderful. See you then."

I made my way back to where the car was parked. It started right up and I backed out into traffic. I drove past the turn-in to the grocery store and headed out onto the highway, out to Firefly Lane.

Robin Goodfellow was waiting for me at the top of the hill. I stopped before the engine could die and then got out of the car and called up the hill, "I'm ready to make a bargain."

His lips curled up. "Music to my ears." He held out a hand. "Just come with me, my dear Joey, and I'll show you how to make all of your dreams come true."

I shut the car door and climbed up to the top of the hill where he stood. His sapphire eyes glowed with an ethereal light and swirls of amber light spilled from his hands until they created a corona with him at the center.

All the small hairs stood up on my arms as I reached through the eddying magic. Our hands touched.

"A favor for a favor?" Robin asked.

I nodded. "A favor for a favor."

"A bargain is struck." He grinned and I knew there was no turning back.

CHAPTER FIVE

"There's no such thing as a free lunch. Some poor bugger somewhere had to pony up for it."
-Notable quotable from Granny B

"So," I said, looking around at the hilltop. "Did it work?"

Everything looked the same as it had before we struck the bargain. The amber motes had vanished as though they had never existed. The world around us appeared exactly the same as it had when I arrived.

"Did what work?" Robin raised an eyebrow at me.

"Um…did we travel back in time?"

He laughed. "Oh no, lamb. You can't simply just pop backward and start mucking about with the timeline. You haven't been trained yet."

"Trained?" Alarm spiked. "You never said anything about being trained."

"Didn't I? A minor oversight." He waved it off like it wasn't a big deal. "Have you had lunch? I'm starving."

"Lunch?" I blinked. We'd just made an open-ended magical bargain and he wanted to have a nosh?

"Of course. Let's go to that little greasy spoon where you were previously employed and we'll hash out the details." He raised his hand. The world tilted sideways as if it were being squeezed flat and the landscape shifted from the chill mountaintop to the parking lot.

I staggered and Robin caught me. "Easy, lamb."

I scowled up at him. "Why do you keep calling me lamb? I have a name."

"Are you one of those tiresome females that sees an endearment as some sort of masochistic plot to demean your identity?"

"That would be my mother." She'd geld him with a butter knife if he ever called her by a name other than her given one.

"I assure you, Joey, I meant no offense." His voice took on a husky note. "I call you lamb because it reminds me of how you looked in the bath, all covered in fluffy white bubbles."

"Sshhh," I hissed at him.

Reverend Phillips and his wife, Emily, exited the café and were passing us in the parking lot and casting us a strange look. "Lower your voice or the whole town will be speculating by supper."

"Joey? Is everything all right?" Reverend Phillips called out.

"Fine, thanks. Just having lunch with my...," I trailed off, not knowing how to finish that sentence. Coworker didn't fit. Neither could I pass Robin off as a family member since the Reverend knew the entire Whitmore-Blackthorn clan. I certainly wasn't going to say boyfriend. That would set tongues waging faster than that time the real estate agent Merrilee Higgins got caught hooking up with Coach Calhoun in the vacant bungalow over on Pemberton Road.

"Friend." The word slipped out. "My friend, Robin."

Emily's blade thin nose crinkled as she studied my wardrobe, taking note of the too-long men's sweatpants. A knowing light lit her eyes as she studied Robin.

"Well, see you at Sunday service," the Reverend said and he and Emily hustled to their station wagon, either to escape the cold or to run home and start burning up the phone lines.

"Your friend?" Robin asked and, for a moment, his voice lost that snarky edge of detached amusement.

My shoulders did a quick up and down. "I panicked. I wasn't expecting to just poof on over here. Give me a little warning next time and I'll come up with a better fib."

"I see." He gestured toward the door of the café.

"Oh no," I balked. "I can't go in there, especially not dressed as I am." I gestured to my borrowed sweats.

Robin rolled his eyes. "I've seen how people dress in this town. Believe me, if you're not covered with either engine grease or manure, you're ahead of the curve."

He wasn't wrong. Still. A woman didn't want to show up looking homeless the day after she'd been sacked. "In case you forgot, I was just fired from here yesterday. And the food really isn't all that good anyway. Not since cheapskate Rodney took over."

He didn't bother arguing with me, just pulled open the door and headed inside, leaving me out in the cold with no purse, no phone or car. Before the door closed, I caught a whiff of chili and my stomach growled. Okay, some of the food kicked-ass. Besides, I hadn't had anything solid since the day before.

Fine, better to go into the café dressed in too large sweats and eat a hot meal than to stand in the parking lot waiting for Robin to poof me back to my mother's car.

The bell above the door jingled, announcing my entrance

to the patrons and staff. Rodney sat behind the counter and his eyes nearly bugged out of his head at my arrival.

"Joey?" he asked a tad nervously.

"Just having lunch with a friend." I could feel every eye in the place looking at me and blood rushed to my cheeks. There was a world of difference between having people watch me perform a well-rehearsed gymnastics routine in a competition and being fodder for the gossip mill.

Robin was seated at a booth in the far back section of the café. He was chatting up a woman I didn't recognize. A pretty young blond girl wearing a tight sweater tucked into skinny jeans. She must be my replacement because she wore an apron and held a pad and pen, though she wasn't making any effort to write anything down.

Feeling like a schlub, I sidled my way over to the table. I had to squeeze past the waif to slide onto the duct-taped vinyl bench seat.

"Ah, and here she is, my lovely *friend*." Robin snagged my hand and brought it to his lips. "What will soothe your soul on this blustery midwinter day, Joey? Perhaps something hot to fill you up?"

Was he *trying* to start gossip? I could see Winnifred Bates and her sister Flo staring at us from the counter. He might as well chum the waters for sharks the way he was carrying on. I kicked him under the table even as I said, "A bowl of chili and a coffee, please."

"Make that two," My companion dimpled at the girl.

"What the hell, Robin?" I hissed at him the second she was out of earshot. "That little speech of yours is going to be greasing the gossip wheel for months."

"Probably," He nodded. "You're welcome, by the way."

"For what?" I hissed, jerking my hand back. "Making me seem like the town slut?"

"Making you appear *desirable*. You were concerned they

would be gossiping about your apparel. I gave them something else to focus on. Honestly, lamb. Aren't you too old to worry so much about other people's perception of you?"

"Too *old*?" I huffed. First, I was dubbed fat and now old.

He waved it away with an easy gesture. "I simply meant that you should be past the point in your life where the opinions of those around you ought to sway your perception of yourself so easily."

Only slightly mollified by his answer, I leaned back and allowed skinny jeans blonde to set a mug and saucer before me and fill it up with steaming java. She kept casting surreptitious glances at Robin, which he didn't seem to notice. All his attention was on my face.

When she was gone, I asked, "What? Why are you looking at me that way?"

"What way?" He tilted his head to the side.

"Like I'm a puzzle you're trying to solve."

His lips twitched. "Perhaps because you are more complex than I first believed. You fascinate me, Joey Whitmore."

I blushed and tucked a strand of hair behind my ear.

"Tell me about October 3, 1996," Robin said. "Specifically, what is it you want to change?"

My gaze drifted over the café, the familiar sights, and smells. "The accident that ruined my career in elite gymnastics before it ever really began."

Robin waited for me to gather my thoughts.

"I was a level ten gymnast. My"— harridan hardass —"gymnastics instructor was helping me reach elite status. I'd been doing it since I was a kid and the gym was always my favorite place to be. My family and I had gone to the '96 Olympic Games in Atlanta. That was the year team USA, the Magnificent Seven, took home the gold. I was sitting right there when Kerri Strug did the second vault on her injured ankle. No one realized how badly she had been hurt until after she won." My heart still raced a little as I thought about it. She could have crippled herself, but she did it anyway, almost without thought. Because losing was not an option.

"So, after we got back home, I upped my practices all summer. Forty plus hours a week. I was actually considering homeschooling so that I could spend more hours in the gym. Training harder, getting better. I was working on my parents, trying to convince them it was the right way to go. But I had a bad fall near the end of August. Off the balance beam. It spooked my mom and she said I should stay in high school at least until I recovered fully. And then a senior boy asked me out." A lump formed in my throat as I remembered the day. "He wrecked his car. With me in it."

Robin's gaze fell to my wrist. "That's the source of your injury?"

I nodded. "I'd been hurt before. Badly. But this…this was different. The wrist is made up of eight small bones. Six of mine had been broken, two shattered beyond full repair. I couldn't do handstands, cartwheels, nothing where I held weight on the joint. Even with months of physical therapy, there would be no way I would ever make the Olympic team. It was a career ending injury."

"So, you stopped competing altogether?"

I shifted under his assessing stare. "Why do it if there's no way to win?"

"Joey?" Another voice called.

I glanced up and froze in place. Total deer in the headlights.

"Twice in as many days." Georgia approached on her way back from the restroom. Her smile was turned on full.

"What are the odds?" My voice sounded weak and reedy.

"I can't believe you're here." She lowered her voice and then cast a dark look over to where Rodney perched on his stool like a homely toad on a wobbly mushroom. "After what went down yesterday. And who is your charming companion?"

Georgia looked pointedly at Robin who was glancing back and forth between the two of us like he was watching a tennis match.

I really didn't want to introduce the two of them, and not because Robin wielded magic. But I was raised in the South and manners weren't something a woman like me could get around, regardless of the circumstance.

"Georgia, this is Robin Goodfellow. Robin, this is Georgia Knox."

"A pleasure," Georgia said and extended her well-manicured hand.

For a moment I was afraid Robin was going to refuse to shake with her. And that simply wasn't done. A woman could refuse to shake hands with a man, but when she offered, he was obliged to accept. It was a silly, out-of-date custom, but again, we were prisoners of our upbringing.

Finally, after what felt like a full minute of awkward silence, Robin took Georgia's hand and shook. "Nice to meet you, Georgia. Joey hasn't told me a thing about you."

I buried my nose in my coffee cup and wished the cracked linoleum floor would open and swallow me whole.

Georgia shifted, a little uncomfortable. "Well, it is a bit of a roundabout tale. You see, we used to be married."

"Really?" Robin's sapphire eyes had a predatory glint. "And would your ride be the tow truck parked over there?"

I'd been so flummoxed about popping from the hilltop to the café that I hadn't noticed the tow truck.

"It is."Georgia nodded.

"Fascinating." Robin's gaze was locked on me. "This explains a few things. I must say, my dear, that you are without a doubt the most well put together tow-truck driver I've ever encountered."

"I work with what I've got." Georgia preened.

I slunk further down in my seat. Was this really happening? My ex flirting with my...my...whatever the hell Robin was?

"Georgia, your meal's up," Rodney called from the counter.

"I better go eat. It was good seeing you, Joey." Georgia put a hand on my shoulder and squeezed lightly.

"Yeah, you too." The lie spilled from my mouth automatically.

As she walked away, I decided to be blunt before Robin could make the situation even more uncomfortable. "She used to be a man. George."

"I know." Robin nodded.

I frowned. "You do? How?"

"It's difficult to explain. There's an aura around some people that signifies great change. You have it. So does she." He nodded to Georgia.

"An aura. You read auras?"

He nodded. "It's what allows me to enthrall mortals."

"So, Georgia and I have the same sort of aura?" Was that because we were both meant for different lives than the ones we'd been born to?

"Not exactly. Hers is dappled with light. Yours has a thick layer of dust which dulls it."

"Fabulous," I said and was relieved to see the server carrying two bowls of chili in our direction. I didn't want to talk about Georgia or my dusty aura anymore.

The scent from the chili spices soothed my ragged nerves. The café served the chili with a side of corn chips as well as little containers of shredded cheese and sour cream. I dug in, not looking at my companion or meeting his inquisitive gaze. I knew he had questions. People always did when they found out I had been married to a woman who used to be a man.

Questions I didn't know how to answer. Like, did you suspect anything was off about him when you were married? When you found out, did you consider staying married? Or the even more invasive, how were things in the bedroom?

Because the truth was, I didn't know a damn thing was wrong with our marriage. Sure, there were times when George had been quiet and withdrawn. Then again, I had those periods too.

As for staying married, well, the truth was that I had considered it. I hadn't been in the marriage for sex, just companionship. But Georgia's hormone therapy kicked in and she wasn't attracted to me anymore. Every time our paths crossed, I remembered the last night we'd shared a house. Her telling me that she wanted to date men, but wouldn't cheat on me. That was probably the second most difficult conversation of my life. Right after the doctor told me that the Olympics were no longer in the picture.

Thankfully, Robin held his tongue and tucked into his food. I added a dollop of sour cream and swirled it into the chili and then topped it with cheese before scooping the mixture up with a corn chip. Delicious.

Robin was staring at me again.

"What?" I shifted, feeling self-conscious under such scrutiny.

He smiled. "You're enjoying yourself. You enjoy this food despite the trials in coming here."

"It's one of my favorite meals. Try some." I nodded to his untouched bowl.

He did and a look of surprise crossed his face. "This is excellent. The best I've ever tasted."

"And I bet you've been around some. What with your line of work and all," I fished.

"That's putting it mildly." Robin was eating his chili with a spoon, which, in my opinion, took something away from the experience. Though I probably didn't need the empty carbs.

In my mind, I could hear Alina's words. *You got fat.*

I wiped my hands on a napkin and then reached for my own spoon.

"Why did you do that?" Robin frowned.

"Do what? I'm just sitting here eating my lunch."

Those blue eyes narrowed to slits. "Yes, but you changed how you were eating."

"So?"

"So, when you did that, something diminished in you. It was like watching a candle die out and you are left in the darkness."

My lips parted. "How is that even possible?"

"Go back to the way you were eating before," he ordered.

I bristled at the domineering tone. "You can't tell me what to do."

He snorted. "Then I'm the only one."

I clutched my spoon tighter, as though it were a weapon, I could use to attack him. "What exactly is that supposed to mean?"

He opened his mouth to retort but the blonde waitress approached. "Is everything all right over here?"

"Fine." Setting down the spoon, I turned to face her. "We're ready for the check, though."

She nodded and headed toward the register.

Robin had set his spoon down too. Without looking at me, he scooped some chili up on a chip, stuffed it into his mouth, and chewed.

I folded my arms over my chest and waited.

He swallowed and then reached for the water glass.

Didn't say a word, just picked up another chip and repeated the process. An olive branch of sorts I guessed.

After a moment, I did too. Our spoons stayed on the table and yet all the chili disappeared.

❄

"Oh shoot, is that the time?" My gaze had, out of habit, fallen on the cheap plastic clock behind the register as we went to pay. The face of it read 1:45.

"A hot date?" Robin asked as the waitress handed him the bill. He didn't even glance at it as he forked over his credit card but I did. The name Tammi and a phone number scrawled on the bottom. The i on her name was dotted with a heart. What was she, twelve?

"Speaking of dates," I nodded to the bill and the girl who was trying to get his attention.

Robin glanced down at it and his expression darkened. He looked back to the girl and to my horror, stuck a finger in her face. "Is this something you do often?"

"Nnnnno," she stammered and I could tell it was a lie.

"Did I come on to you in any way? Or send out any signals that I was interested in anyone but my companion here?" he pushed.

"You were flirty," she insisted.

"I was friendly," he corrected her.

"Robin," I tugged on his arm but he was intent on his task.

"Do you really think that I would want to spend time with a female who has all the life experience of single-celled protozoa when I have a former gymnastics champion by my side? What have you ever done except grow a set of mammary glands and take up space?"

Over by the counter, I saw Georgia's fork pause in midair. The rest of the diners were watching us as well.

The server straightened her shoulders and her eyes flashed as she eyed me up and down. I could read her face. Former champion or not, I was a fat, middle-aged has-been who came to lunch in a man's sweatpants. I was no threat to her youthful beauty. "You're a dick."

Rodney hurried over. "Is there some sort of problem here?"

Robin opened his mouth to reply but I blocked the path. "No, no problem. If you could just swipe the card there. We have another appointment."

"It's on the house." Rodney practically shoved Robin's credit card back at him.

Robin pocketed it and glared down at the server. "No tip."

She gave him the finger. Rodney's eyes bulged and he hustled Tammi with an i into the back.

I practically dragged Robin out the door. "Come on, we need to go. Poof us back to the hilltop where my car is."

"What's your hurry?" He folded his arms over his chest, obviously not in a poofing frame of mind.

"I have an appointment at the vet's office at two."

"Excellent." Robin rubbed his hands together. "This is the perfect time to practice with it."

Before I could ask what he meant, he snapped his fingers, the world narrowed and shifted around us again until we stood inside his impressive treehouse. We were in a different room than we had been before. This one had free-floating shelves along the walls littered with various objects. I spied a hairbrush, a mirror that looked to be surrounded with thorns, a ball of golden string. A golden and purple pocket watch. A big black book that seemed to absorb the light from all the things around it. Despite my rush, I spun in place, taking it all in. "What is all this stuff?"

"A faery's hoard. Unlike living things, items don't have auras. But they can hold magic. Smaller items are best suited to hold magic akin to whatever it is they were created to do. The hairbrush for example." He picked it up and held it out to me.

Gingerly, I took it. "Is my hair a mess?"

"Just try it, lamb." He made stroking motions with his hand, mimicking the act of brushing.

I turned to face the thorny mirror. My reflection stared back at me, dark, graying hair in a total rat's snarl. Crap, even worse than I'd thought. I pulled free the elastic band and let my hair spill down my back.

I ran the brush through my hair once and something shimmered from the bristles. I repeated the motion again, and again and again. My hair didn't snap with static electricity the way it normally did when I dry brushed it in the winter. Instead, with each stroke of the brush, it smoothed and straightened.

I paused and turned my head from side to side. "Is it just me or are my grays going away?"

His smile radiated satisfaction. "That's what this object does. Restores your hair to its youthful glory."

I touched the silky strands of brown that glittered with the ambient amber light. It looked better than the best haircut I'd ever had at a salon. "You're telling me that every day could be a good hair day?"

He raised a brow. "How do you think my hair remains so youthful and amazing?"

"Where can I get one of these?"

He plucked it from my hand. "I'm afraid it, much like you, dear Joey, is one of a kind."

I turned to face him. "Do you have anything that could make me not be fat anymore?"

He glowered down at me. "You aren't fat. Is that why you stopped eating the chips earlier?"

Unable to meet his gaze, I nodded. "It's something my

former trainer told me today. That I'd let myself go. And she was right."

He curled a finger under my chin. "Look at me. You are beautiful, lamb. Womanly. I, a veritable connoisseur of beauty, would change nothing about your appearance."

My heart fluttered at his words. Stupid, stupid heart. Overeager for genuine male admiration.

Look how well that turned out for you the last time! A little voice shrieked. Mentally, I referred to her as the sensible shrew.

I pulled out of his grip. "So, what was it you wanted to show me?"

Robin studied me a moment and then turned to a rough-hewn desk. He opened a drawer and extracted a golden box. He gestured for me to come forward. "This."

I circled the desk and came to stand beside him. "What is it?"

"Open it." His eyes had caught that bright sapphire gleam again that I was beginning to associate with trouble ahead.

A sense of foreboding washed over me. I hesitated. What could possibly be in the golden box? Something magical, no doubt. But why had it been shut away in his desk? Perhaps it was dangerous.

Too late to turn back now. The bargain had already been struck.

I reached for the lid and lifted the latch.

There were no eddies of magic or amber sparks. Instead, there was velvet cushioning to protect the object within.

Inside lay an hourglass filled with purple sand. The sand was evenly divided between the top and the bottom of the glass. Even though it appeared plainer than most of the items in the room, power thrummed off of it in great cascading waves.

"What is it?" I asked him nervously.

"An hourglass."

I shot him a withering look. "I can see that. I mean what does it do?"

He picked it up and oddly, the sand within didn't begin trickling down into the bottom portion. "It allows you to alter the space-time continuum. Want to see how an election turns out?"

"Not especially," I grumped.

He waved it off. "Poor example. How about seeing what your life looks like plus forty years? Or maybe just rewind time an hour to make an appointment that you are fifteen minutes late for?" He unscrewed the lid and removed a single grain of sand. "This can allow you to do it."

"One grain of sand." I eyed it skeptically.

His grin turned wicked. "Better hold on to me, lamb."

The ground shifted beneath my feet. Panicked, I reached for Robin's arm to keep from falling under the motion. The shifting wasn't jarring like an earthquake, more like one of those moving sidewalks at a really big airport. Except it was churning along at an incredible rate. The objects of magic blurred into streaks almost as if they were subjects in a still-life watercolor that were being smeared with a wet brush. It was disorienting in a different way from Robin's magic transporting us from one location to another. I felt unsteady and displaced. Like my essence was barely clinging to my body.

And then it stopped.

The lurching momentum killed the little that was left of my equilibrium and I would have sprawled face down on the floor if Robin hadn't snagged me around the waist.

His body was warm and hard and he smelled of cedarwood and male spice. I clung to him, urging my heart rate to slow. It wasn't cooperating.

"Are you all right?" he murmured in my ear.

"What just happened?" The weird streakiness had dissipated. All the objects in the room were exactly where they had been.

"We traveled back in time exactly one hour." He wasn't releasing me and I hastily moved away, needing a minute to process without his heated touch distracting me.

I looked up into his eyes to see if he was teasing but could see no sign of his standard humor. "Back in time? You're serious?"

"Absolutely. There are now two versions of me here as well as two versions of you. Our echoes should be leaving for the café right about now. Take a look."

"Echoes?"

Robin moved over to the window and beckoned for me to follow. "Quickly."

I moved up to his side and looked down from the tree and to the top of the hill where I could see another Robin holding my hand. My lips parted. An instant later, the two figures vanished.

"How...how is that possible?"

"Time is a river. Normally we flow along with the current. But the sands of time allow us to walk against the current, back the way we came."

"Okay." I nodded. "So, you and I are in the parking lot in front of the café. Then how can we also be here?"

"Our younger selves are called echoes. Eventually, the echoes will catch up to the current version of ourselves. At that point, the sand will combine our echoes with our bodies, in this case in less than one hour. That is when we regain our normal place in the river. The echoes will be absorbed, allowing us to take their place and them to have our newly made memories. The longer we travel back, the more history the echo will have to absorb. An hour isn't much, but a month or a year takes some time. Come, lamb, the river is flowing." He moved away from the window and strode out of the room.

My head was spinning with information as well as the aftereffects of the magic as I stumbled along behind him. "But I still don't see how—?"

He continued on through his living room and down the stairs, barely looking back at me. "Joey, I can either give you lessons on the fundamentals of the space-time continuum or you can make it to your appointment. Now go. I have things to accomplish this hour as well. I'll meet up with you after we have reabsorbed our echoes."

I followed him out into the air. "Wait! Is it dangerous? I mean, what if I run into the other version of me? Will I like, wipe out my own existence or something?"

He rolled his eyes at me. "You've watched too many science fiction movies. No, you can safely interact with your echo. Pulling a few strings will not hamper the fabric of the space-time continuum. Now go on. We have less than an hour before the current catches us up. Use it to your advantage." Robin snapped his fingers and before I could ask another question, he vanished.

I blinked and then shook my head, unable to believe he'd just abandoned me in the wrong time.

Then again, what else could I expect from a mischievous fae bargain?

CHAPTER SIX

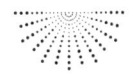

"If it seems too good to be true...it's probably a big, fat lie."
—Notable quotable from Grammy B

I called Darcy the second the tires of my mother's car left Firefly Lane. "What are you doing right now?"

"Dealing with a brutal hangover," she kvetched. "Why did you let me drink so much last night?"

"Like I could have stopped you. I'll be there in five minutes to pick you up. Be ready."

"Ready for what?"

"Just do it!" I barked.

She blew out a breath. "Fine, bitchy briefs. I'll be all set for my abduction. I should warn you though, my care and feeding is hella complicated."

I hung up the phone and concentrated on driving, not allowing myself to think about what was going on.

Exactly four minutes and fifty-seven seconds later—I'd been counting—I slammed on the brakes in front of Darcy's house. She was standing outside, wearing a giant pair of sunglasses along with her baby blue parka and flannel lined jeans.

"What gives, Joey?" She climbed in and gave me a sour look. "And wow, your hair looks amazing. Did you have it done?"

"In a manner of speaking. Buckle up."

She reached for the shoulder harness. "What is this urgent mission?"

"We're going to the café." I waited until she'd buckled her seatbelt and then peeled away from the curb.

"Slow down! And the café? Ugh. I can't eat there today. All the smells and grease will make me vomit."

"You're not going there to eat." I took a hard right and Darcy slammed into the door. "You're going to be my witness."

"Um, like an alibi? Because if you hired some goon to off Rodney, I fully approve."

"No one is being murdered. I just want to see if I'm in the café."

"Huh?"

"You'll see."

I pulled up to a vacant spot at the back of the lot, far enough away that no one would spot my mother's car. "Now... go on in and see if I'm sitting at a table with a good looking, if arrogant blond guy."

Darcy's eyebrows had migrated halfway up her forehead. "Um, Joey? How could you be in there when you're right here?"

"Just go look." I huffed.

"I am getting you massive doses of therapy for your birthday. For real." Darcy snarked and then climbed out of the car.

I stared at the clock in the dashboard, the numbers a

bright blue. 1:27. Blood pounded in my ears. When I'd looked at the time in the café it had been 1:45. Were the echoes of myself and Robin actually in there eating chili right now?

Darcy reappeared at the door to the café. Her sunglasses were perched on top of her head and she didn't bother to replace them as she marched with purpose toward the car.

"Well?" I asked as she climbed in next to me. "Was I there?"

Slowly, she nodded. "Only your hair looked like hell."

A rush of dizziness washed over me. It had worked. Darcy had seen me sitting there with Robin.

Not me. My echo.

"How did you do that?" she asked. "Is it some sort of actor dressed like you or...?"

"No." I swallowed. "Would you believe me if I said magic?"

She stared at me. "You're serious?"

"The guy I'm with...he's a faery."

"A faery," she repeated, her tone flat. "You mean like he's batting for the home team? Because the way he was looking at you—"

"I mean he's a legit full-sized fae. And I made a bargain with him. Three trips back through time in exchange for a favor."

One of her eyebrows went up. "And you used one of those trips to drag me out here to watch you eat chili?"

"No. I mean, not really. This doesn't count because I didn't ask him to bring me back here." At least I'd hoped it didn't. Robin hadn't said that this was one of my three trips back in time so I had assumed it was a demonstration.

Darcy pinched the bridge of her nose between her thumb and forefinger. "I need a minute here."

"Sure." I put the car in drive and headed to Grammy B's.

I'd make that vet appointment no problem, now that I had all the time in the world.

I ran into the house, got Puck into the cat carrier with only one set of claw marks to show for my efforts, kissed Grammy on the cheek, and was back out in the car and was halfway to my destination before Darcy spoke again.

"So, let me get this straight. You bargained with a fae and traded an open-ended unnamed favor in exchange for three trips through time. And you aren't worried about what aforementioned favor might entail?"

"Not too worried." I was trying not to think about that part.

"You're a little too old for him to claim your firstborn. Maybe he'll demand sexual favors." She made one of those stupid fanning motions with her hand.

I shivered a bit at the thought. "You did see him, right? He wouldn't need to bargain for sexual favors. Most women would give it up without a valuable time travel incentive."

"Maybe he's into some twisted kink," Darcy suggested. "Something no normal woman would give him without the big bargain."

I cast her a sidelong look. "You're being ridiculous."

"Joey, this is the most reckless thing I have seen you do in years!" She sounded excited. "So, what are you going to change?"

I raised an eyebrow. "Do you even have to ask?"

"The accident." She nodded. "Makes sense. So how, exactly?"

"I haven't worked out all the details yet." Though I did recall that day and my movements very clearly. School, gymnastic practice, and then the date I'd been so excited to have that ended in tragedy.

"What about George?" She asked as I pulled up to the vet's office.

"George didn't move here until after high school." I pulled into the parking lot of the vet's office and put the car in park.

"Are you going to undo your marriage?"

"I'm going back to avoid the accident," I explained to her. "If I do that, then I'll make a name for myself, maybe even the Olympic team. So I won't be schlepping around this mountain top until I'm thirty-five. I won't be so lonely that I latch onto George when he pays attention to me and decide it's now or never. Don't you see? The marriage to George will *never* happen."

"Wow," Darcy looked impressed. "You really thought this through."

I nodded, unwilling to explain that I'd been imagining the way my life could have gone if only I hadn't broken my wrist every day for the last twenty-four years.

I popped the car door and climbed out and then reached into the back for the cat carrier. Puck glowered at me, obviously annoyed that she had been carted around in such an undignified manner.

"It's okay, kitty," I soothed. "Dr. Green is just going to make sure you're healthy and find out if you have an owner."

Darcy held the door for me as I humped the carrier into the office and then set it down. Ursula Levey sat behind the reception desk, filing her nails. Her long red hair was pulled up into a high braid that enhanced her facelift.

"Joey," Ursula's smile was predatory. "I hear you got fired from the café. Nice homeless sweats look by the way. You practicing for the inevitable?"

"Ursula, I hear your husband left you for another man." Darcy wore a sweet smile on her face. "Funny how gossip spreads around a small town."

"Well, at least he didn't decide to become a woman first," Ursula snapped.

"Leave Georgia out of this," I warned. I had heard all of

her barbs and was used to them but I wouldn't tolerate her trash-talking Georgia.

"Yeah, just because her boob-job is better than the one you're sporting," Darcy nodded to the exposed cleavage. "It looks like you have an ass on your chest."

Ursula's face flamed and she pushed herself out from the desk. "I'll let Pete know you're here."

"What a passive-aggressive hose beast," Darcy shook her head. "Her twin brother is the nicest guy in town and she's his emotional photo negative. She hasn't changed at all since high school."

I had to agree. Ursula Levey was not the sort of person normally found working at a veterinarian's office. She was mean and spiteful and for some reason, she'd had it out for me since we were kids.

"Did Tom really leave her for another man?" I whisper-hissed.

"Yeah, their accountant." Darcy was always up on the latest gossip. "Cleaned out the joint bank account and headed for Aruba. Or maybe it was Jamaica. I don't know, one of those tropical places my pasty hide never gets to visit."

Ursula pushed her way through the swinging door and reached for the cat carrier.

"*Rooooweeeer,*" Puck screeched and swiped a paw out through the bars of the kitty jail, nearly costing Ursula one French manicured index finger.

"It's true," Darcy had a note of awe in her voice. "Animals can sense evil."

She swore and jumped back. "Is that thing rabid?"

"No more than you are," Darcy said with a sweet smile.

I picked up the carrier and said, "I've got her. Lead the way."

With one more killing glare, Ursula minced down the hall

and gestured to a small room on the left that smelled of woodchips, disinfectant, and dog.

She didn't say anything as we set Puck down on the metal exam table and then seated ourselves in uncomfortable plastic chairs.

I squirmed. "Do you think…never mind."

"What?" Darcy asked.

"Well, it's just that I was wondering about when I go back, do you think I can change other things?"

"Like what?" Darcy raised a brow. "Do you mean—"

There was a knock on the door and a moment later Pete Green stepped in. His smile crinkled the skin around his baby blue eyes. His thick sandy brown hair had just a slight hint of red and his skin held a deep golden tan. He wasn't as good looking as Robin, but he was a close second.

I nearly sighed when he turned that smile on me. "Joey, Darcy, how are you, ladies? It's been a long time."

I mumbled something incoherent.

Darcy did what she always did and came to my rescue. "Hi, Pete. How's the family?"

He grinned and took out his phone, swiping to display a picture of himself, a pretty blonde woman and two golden-haired cherubs as well as a beagle puppy.

"Wow, they're getting big." Darcy elbowed me in the ribs.

"Congratulations," I coughed up and looked away.

"So, who do we have here?" Pete stashed his phone and headed toward the carrier.

I jumped out of my seat. "Careful!"

But Pete unlatched the door and Puck strutted out like she owned the place.

"Hey there, pretty girl." Pete stroked along her back and she arched into his touch and then began to purr.

Too low for Pete to hear, Darcy sighed. "He always did have a way with the pussies."

My hour of pilfered time was up when we left the vet's office, still with Puck in tow. There was no weird magical conveyor belt feeling, nothing at all other than a slight dizzy spell as we were walking out the door.

I staggard and Pete reached out and put a steadying hand on my arm. "You okay?"

"Yeah." I suddenly felt…whole. There was no other way to describe it. As though a hunk of me had been missing. "Sorry, just got a little woozy there."

"Maybe you ought to sit down in the waiting room for a bit." He offered.

With Ursula sniping at me the whole time? Hard pass.

"It's okay, I can drive." Darcy offered.

We discussed Puck for a few. She wasn't chipped and, according to Pete, no one had reported a missing mackerel tabby. He promised to be in touch if he heard anything. He'd already given us a bag for the flea prevention treatment and checked for ear mites, which thankfully, she didn't have.

"So, what was it you were saying about making other changes?" Darcy asked when we were alone in the car once more.

I sighed as she turned into her driveway. "I never told you but…Pete asked me out once."

She put the car in park and turned to face me with her mouth hanging open. "What? When?"

"After my accident." I sighed. "He brought me flowers in the hospital."

Darcy shook her head. "So why didn't you ever go out with him?"

I stared out the window at the snow-covered crab apple tree in the neighbor's yard. "I was still hoping Bill Tucker would show up. Say he was sorry for what happened and ask me out again."

Darcy shook her head. "I didn't realize you were that hung up on him."

I didn't want to think about Bill, the boy who had ruined my life. "Besides, I didn't want a pity date and that's what it would have been with Pete. By the time I was out of rehab, he was about to head off to college. And it didn't seem like the time to start something, you know?"

Darcy *thunked* her head back against her seat. "Jeez, Joey. Why would you throw a guy like that back?"

"It's not like I caught him or anything. And he sure moved on fast enough. He got married when he was studying to be a vet, But I can't help wondering…." I trailed off, unsure of how to finish.

"What if things were different?" Darcy guessed. "I guess you'll find out. When are you going to do it?"

"As soon as possible."

"You okay to drive home?" She studied me. "What was that little episode earlier. Or were you just pretend tripping so Pete would show concern? Because if you were, props."

"You know I can't flirt worth shit. No, I got a little dizzy when the time spell ended was all."

Darcy studied my face. "You sure this is a good idea? Every time travel story I ever heard of warns us not to muck around with time."

So I wasn't the only one worried about wiping out my existence. "Robin implied that it was safe."

"That's the other thing." Darcy bit her lip. "Are you sure you can trust him?"

No. In fact I harbored a gut-twisting sensation that I absolutely couldn't trust him. "It's done, Darcy. We made the bargain." And I had a feeling that getting out of a magical deal wouldn't be easy.

"Okay, well, if you're sure," she sighed. "I better get back to work. I've got a Count of Monte Cristo for a Chihuahua that needs to go out in tomorrow's mail."

"Where do you find these people?" I shook my head.

"Word gets around. Hey, do you think Pete would let me put up a flyer in his office?"

"Maybe. You should call him and find out."

"Maybe you should call him. Like, say, twenty-three years ago?" She waggled her eyebrows.

I got out of the car and then took the keys before giving her a hug. "Thanks for having my back. And believing my crazy story."

"Anytime." Darcy winked and then headed into her house.

I drove home and parked in my mother's usual spot. After unloading Puck and setting her free to wander, I called Grammy B to let her know the cat was free to a good home.

"Did you want me to drop her off with you?" It would be hell putting her back in the cat carrier but I'd do it for Grammy's sake.

"Thanks, but no. I just don't think I'm up to doing all the caretaking. She's good company. I don't mind watching her while you're at work."

I screwed up my face. Work. Right. I'd better get a jump on changing my past because I really didn't want to job hunt anymore.

Grammy cleared her throat, a horrible phlegmy sound that made me shudder. "Those cookies were terrific by the way."

My jaw dropped. "Please tell me you didn't eat them all already."

"Well, I would, but it would be a lie." She didn't sound the slightest bit sorry. Grammy B really had no shame.

She was my personal hero. "I'll see you tomorrow, Grammy."

I hung up and sat on the fainting couch in the parlor. Puck jumped up beside me and rubbed against my hand until I started to pet her.

Robin had said he would see me soon. How soon was soon though? And though I didn't want to admit it, Darcy's concerns about my end of the bargain had affected me. What did the fae want from a middle-aged divorcee anyway?

A flush stole over me as I recalled the way he had studied me and called me fascinating. Nothing about my current life was fascinating. In fact, I knew the opposite was true. My mother had lived an incredible life as had Grammy B. They were fascinating. By comparison, I was a real dull stick.

"A dull stick who time-traveled today," I muttered and scratched Puck between the ears. Her eyes closed to slits as she leaned into my touch. "And look what I did with it. I spied on my echo self having lunch at the cafe and took you to the vet. Such a wild woman."

Was I thinking too small? Perhaps I ought to try to use my time traveling trips to do something amazing. That's what my mother would do. She'd save JFK or warn the crew of the Challenger that the shuttle was going to explode.

But avoiding my accident wouldn't just benefit my life, I assured myself. Dad had said as much. Maybe I would be giving my parents the space they needed to grow together instead of apart. And Georgia too. Without our marriage interfering, she would be free to be herself that much sooner.

The doorbell rang, breaking me out of my musings. I got up. Puck, clearly irritated that petting time had been interrupted, weaved through my ankles as I moved to the door.

At first, I didn't recognize the creature standing on the other side. She wore black leggings with a black tunic on top with a black puffer vest over that and black combat boots on her feet. Her dark hair was shaved on the left side and the remaining sections had been streaked with a blue that matched her eyes. It was her eyes, same shape, and shade as mine and my mom's, that finally clued me in.

"Diedre?" I asked.

Her expression didn't change from the resentful scowl that added to her menacing air. "I go by Dragon now."

"M'kay, Dragon." I pushed the door wider and gestured for her to come in.

She did, carrying a green army duffel. The last time Diedre—aka Dragon—had come for a visit, she'd been carrying a pink suitcase covered with cat stickers.

Speaking of cats, Puck had abandoned her efforts to trip me up and rubbed up against the new arrival, purring up a storm. My cousin's expression softened as she crouched down to pet the insistent critter.

"Her name's Puck," I offered.

"Like from A Midsummer Night's Dream?" Dragon's attention remained on the cat.

Had everyone seen that play except me? "That's right. I found her out on the hill behind the house this morning and she followed me home."

Nothing, no reply.

"So, I hear you're going to be staying with us for a while."

She stood up. "Which room is mine?"

I wished I had a chance to talk to my mother a little bit more about the plans for my cousin. She'd sprung this on me at the last minute. "Um, maybe the blue room? It has its own bathroom. And a nice view. Though I'm not sure if it's ready for company."

Again, no response. What was it about talking to teenagers that made a full grown woman feel like a babbling idiot?

"Come on, let's go check it out," I said and then reached out to take her bag from her.

She shrank away, glaring at my outstretched hand as though I'd offered her a poisonous viper.

My hand fell to my side. "Okay, then. I guess you can carry it."

We trudged up past the second floor that held my bedroom and bath as well as a tiny bedroom that had become a storage room for mom's pornographic art. Mom's room was on the first floor. Diedre would have the third floor all to herself.

We trudged up the final set of stairs and saw the door to the blue room stood wide open. Mom had definitely intended to put Diedre in the space. I could smell lemon cleanser and the scent of fresh from the dryer linens. The double bed had been made and a pretty purple candlewick bedspread had appeared as well as a blue lamp that I had never seen before. The shade was fairly standard but the base looked lopsided. Instead of one round globe for the base, it looked like two uneven lumps. I frowned and stepped closer to examine the top part of it.

On no. Mom had made the lamp. Which meant….

"Is that a dick?" Dragon asked.

I winced. "Technically, it's a lamp. Your aunt has been expressing herself creatively and all her creations come out with a similar shape."

"Like dicks?"

"Yeah pretty much. Though the lamp part is new." At least the shade covered the head. I was going to have to tell my mother that her art was getting out of hand because her niece would be sleeping beside an enormous set of blue balls.

Diedre stared at me and I realized I was just standing there, taking up space.

"Um, I'm not sure when your aunt Prudence will be back. I was just about to go into town and get groceries. Do you want to come with me?"

She shook her head.

"Any requests?"

Another head shake.

"Okay well, um. I'll leave my cell phone number and mom's down on the fridge, in case you need to get a hold of us. There are some cookies down there, apple oatmeal that I just made this morning." Better Dragon eat them than Grammy.

"Okay."

I was getting the impression she couldn't wait to be rid of me. "And I guess, I'll just leave you to it. See you later."

I backed out the door and hadn't reached the top of the stairs when I heard it slam behind me.

I looked down at Puck. "That could have gone better."

"Meow," she agreed.

I picked her up and then carried her downstairs. I found a small ceramic custard cup and filled it with the food that Grammy had given me. I filled another with water and set both in the corner of the kitchen on an old mat.

The cat seen to, it was time to start thinking about the people. What did teenagers eat? Rumor had it, everything, but I'd been on a very restrictive diet when I was Diedre's age. Whatever I made, I needed to make enough for four and I liked to have leftovers for Grammy to heat and eat.

I found a frozen container of tomato basil sauce that I'd made last summer after harvesting tomatoes from my garden. I set it on the counter to thaw, deciding to make lasagna.

There was always plenty left over. I'd grab a bottle of wine and a fresh loaf of Italian bread along with makings for salad. That should cover all the basics.

I scribbled my phone number down on a post-it and stuck it to the fridge. Then I repeated the process with mom's number. Where was she anyway? I'd had her car all day. Maybe she was at Grammy's? Somehow, I doubted it. Mom and Grammy's visits were usually brief and filled with judgmental harumphs coupled with awkward silence.

"You're in charge, Puck," I said to the cat who was bathing her tail. "Make sure Dragon doesn't burn down the house."

I grabbed my purse and flung open the back door.

And screamed.

CHAPTER SEVEN

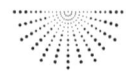

"If you love something...set it free. If it comes back to you, that's a'cause no one else wanted to clean up after it."
–Notable quotable from Grammy B

"What are you doing here?" I hissed at the tall form lurking just outside my door.

"You were irritated when I popped in earlier so I decided to knock." Robin stood on the doorstep, looking windblown and sinful.

I put a hand over my still racing heart. "I was irritated because I was naked in the bathtub when you decided to *pop in* for a visit. And you just scared the hell out of me."

"Apologies, lamb." He took my shaking hands in his and brought them to his lips. "I didn't mean to frighten you."

"Well, you did." I huffed out a breath. "I'm glad you're here now though."

His full lips curled up in a predatory smile and he moved

in closer until I could feel the warmth radiating off his big body. "Miss me, did you?"

I blushed to the roots of my hair. Why did he have this effect on me? It was as bad as earlier with Pete. Worse because while Pete was just a nice guy who I'd been crushing on since high school, he didn't make me feel all fluttery inside. Not the way Robin did.

Then again, Pete was human.

"Joey?" A feminine voice called from behind me. "I heard you scream. Who is this guy?"

I turned and saw my cousin standing in the doorway, armed with a pull trigger canister of...something. "Is that pepper spray?"

"Is he attacking you?" Dragon looked ready to spit fire with a little help from her device.

"No, no. He just took me by surprise. Put that away." Now I had to introduce the faery to Dragon. Skippy.

But Robin took the lead. "My apologies for startling you. I'm a friend of Joey's. You can call me Robin. And you must be her fierce...?" He trailed off, one eyebrow raised, waiting for her to fill in the blank.

"Cousin," I supplied. "This is my cousin, Dragon."

"Indeed," Robin raised a brow. "Your cousin is in town for a visit? You never mentioned it to me."

"My mom dumped me here because she's embarrassed by me." Dragon lifted her chin defiantly, as though daring us to pity her.

I opened my mouth to reassure her that that wasn't the case, that her mother loved her and wanted what was best for her. But was that the truth? Before I could decide, the fae took over the conversation. "I am a grave embarrassment to my mother as well."

"You are?" Dragon tilted her head to the side as she

studied him. "Did she dump you in the middle of nowhere too?"

Robin shook his head. "No, she simply exiled me from her presence until I abide by her edicts."

How could that be possible? He was beautiful and charming and had gotten me to sign up for an open-ended favor against my better judgment. I wasn't sure what the requirements were to be a good faery son, but he must be one of the best at what he did.

"And what about you, lamb?" Robin turned those sapphire eyes on me. "Are you also an embarrassment to your mother?"

I snorted. "Are you kidding? I'm a washed-up former gymnast that never fulfilled her potential. A forty-something divorcee who lives in her house. My longest run of employment was six months at a temp agency. *Of course*, I'm an epic embarrassment to my mother. How could I not be?"

"What?" A new voice said from behind me.

I cringed. Shot a poisonous glare at Robin and then turned to face the music. "Hi, Mom."

She was carrying two big bags full of what appeared to be pillows. Though her cheeks were reddened from being out in the cold, she looked pale.

"Let me help you with that." I took the bags from her hands and retreated into the house cursing my runaway mouth with every step. I bypassed the kitchen and moved down the hall to the alcove at the base of the stairs and plopped the bags down on the shaker bench where we sat to put on our shoes. My gaze fell on Puck, who'd curled up in a patch of sunlight and was resting peacefully.

I closed my eyes and took a deep breath. Okay, things weren't so bad. I'd get through dinner and then Robin would show me how to go back in time to undo my accident. Then I wouldn't be a colossal failure and the conversation that had just happened would be erased.

"I hope," I muttered and then returned to the back door. I didn't slow, just snagged Robin's arm as I passed through and towed him to the car. "Going to the store. Text if you need anything."

"Wait!" Mom called but I pretended I didn't hear her as I cranked the engine over.

Robin slid into the seat beside me. "If you want to go back to avoid that conversation, that will count toward your three trips."

I glared at him as the car turned off the street. "You set me up."

"Me?" He pressed a hand to his chest and blinked. "How is what just happened my fault?"

I paused for the traffic light. "It's what you do, isn't it? Create chaos wherever you go for your own amusement?"

He frowned. "Well, admittedly, I have played a few pranks in my day. But you're the one who was ranting about what a worthless daughter you are."

"Because you brought it up!" A horn blared behind me and I pounded on the gas. "You might as well have jumped on my insecurity button with both feet!"

"Technically, Dragon brought it up. I was only trying to help you relate to her." Robin's tone was quiet. "I apologize if I overstepped."

If I hadn't been behind the wheel, I would have closed my eyes. As it was, I turned into the market's parking lot and backed into a free space. I shut the engine off and sat quietly, staring at the sign advertising BOGO tomato soup cans and 2 for $5 coffee creamer.

"It's not your fault," I admitted on an exhale. "Sorry for blaming you. I know that I'm just…."

"Just what?" he prompted.

"Mom and I aren't the world's best communicators. We live in the same house and get along but that's because we don't spend much time actually together, you know? Not since my accident."

"It always comes back to that doesn't it?" Robin reached into his pocket and pulled out the little hourglass. "Are you ready for your next lesson?"

I popped the car door and climbed out. "I don't recall having the first lesson."

"The first lesson is that time is the one resource most will never get back. Yet is the one all mortals insist on squandering. How did you spend your extra hour?" He stepped in front of me to hold the old-fashioned glass door to the market, allowing me to enter.

"Thank you." I snagged a buggy from the nested row of them and pointed it toward the produce section. "Well, after you abandoned me at your place, I picked up Darcy and we drove to the diner to spy on the...what did you call the earlier versions of us. Our echoes?"

He snapped and pointed at me. "Ah-ha. Exactly my point. I gave you a free trip back in time and you felt the need to verify that which was already verified. You'd seen the echoes on the hill and yet you demanded verification from a third party."

I snagged a plastic bag and a head of green leaf lettuce. "I needed to talk to someone about it. Someone other than you. Because I wasn't one hundred percent sure that you're real. Would you get a bag of carrots for me, please?"

He retrieved the carrots and placed them carefully in the bottom of the basket. "Of course, I'm real. And you know, you really shouldn't be saying please and thank you to fae royalty. It could be interpreted as a sign that you feel indebted to them."

How was he so handsome, even under the horrible fluorescent lights of the super market, it was easy to believe he was a fae prince. That would make his mother….

My cart crashed into a stand of apples and several Golden Delicious went rolling onto the floor. I bent down and started collecting the bruised fruit.

"Are you well?" Robin asked.

"Your mother is a fairy queen," I breathed. He'd told me earlier that he was a fae prince, but I hadn't believed him.

"What of it?" Robin crouched down next to me and collected a few of the apples. "I was just cautioning you, lamb, in case you ran across any more of my kind."

"When would I?" I stood and replaced the apples back on the display pile. My heart thudded and I tried to calm myself even as I kept sneaking glances at my companion.

He didn't answer. Instead, he perused the market shelves with interest. Picking up a jar he asked, "What is peanut butter?"

My mouth fell open. "You've never had a peanut butter and jelly sandwich?"

"No." He frowned and rolled the jar around in his hands. "When would I have?"

I guess the fae queen wasn't big on brown-bagging it. I took the jar out of his hands and added it to my haul. "Grammy says peanut butter and strawberry jam is the way to go. Personally, I like the classic version. PB&J on worthless white bread. I'll make one for you and you'll love it."

"You're offering me gifts?" he asked quietly.

"It's just a sandwich. Besides, you bought me lunch today. Fair's fair."

"Technically your lunch was on Rodney."

I pawed through the baked goods, looking for a loaf of Italian bread that could pass for fresh. "Which reminds me, I have to go back over there and tip the waitress you stiffed."

"Why? After what she pulled?"

"Because she brought us food and it's what decent people do when they dine out."

"So she took your job and tried to steal your companion and yet you still feel the need to dip into your meager reserves and gift her with currency?" The intense way he was staring at me as though trying to figure out what made me tick was unsettling. I refocused on my shopping and our earlier conversation.

"So the first lesson is that mortals always squander time even though we will never get it back. What's the second lesson?"

"That the mortal mind will explain away whatever it can not comprehend." He snapped his fingers and all the items on the shelf we were facing rearranged themselves in a seemingly random way.

"Why did you do that?" My tone was horrified. None of the items matched the pricing labels.

"Just watch." Robin stepped back as a harried-looking young woman rushed into the aisle. She studied the mess the faery had just made, frowned, stepped back and scanned the aisle again, hurried several steps down, plucked a jar of honey off the shelf and then rushed off.

"It's how the space-time continuum protects itself. As the mortal population has increased, the mortal attention span for anything outside of its own pedantic existence decreases. Most don't stop and question why things are done the way they are, even when it inconveniences them. They accept it and move on. Some in pursuit of money or power or fame. Others perhaps seek inspiration or even a sliver of time where they can simply be not in demand any longer."

"That's…" I wanted to say not true, but could I? I'd just seen an example of what he'd done. "Just put it back the way it was, please."

"Lamb, honestly, you can be such a wet blanket." But he snapped his fingers and the shelf returned to its previously organized state. "You see my point. Look at time like you would an organic creature. It has a built-in sense of self-preservation. It will protect itself at all costs. Only a pivotal shift can unmake it."

I thought about that while I detoured through a few more aisles than normal, picking up things I thought Dragon might like to have around the house and thinking about what Robin had said. "So, you're saying travel through time is possible because no matter what, people will rationalize any weirdness they see and write it off as something other than me tampering with time?"

"Exactly. It's self-protection as well. No one wants to be singled out as weak among the herd. Historically, seeing or hearing things other mortals can't hasn't gone well for members of your species."

"True that." We were in the frozen food section when I spotted him. Oh no, not twice in one day. I wasn't *that* unlucky, was I?

"Turn around," I hissed at Robin who was busy frowning at a bag of tater tots he had retrieved from one of the glass cases. "And put those back."

"These appear to have no nutritional value whatsoever. Yet I see people eating them all the time. What's the point?"

"The point is they're good. Now shake a leg before he sees—"

"Joey?" Pete called out to me. "Twice in one day, how's that for luck?"

"—us," I muttered then turned to face the veterinarian. "Hi, Pete. How have you been?"

"Since two?" Pete laughed. "I honestly can't complain."

"Two?" Robin raised an eyebrow at me. "I thought you said you went to the diner with Darcy?"

"I did. Then I took the cat I found to the vet's office to see if they could help me find her owner."

Pete's golden-brown gaze went from me to Robin, who was still clutching the tots and then to the cart full of food. I could see the wheels churning and see him putting one and one together and coming up with sixty-nine.

Robin was scrutinizing Pete as well and I wasn't a fan of the speculative gleam in his eyes.

All we needed in the frozen food section was Georgia and Bill Tucker and we'd have the entire collection of Joey Whitmore's tragic dating history aka people I avoided whenever possible.

"I'm sorry again about Ursula, Joey," Pete said before I could think up a good excuse to use as an escape. "She's been having a tough time lately but that's no excuse for her to take out her unhappiness on you."

"Forget it," I murmured and waved it off. "I already have."

Robin chose that particular moment to sling an arm over my shoulders. "We should probably get going. Your mom and cousin will be waiting for us, don't you think, lamb?"

I cringed.

Pete looked surprised for a minute but recovered so fast I figured I must have imagined it. "Okay, well, I'll let you know if I hear anything about the cat. See you around, Joey."

I waited until Pete rounded the corner before shoving Robin's arm off of me. "What was that?"

"I'm saving you from further embarrassment. Your flirting needs some work, lamb."

"I wasn't flirting with Pete," I huffed.

"No, but he was undressing you with his eyes."

"He was not! First of all, he's married, therefore off-limits."

"Oh really?" Robin asked. "Then why wasn't he wearing a

wedding ring? And did you see the contents of his cart? Stack of microwave dinners for one."

I blinked. What with being so busy trying to extract myself from the awkward situation, I hadn't noticed. "He's a vet. He probably can't wear the ring if he's doing surgery."

"And the lonely heart's special?" Robin asked.

"Maybe he just likes them," I insisted. "He was showing me a picture of his family earlier today. And his wife is about ten years younger than I am, a slim, pretty blonde. If he had that at home why would he look at me?"

"Because," Robin said slowly as though explaining a very basic concept to a complete dimwit. "Mortal men always crave what they don't have. And I'm getting these."

He dropped the tots onto the pile of groceries.

※

"So, why didn't you stay married to Georgia?" Robin asked as he leaned on the counter while I washed the lettuce.

"Keep your voice down." I cast a surreptitious look at the closed door to my mother's art studio. Strains of Bobby Darin's *Dream Lover* were barely audible.

"Why? Is that a taboo topic as well?" Robin moved over to the pot of bubbling sauce. "I'm going to need a list."

"Not taboo, just uncomfortable." I sighed and reached for the vegetable peeler. "I knew almost from the beginning that marrying George was a mistake. We were very good friends and had been dating for two years. Getting married was the next logical step, at least the way I saw it." Mostly because unlike my mother, I wanted to be married.

Attacking the carrots with a vengeance, I summed up, "So we got married. But things weren't great in other…er… areas."

"You mean sex." Robin raised a brow.

I glanced up at him sharply. "What makes you think that?"

"Lamb, you are a bubbling cauldron of carnal lust about to boil over." His lids lowered to half-mast. "I sense that you have never been truly satisfied."

"Ow," I dropped the peeler which had just accidentally taken a layer of skin off the back of my thumb. "Damn it, that stings."

I moved to the sink to rinse it off but Robin caught my hand.

"What are you doing?" I blinked up at him in surprise.

He didn't answer. There was a swirl of amber and gold lights coming from his hand and he placed it directly over mine. Not touching, but near enough that I could feel the warmth.

Then, my skin began to glow with the same golden hue. The pain eased and the blood evaporated into mist leaving only unblemished skin behind.

Robin released me and I studied my hand, front, and back. "That's some talent you have."

"That's not even my best one," he crooned.

"Thank you." I smiled up at him.

"What did I tell you? Never thank a fae," he warned.

I shrugged. "I didn't. I thanked my friend for patching me up."

"Joey," he murmured and moved even closer until we shared the same airspace.

I lost myself for a minute in the sapphire depths of his eyes. My heart thudded against my ribcage. Was Robin about to kiss me? What would it be like to kiss a fae prince?

I was mentally preparing myself to find out when his gaze shot to the kitchen door and he vanished. A moment later, Dragon came in carrying Puck in her arms.

I thumped back down hard on my heels, not realizing until I landed that I had been up on my tiptoes. So close. I had been so damn close to kissing the hell out of Robin. Which would have been wrong. He wasn't even human!

No, Robin Goodfellow was a distraction I didn't need right before I rewrote my life for an honest-to-goodness happily ever after. This was no time for a detour.

"What's for dinner?" Dragon lifted the lid on the bubbling pot of sauce.

"Lasagna." I made an effort to smile at her. "Sound good?"

"I don't eat meat." She lifted her chin as though I was about to challenge her on her diet.

"Well, that's good to know." I had been just about to fry up some ground beef to add to the sauce. "But cheese and dairy are okay?"

When she nodded, I busied myself with layering the no-bake noodles, cheese, and sauce into a ceramic casserole dish. Dragon set the cat down, washed her hands, and then took over the salad I had left unfinished.

It was nice to have help. Normally, my mother and I took turns making dinner. I couldn't recall the last time I had prepared a meal with someone instead of for them.

The oven beeped, indicating it had come up to temperature. I wrapped the lasagna securely in tinfoil and picked it up. My bum wrist chose that moment to cramp up. I dropped the heavy metal pan and it clattered to the floor. The tinfoil was jarred loose and noodles and sauce spattered the black and white floor.

"Damn it." I closed my eyes, trying to block out the mess.

"Are you all right?" Dragon put a tentative hand on my shoulder.

No, I wasn't. I was embarrassed because one stupid mistake had consigned me to a life of misery. But I didn't want to lay that all out for my cousin, who was having her own rough time, so I said, "Old injury."

My mother chose that moment to pop her head out of her studio. "What happened?"

"My wrist seized up." I turned to the sink and retrieved a dishrag. When I spun back around, Puck was there, licking sauce and ricotta cheese off an uncooked noodle.

"Let me get this. You ought to ice that wrist." My mother reached for the cloth.

I snatched it away. "I said it's fine." I dropped to my knees and after shooing the cat away, scooped the mess into a dustpan and then directly into the trash.

My mother stood there and I knew she wanted to say something. At that moment, I was incredibly grateful for Dragon's presence. Mom would curb her tongue with her niece in the house.

Dragon was looking at the pot of sauce. "There's still some left. Maybe we can just do spaghetti instead?"

A lump formed in my throat. She was a good egg, stepping up with a solution to help diffuse the tension.

"Sure." The ceramic dish was cracked beyond salvation. I added it to the garbage bag and then tied it up. "I'm just going to take this out to the trash."

I stood up and, feeling like I was a hundred years old, shuffled out the back door.

"What just happened?" I heard Dragon ask my mom.

Against my better judgment I paused, wondering how Prudence Whitmore would respond. We didn't talk about what had happened. Not ever.

My mother cleared her throat. "You know Josephine was in a car accident when she was a teenager? Well, that accident cost her the chance to become an elite gymnast and her shot at the Olympic team. She never got over that. Sometimes she pushes too hard and the wrist gives out. And every time it happens, it reminds her of what she lost."

"You mean going to the Olympics?" Dragon asked.

My mother sighed. "The Olympics, being able to do gymnastics. Everything she had worked and sacrificed for. The way she saw it, all of her hard work came to nothing. It was all snatched away in a moment. And she's never let herself try for any new goal since."

I moved away from the door. We had several bricks set on top of the trash can lids to keep the raccoons out of the garbage. I picked one up and hurled it into the trees behind the house with all my strength.

That felt good, so I did it with the other one. Then I sank to my knees on the frozen ground and sobbed.

My mother was wrong. I had tried to make my life better. To find a new path. I'd gotten married, worked all sorts of jobs, but it didn't change the fact that I could no longer do the one thing I had been put on the planet to do. The only area in which I'd excelled. The universe had cursed me with bad luck because of the gift I had squandered.

"I have to fix it," I whispered into the night. "I have to make it better, no matter the cost."

It was time.

CHAPTER EIGHT

"A real man knows what to do in every situation...exactly what his wife tells him to do."
-Notable quotable from Grammy B

After dinner, I volunteered to take a plate of spaghetti over to Grammy's, knowing mom wouldn't think anything of it if I was gone for a while. Grammy B was asleep in her recliner. I shut off the forensics crime show, stowed the spaghetti in the fridge, and left her a note telling her what I'd left her and how long to reheat the plate when she felt like eating.

Then I drove out to Firefly Lane.

There was no sign of Robin though all the lights were on in his treehouse. I hunted around until I found the knot that caused the door to the tree to swing inward. Any other time, I would have waited outside until the owner came home even though it was starting to snow. But Robin had no problem letting himself into my space—including my bathroom while I was naked in the tub—so fair was fair.

I climbed the stairs and moved into his living area and then through it toward the magic artifact room. The hourglass full of purple sand sat on his desk as though it were waiting for me. My heartbeat accelerated and without conscious thought, my feet carried me across the floor and over to the desk.

The sands of time. How did they work? And where had he gotten them from? And would I really be able to keep the accident from happening?

"What are you doing, lamb?"

I spun around and put a hand over my heart. "You scared me."

He studied my face. "You weren't thinking of traveling back now, were you?"

"Why not?" I raised my chin. "We struck a bargain. It seems to me that I ought to be able to go back whenever I want."

His blue eyes glittered. "And what if you do something unintentional when you go back? Without completing your training, you wouldn't know how to undo it."

"What training?" I threw my hands up in frustration. "So far all you've taught me is that people waste time and are too preoccupied with their own lives to question random changes. It's starting to feel as though I'm taking your course in mortal bashing 101."

The light in the room flickered and the tree shook. Was it an earthquake? In the mountains of North Carolina? Whoever heard of that? It took me a moment to realize the house was responding to his dark mood. His blond brows pulled down over the bridge of his perfect nose. He snapped his fingers and the tree stilled.

"Lesson three," he said. "Mortals are unfailingly impatient. To their *detriment*."

He held out a hand and after a long moment, I gave him

the hourglass. He took it back to the desk, placed it in the box, and shut the lid.

He ran a hand through his hair. "Believe it or not, I'm trying to help you. I want you to get everything you want out of your three trips back and nothing else because, lesson four," he paused for dramatic effect.

I rolled my eyes. "Lay it on me."

"Lesson four, when the faery dust hits the fan, everyone looks for someone else to blame."

"You're basically teaching me about human nature, not time travel." I sagged into one of the carved chairs in front of his desk.

He leaned back against his desk and crossed one long leg over the other. "That's right. I am."

"But why?" What could one possibly have to do with the other?

"Because to successfully travel through time, you need to *understand* human nature. Would you like deaths on your head? How about unintentionally causing your own?"

My lips parted. "You said when we went back earlier that it wasn't dangerous."

He nodded. "That's right. It's not dangerous to go back a single hour. But we're talking about something bigger than that. You want to reverse something that happened over two decades ago. That's a long slog against the current. Do you have a plan as to how to enact the change you desire?"

I closed my eyes and recalled the scene as vividly as if it had happened yesterday. "I have to keep from getting in that car."

"But *how*, Joey? Will you kill the driver?"

My mouth dropped open at the suggestion. "What? No! I could never kill anyone."

His fingers drummed on the edge of the desk. "Then

maybe tamper with the car. Steal the distributor cap so it won't start?"

I nodded. "Okay, that sounds good."

"And what if the vehicle's owner sees you and calls the police? How will you identify yourself?"

I opened my mouth to answer that the people in town knew me. But they wouldn't. In 1996, Joey Whitmore was a teenage gymnast. I couldn't use my own name.

Robin continued to drive his point home. "Who will you call for bail? Your father?"

"Of course not." Then a thought occurred. "Wait. Won't I come forward to this time again after I prevent the accident?"

Robin shook his head as though dealing with a difficult child. "Again, too much television. No, Joey. Though the moment you wish to change is pivotal *to you*, it is meaningless to the space-time continuum. Don't you recall what I told you would happen earlier?"

"That we would reabsorb our echoes and they would get our memories of the extra time that we had."

Robin folded his arms over his chest and nodded once. "Correct. And did you notice anything different when time caught up?"

I thought back to that afternoon. "I got a little dizzy, but nothing else."

"Right. Because you didn't travel forward again, you lived that hour over in a different way, essentially doubling your time."

I stared at him. Surely, he wasn't saying what I thought he was saying…?

Though I hadn't spoken a word, Robin nodded. "If you go back to 1996, the day you arrive will be your starting point. It's a one-way trip. You go back and live it over until your echo catches up to you twenty-four years later."

"But I'll be sixty-six!" I shook my head. "What good will changing the past do if I don't get to live my life over?"

His lips twisted in something that was halfway between a smirk and a grimace. "You could use another trip to come forward into the new fork in the river. But I wouldn't recommend that."

"Why not?" That sounded like the perfect solution.

"You won't have your echo's memories. You won't know what is the same and what changed. All your memories will be from this life, not the one in that altered timeline."

I considered for a beat. "Lesson two says that no one will notice if I'm a little off, right?"

"Yes." Robin nodded as though he didn't like the direction the conversation was taking us.

I shrugged. "I can fudge it."

"Fudge it?" Robin stared at me incredulously. "Fudge over two decades of life experience?"

"Why not? Not that much will change for anyone other than me." Except maybe my parents would be together.

"Lamb, you are ridiculously naive." Robin sighed. "All right, your homework for this evening is to consider how you will prevent the accident in a way that won't get you incarcerated or maimed."

I flinched. "Maimed?"

"It's a possibility, especially if you do something foolish like throw your current self in front of the car." He pushed off the desk and then reached for my hands.

"Because Joey, if you are killed in the past, that is where your story ends."

❄

"Three trips," Darcy scoffed as we sat on the front steps of her house, our hands wrapped around mugs of steaming hot cocoa as we watched the snow come down. "Sounds to me like a casino game where the house always wins. If you have to use one trip to go back and another to come forward and it blows donkey sac, there's no way you can use the third trip without getting stuck."

I took a sip of the cocoa, which she had added a shot of whipped cream vodka to. "This means I only have one chance to fix the past. I need to make sure everything is perfect before I come back."

"Perfect." Darcy sighed. "Joey, I don't know about this. It's one thing to snag an extra hour. Hell, I wish I had more of them in the day. But you're talking about redoing your *entire adult life*. Are things really so terrible?"

I held up a hand and began ticking off facts. "I can't hold a job. My ex-husband is a woman, my car is impounded and I live with my mother."

She winced. "At least you have your health?"

I pointed to my wrist. "Except for this. And the fact that I am fat."

"You're middle-aged. And you can change the stuff you don't like about yourself," she insisted. "Maybe Robin has something in his bag of tricks like he did for your hair. It still looks amazing by the way."

"Thanks. And that's what I'm trying to do, change things for the better," I insisted. "Not just my life, but my mom's and dad's as well. They can focus on each other instead of piecing me back together. And if I'm whole, I can pursue my dreams. Have a real career, not a series of dead-end jobs. My marriage to George never would have happened. That's the moment, Darcy. It's the point where everything went wrong."

Darcy drained her mug then rolled it around in between her palms. "Have you ever considered, I don't know, just moving forward with time?"

"It's what I've been trying to do for the last twenty-four years." I put my head in my hands. "Trying and failing."

She set her mug down and then reached out and gripped my hand in hers. "I just want you to be happy, Joey."

A crash sounded from inside followed by an ear-splitting wail.

"Dar-ceeee," Mike's frantic face appeared at the window. "Where are the Band-aids?"

"In the medicine cabinet where they always are." Darcy rolled her eyes. "It sounds like all hell is breaking loose. I better get in there. Thanks for the sanity break."

I snorted. "If me talking about time travel is sane, then I don't want to know what you consider insane."

"Having five kids in your thirties?" She raised a brow. "Six if you include Mike. Want me to send the man-child out to walk you home?"

I shook my head. "Nah, I need a little time to come up with a plan."

She gave me an impulsive hug, rare because Darcy wasn't a hugger. "Okay. Promise to call me before you, you know."

I stuck out my gloved hand and crooked my smallest digit. "Pinky swears."

She hooked hers around mine.

"Dar-ce*eee*!"

My bestie shook her head, collected the mugs, and then headed back into the house.

It was a cold and quiet slog up the hill to the Victorian. My breath came out in little puffs as I stared up at the moon and thought about what Darcy had said. I could change. People did it all the time. Wake up one morning and decide it was time for something new. Hell, isn't that what the midlife crisis was all about?

But changing who I was now wouldn't fix the past or the bad luck that came from squandering my gift. How would I break the cycle of bad luck, garbage choices, and a life that had led me on a wild goose chase to absolutely nowhere?

The things Robin had told me were admittedly scary. My three trips were really one and a half. That when I went back, I would be completely on my own because I couldn't tell a single soul who I really was or what I was doing. If I went back and died, that would be the end. And even if I did succeed, I would still be stuck with memories of failure because it would take over two decades for my echo self to catch up.

And there was still Robin's favor waiting in the wings.

I was so lost in thought that I didn't notice Dragon sitting on the porch swing wrapped in an Afghan until she sent the glider into motion.

"And here I thought I was the only one desperate enough to be out in these temperatures." I made a shooing gesture and she slid over to make room for me.

She didn't say anything and we rocked in silence for a time.

"Are you nervous about starting at a new school?" I asked her.

She shrugged. "A little."

What did one say to a taciturn teenager anyway?

"Is that guy your boyfriend?" Dragon asked.

"What guy? You mean Robin?"

She nodded.

"No, he's just a friend." In the oddest sense of the word.

"Do you have a boyfriend?"

"Nope. I'm as single as they come. What's with all the questions about my love life." Or lack thereof.

She took a deep breath. "Mom said once that you were a lesbian."

My eyebrows went up to hit my hairline. "Did she."

"Not to me or anything. I just overheard her while she

was talking to someone on the phone. But that's not true is it?" Her tone sounded almost hopeful.

"I'm not a lesbian," I told her softly. "I'm not attracted to women."

Dragon pushed the swing with her foot. "I didn't think so. If you were a lesbian you would have stayed married when your husband became a woman, right?"

"Not exactly." Why was everyone on my case about my marriage today? First Robin asking about our sex life. Which had been fine and never more than that. And now Dragon.

I needed to do better explaining it to her than I did Robin. I could brush him off because he wanted to be nosy and shocking. A general pain in the rump. But my gut was telling me Dragon needed something, though I had no idea what.

"The thing is, George always needed to be Georgia. I didn't know that when we got married. He didn't tell me that."

"So he lied to you?" Dragon asked.

I wrinkled my nose. "More like he was lying to himself. You ever hear the saying fake it 'til you make it? I think that's what both George and I were doing in our marriage. Faking it for our own reasons. We wanted to work out."

"But, like, did the idea of being with a woman disgust you? Sexually, I mean." Her voice had taken on that intense note.

"I wouldn't say disgust. More like it's not really what I wanted." A thought occurred and I cleared my throat and asked, "Dragon, honey. Are you gay?"

She looked away so I could only see her profile. A muscle jumped in her jaw. "I like guys."

"But like, do you want to date guys?" I pushed. It was a nosy question but she was practically vibrating with intensity.

She shook her head. It was a quick, jerky movement.

"Do you have a girlfriend?" We were in uncharted waters and I didn't know what precisely right thing to say. I'd never been around teenagers, at least not since I'd been one. But she was talking. That had to be better than the defensive silence.

"I did. Back in Baltimore."

"And did your mother know?"

A quick, jerky nod. "She said Tasha is a bad influence. That's why I'm here instead of staying with the housekeeper the way I usually do when she's overseas. She said I needed the family to keep an eye on me."

I started to piece it together from there. Dragon saying her mother was embarrassed by her. Being shipped off to us suddenly when her mother traveled for work wasn't about reconnecting with her roots. We were supposed to be some sort of wardens over the teenager. No wonder she'd shown up looking at us and the house as if we were a prison sentence.

I was going to have a little chat with my aunt.

In the meantime…, "It's okay." I put my arm around my cousin. Her shoulders were stiff as line-dried linen. "It's who you are and it's okay. You have to be who you are, no matter what anyone thinks. Like Georgia did."

She turned back to face me and I could see her eyes lined with silver moisture. "But like, you don't hate Georgia for tricking you?"

"No, I don't hate her." The only person I blamed for the failed marriage was me. "Look, some people who were in our situation would have stayed married because they were friends and were happy together. And while George and I had fun together, I didn't really know Georgia. It would have been like being married to a stranger. Awkward, you know?"

I kept the last little bit to myself. That Robin was right. I wanted sex. Hot, lusty, make your eyeballs roll back up in your head and leave the sheets in a sweaty tangle sort of sex. With a man. Who loved me and only me. And if I couldn't have that, I'd rather go without.

I pushed off with my foot and the swing started to rock again. "Besides, I hear Georgia dates guys now."

"Really?" She asked.

"Yup. Big, hairy trucker types that smash beer cans on their foreheads."

She wrinkled her nose. "Gross."

Pretty much my opinion too. I preferred charismatic men who told me I was beautiful.

Shoving that thought back into a mental dark corner, I winked at her. "Different strokes for different folks. There's someone out there for everyone, Dragon. You don't need to approve, just accept."

She let out a sigh. "Don't tell Aunt Prudence okay?"

"It's not my story to tell," I promised. "But if you feel like talking to her, she'd probably like to know. And maybe you could even get her to take the big blue dick lamp back."

"Oh no, I like it." She grinned.

I gaped at her. "How is that even remotely possible?"

She winked at me. "Different strokes for different folks."

"Touché." A gust of icy wind cut through my clothes. "Okay, well as much as I love girl-talk in the moonlight, I think we both need to head to bed."

I rose and was surprised when she wrapped her arms around me. "Thanks, Joey."

I hugged her back. "Anytime. Want me to drive you to school for your first day?"

She nodded. Dragon retreated to her room and I entered mine. After crawling into a pair of flannel PJs, I snagged my laptop and fired off an email to dear old Aunt Hannah, telling her what an uber bitch she was for abandoning her daughter, who she hadn't checked on to make sure that she had arrived fine after her long trip via the bus. In winter.

Satisfied, I closed the laptop and stared out the window while mulling over how exactly I was going to prevent my accident. I needed a plan, a way to approach myself that wouldn't come across as all creepy stalker weird. And above all, I needed to convince the teenage Joey Whitmore not to get in the car that would crash at 7:18 PM on October 3, 1996.

One task. One very simple, time-specific task. I could do it. And then I could travel forward to this time and be a success story instead of the black sheep.

Two trips through the river of time and I would be living the life I had always imagined.

A soft thump at the end of my bed startled me. I glanced down to see Puck's large green eyes of staring up at me.

"Hey girl," I said, reaching down to scratch between her ears. "Where have you been?"

"We need to talk," the cat said. "You're in great danger."

CHAPTER NINE

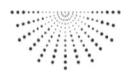

"Believe everything a man's ex says about him."
-Notable quotable from Grammy B

"Excuse me?"

It was a stupid thing to say to a cat. But I wasn't sure that I had heard her correctly. Or maybe I was asleep and all the other weirdness had seeped into my dreamscape.

"I said you're in danger." Her tail twitched and her eyes glowed in the dim light of the room. "I've been trying to warn you all day, but this house is like Grand Central before a parade."

"Sorry?" I shifted, unsure what I was apologizing for. It was one of those knee-jerk habits that I was still trying to break. "Who am I in danger from?"

"Robin Goodfellow." The cat batted at the air with claws extended. "I know he's been lurking around you. I can smell his stink all over you and your house. He's wily though. Have you struck a bargain with him yet?"

My lips parted. "How do you know about the bargain?"

"Because I was once foolish and desperate enough to bargain with him." She arched her back and hissed, "As you can see, it didn't end well."

My eyes went wide. "Robin turned you into a cat?"

"He turned me into a puck," Puck grumbled. "The cat is just the easiest shape to use so I blend in. I'm essentially a house spirit. Have been for the last two hundred and fifty years."

My lips parted. "You're telling me that you're over two and a half centuries old?"

Her eyes narrowed. "Yes. Longevity can be one of the side effects when you bargain with the fae. Answer my question, Joey. Did you strike a bargain with Robin Goodfellow?"

I swallowed and nodded.

She spit a series of curses and then hopped off my bed and began to pace. "And what were the terms?"

My lips parted but no sound came out. She was so insistent, so forceful and full of conviction that I had almost answered without thought. "Why should I tell you anything about my private business?"

"I let you take me to the vet, didn't I?" she asked in return.

My jaw dropped. "You *let* me?"

"Your nana thought I had fleas." She sniffed indignantly. "Or ear mites. What I have is a two hundred and fifty-year-old case of I don't want to be a pawn anymore," she huffed.

"Okay. So, what can I do to help?"

She blinked at me. Her big cat eyes wide with very human expression. "You want to help me?"

"Well, sure."

"The best way to help is to not bargain with the fae. Since we can't unring that bell the only way to go is forward. Have you begun redeeming your favors? Whatever it was that you bargained with Robin for, can you get out of it?"

She must have meant my trips through time. "Um, no,

actually I haven't redeemed any of my favors. He's still teaching me the basics."

Puck sighed in relief. "Okay, good. There's still time then."

"Time for what?" I shook my head. "I don't understand what it is you want me to do?"

She sat down and stared at me. "I was the first woman in this land, before it was called America, the very first to offer him a bargain. In doing so, I became his anchor into this world. You know that magic and technology do not mix, yes?"

When I nodded, she continued, "For Robin, or any of the fae really, to stay on this side of the mortal plane, they require an anchor. Also known as a familiar. A presence that can see both sides and allow his magic to flourish here. That was the price of the magic he worked for me. I became his living anchor, a mortal female turned immortal. I've been looking for a way to stop him ever since."

I blew out a breath. "You've spent the last two and a half centuries trying to what…?"

"To stop him." She began bathing her tail.

"Right, and how do I fit into this scheme?"

She paused in her washing. "If Robin has no one to bargain with, it will loosen his hold on the mortal plane and force him to go back to his own place. He needs three things. An anchor such as myself to ground him in time and location. To be under a contract with a mortal and to fulfill that contract in its entirety within a certain amount of time to stay here. My guess is that he's had you on his radar for a while. Probably pulling a few strings to make it look as though you have no other choice but to cash in his favors. And he's working others too."

"Others?"

"Other victims," She huffed. "His MO is usually desperate women at the end of their rope. You're totally his type.

Middle-aged, no husband or kids, dead-end job. I've learned to see the pattern and try to get close to the next target, to warn her off whenever possible."

I shook my head, not willing to believe her. "But that's so...manipulative."

She gave me a *don't be stupid* look. "He's a fae prince. It's what they do."

My throat felt as though it were closing up and it took effort for me to swallow the scream that was building in my chest. Yet what the cat said made a sick sort of sense. All the compliments, all the push-pull, the seductive charm. He wasn't my friend. I was his freaking *mark*.

Stupid, sad, gullible, Joey. Desperate for affection. For respect and male admiration. Had I learned nothing since I was a sixteen-year-old dimwit?

Oh, how he must be laughing his faery ass off.

Taking a deep breath to steady myself, I foraged for more information. "You said there is a pattern?"

She nodded. "Since he has you under a magical contract, chances are he'll have one ready to tip over the edge into the next."

I don't know why her words hurt, but they do as I recall the pretty blonde woman I had seen him with at the diner that first day. *I'm doing some work for her,* Robin had claimed.

What had she bargained for?

"Tell me, have you pushed him to redeem your desires yet?"

I nodded. "He was warning me about some of the dangers. Gave me homework."

The cat bobbed her head in what I could only assume was a nod. "Classic stall tactic. He doesn't have his next victim lined up yet. When the next is set to tumble, that's when he'll start pressuring you to fulfill his end of the bargain. Then, he's got you with no way out."

"What sort of favor does he ask of the others?" A lump of ice had formed in my stomach as I finally considered what a foolish thing I had done in striking a bargain with a magical creature.

"It depends on what he needs at the time. Some he enthralls and gifts to another fae in exchange for their support. He's working his way through the court system, trying to get back into the queen's good graces."

"Gifts? You mean he *sells* people?" The thought horrified me.

The cat stared at me levelly. "He's fae. It's what they all do."

I swallow hard. "How do I get out of it then?"

"Stall for time. Don't complete your favors. Eventually, the clock will run out on the bargain."

"What happens then?"

Puck shook her head. "I'm not sure. It's never happened before."

I let out a shaky breath. "What if he's got someone else already lined up?" Some other unhappy, vulnerable female desperate enough to take a chance on magic.

"He always does," she murmured. "You should get some sleep. For the time being, pretend to play along. He can't force you to redeem your wish."

I leaned back against my stack of pillows. "No, no he can't."

There's a soft leap and she curled up beside me. "I'm sorry. I know how charming and persuasive he can be. I was half in love with him by the time I entered into the bargain."

"And what did you get in exchange?" I asked.

She let out a sigh. "My child. My only son lived when everyone else around us was dying. Robin protected him."

My wrist was throbbing, the way it often did when a storm was brewing. "And was it worth it?"

She curled into a tight ball and didn't reply. That's okay. I could guess at her answer.

※

I TOSSED and turned until predawn bathed my room in a rosy light. All I had seen all I had learned the night before had played on repeat in my mind. Robin, the two hundred and fifty-year-old tabby cat, favors, and time travel. What good would fixing my life do if Robin was going to enslave me at the end of the journey? If I couldn't actually go and enjoy the changes?

I got up and went into the bathroom. Splashed some water on my face before heading downstairs to the kitchen. The scent of coffee greeted me and I wasn't surprised to see my mother sitting at the kitchen table, laptop open in front of her.

"Good morning." I shifted from foot to foot, uncomfortable after the train wreck from the day before.

"Joey." My mother removed her glasses and sighed. "Honey. Come sit."

That was the same tone she always used when she had to break bad news.

I stalled for time, rummaging around in the cabinets in search of sugar. But eventually, the coffee was poured and I lowered myself onto the seat next to her.

"About what you said, yesterday. You aren't an embarrassment. Not to me or to your father."

I snorted. "Please. I know you're disappointed that I haven't lived up to my potential. You say it almost every day."

"That's because I want more for you." She removed her glasses and spun the laptop so the screen was facing me.

I frowned. "Why are you looking at the community college website?"

"I wanted to see if there was still time for you to enroll in the spring semester. And there is." She bit her lip. "I always thought you would go to college when you were ready. It's a good step to find out what else interests you."

I looked down into my mug. Out the window at the drifting snow. Anywhere but on that computer screen. What else interested me aside from gymnastics? Not a whole hell of a lot.

Oblivious to my mood, my mother pressed her agenda. "This wouldn't be for me, Joey. It would be for you. To help you find your place in the world. You enjoy cooking, right? Maybe you could take culinary arts or…or…" she floundered and then retrenched. "I know you had your dreams crushed and I'm sorry. But I'm not disappointed in you, Joey. I'm disappointed *for* you. Can't you understand the difference?"

"Don't you think I've tried?" I muttered.

"What?" Mom leaned forward.

"I'm cursed. I have been ever since the accident."

"That's ridiculous." She shook her head.

"Is it? Why does everything go wrong for me? I try and try and fail and fail. I have had zero success and all I have to show for the last two-plus decades is fifty extra pounds, a divorce, and a stack of unemployment papers that could choke a donkey."

"That's not—"

"But it doesn't matter, does it?" I asked. "Not to you, not to anyone. I'm just someone to be pitied. Do you have any idea what that's like for me?"

"Joey—"

"And what about you, Mom? What about you and Dad and your life? He's miserable living in that apartment over his office."

Her eyebrows pulled together. "He never said anything."

"Of course not. He didn't want to pressure you. But he's

still there, waiting in the wings for you to finally, *finally* say you want to be with him. Really with him. Not just this lunatic arrangement you two have set up. Maybe you should worry less about my life and more about your own."

With that, I pushed out of the chair and stormed up the stairs.

Only to find Robin Goodfellow lounging on my bed.

"Drama abounds," he said.

I held up a hand. "Don't. I'm not in the mood for your crap. Or for you." I stalked over to my dresser and yanked the drawer open.

"Something distressing you, lamb?" Robin got up and moved to stand behind me.

For a moment I closed my eyes and imagined what it would be like to lean back into him, to let someone hold me because I just couldn't be trusted to hold myself together anymore.

Then I remembered what the cat had told me.

I spun around and jabbed a finger into his chest. "Were you planning to enslave me?"

"What?" He frowned. "What would make you ask that?"

As if in answer, Puck strolled into the room.

Robin made a disgusted noise. "Of course, it has to be you. Still holding a grudge all these years later, Clara?"

The cat arched her back and hissed at him.

Robin turned to face me. "Listen, Joey. I don't know what she's been filling your head with, but let me assure you. Clara here has her own agenda."

"So you're telling me that everything she said to me was a lie? That you haven't enthralled the women you've made deals with in the past and sold them to fae nobles?"

His gaze darted away and he slipped his hands into his pockets. "Those were extenuating circumstances."

"What if I want to call off the bargain?" I raised my chin and crossed my arms while studying his face for a reaction.

He shook his head. "It can't be done."

"Why not?"

He sighed. "We struck a magical bargain. It doesn't just bind me. It binds both of us and will hold us to its terms that we put forth to one another. You use the sands of time to travel back and in exchange, you promised me a favor."

I shook my head. "Which you still haven't told me what it might be. What, will you demand my firstborn child as your "favor"?"

His gaze roved my body. "Believe me, if I wanted a child from you I could think of better ways to go about it than entering into a contract."

I snapped in front of his face. "Yeah, well, I've changed my mind. So consider this contract a bust and get the hell out of my house."

He ran a hand through his hair. "Joey, I've told you I can't do that."

"Why not?"

"Because, lamb. You know too much. Where I live, what I can do, that I possess magical artifacts. I've made you immune to my thrall which means we can't pass this off as a bad dream. The only way to go is forward."

Just as the cat had claimed. I took a step away from him. Was that some sort of threat? My room was sadly devoid of weapons.

"Don't look at me like that." His tone was irritated.

It was the first time I had heard him sound anything but cajoling and playful. "Like what?"

"Like I'm going to hurt you. I can't cause you any sort of harm."

"Can't, not won't?" I asked.

"I am physically incapable of hurting you per the terms of our contract."

"Not because you're a decent person who wouldn't ever hurt a woman?"

"I'm fae. We interpret things differently. I can't tell you I've never hurt a woman because hurt feelings like the hellcat over there would count." He nodded to where Puck sat, watching our exchange.

"What I can tell you is that I have no intention of causing you any sort of harm," he continued.

"It's too late for that," I wrapped my arms around myself and turned to face the window. I wasn't going to admit that I had foolishly begun to have feelings for the trickster. That I enjoyed how I felt when he gave me those heated looks and begun to think that maybe being with him for more than the sake of our bargain was a possibility. When was the last time I had felt appreciated as a woman instead of middle-aged window dressing?

But Clara was right. I'd allowed Robin to charm me into a contract that he was now claiming I couldn't get out of. She hopped up onto my dresser and sat at eye level, the piercing green of her gaze condemning.

Add another regret to Joey Whitmore's ever-growing heap of them.

"Lamb," he began tentatively.

I rounded on him. "Do not call me that. My name is Joey. And I may be trapped in this damn bargain with you but that's where this—" I gestured between our bodies, "—ends. Now, send me back."

"No!" The cat screeched. She lept for me, claws extended.

I ducked, shielding my face from the coming scratches. Robin caught her by the scruff of the neck and walked to the bedroom door. She struggled and hissed and spat, but couldn't free herself from his grip.

"I'll deal with you later." He deposited her in the hall, then shut the door, effectively trapping her outside.

He turned, his sapphire gaze assessing. "Are you all right?"

I put a hand to my chest and could feel my heart thundering. "She really doesn't want this to happen."

As though punctuating my statement, a thud sounded outside the door. And another.

"Is she really trying to break the door down?"

"I told you, Clara has her own agenda." Robin turned away from the door so that he was once again facing me. "Are you sure you're ready?"

I nodded. "If there's no way to go but through, I'm ready to go through." And to hell with the consequences.

Robin reached into the pocket of his dark coat and extracted a familiar looking box. He opened the lid, displaying the hourglass. "Grab a handful of sand, about a third of that in the hourglass. Good. Now, picture the day you want to return to. The sands of time will take you there."

"Just like that?" I asked.

He nodded mutely.

Hesitantly, I reached into the box and extracted the hourglass. Unscrewed the lid the way he'd done. Poured a third of the purple granules into my hand.

I thought about that last morning when I'd awakened in this room, full of easy joy and happiness.

The sands began to do their thing. Swirling, glowing with sparkling amber light. Surrounding me, carrying me back up the river.

The door to my room opened. "Hey Joey, do you know why the cat is freaking out?"

My eyes met Dragon's an instant before the conveyer belt of time yanked me away.

CHAPTER TEN

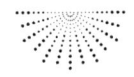

"It's better if you do him right the first time."
-Notable quotable from Grammy B

"Holy hangover, Batman." I put a hand up to my throbbing temple. It felt like a team of gorillas were tap-dancing while simultaneously crank starting a model-T inside my skull. "What was that?"

When there was no response, I dared to crack open an eyelid. I was splayed out flat on my back on my bedroom rug. I sat up. "Hello?" There was no sign of Robin, Dragon, or Puck/Clara the cat. Light spilled into the room through the open window and a warm breeze made the curtains billow inward.

Hang on a second. Warm? It hadn't been warm enough to have the windows open since October.

I stood on shaking legs and then staggered to the window. The mountain hillside beyond the house was dotted with the standard evergreens along with burnt orange, ruby red, and golden yellow leaves. The air suffused with the scents of ripe apples and woodsmoke.

The sound of children laughing and a lawnmower carried to me. Across the street sat a dusty blue pickup truck that old man Tate had sold several years ago when his daughter had yanked his license. It looked a hell of a lot nicer than it had then, far less corrosion in the bed.

A moment later, Mr. Tate himself emerged, looking far younger than the last time I had seen him hobbling into the café. The hair on his head was gray, not white. He bent down to pick up the newspaper, moving with an ease that I hadn't seen him display in years.

My heart hammered against my ribs. Newspaper. We hadn't had newspaper delivery since the town paper shifted to online news more than half a decade ago. The papers were still available but had to be purchased from the grocery or the stand outside the post office.

"It worked." My fingers itched to snag the paper out of his hands and check the date. I'd traveled back in time for sure but to what time? What was the date?

I turned and scanned my bedroom for clues. The trophies were there, but the article detailing my accident was nowhere to be seen. A picture of me, styling with hands in the air with Grammy B and Grandpappy standing proudly on either side. I had given the photo to Grammy after he died.

"Clues clues clues," I chanted and moved to the desk where a physics book sat on top of an SAT study guide. I'd never taken the SATs in my junior year, though I had gotten the book. First training for elite status and then the fallout from the accident had taken up all my time.

There was a poster from the movie *Clueless* taped to the back of the door and another for *Empire Records* on the closet. Both of those movies had come out in 1995. Darcy and I had snagged them from the theater. Getting warmer....

A few miscellaneous titles cluttered the bookshelf,

nothing that was too helpful in grounding me in the date. My Baby-Sitter's Club books had already been relegated to attic storage. Years before *Twilight*, which I was too old for, but had read anyway. No *Harry Potter and the Sorcerer's Stone*. That had come out when I was a junior.

I snapped on the radio. It was set to the alternative station. *One Headlight,* by the Wallflowers. Definitely mid-nineties.

A basket of wadded up leotards and leggings sat in one corner. I picked the top one up. It was still warm and damp as though it had been recently removed. Probably had. To keep up with my elite training, I put in two hours before school and four to six after, with ten to twelve hours on the weekends. I held it to my face and sniffed. The scent of sweat and chalk invaded my senses, so familiar it made me ache.

"Joey, hurry up!" my mother called from downstairs.

My lips parted, an automatic *be right down* on the tip of my tongue when another voice called out, "I just got out of the shower!"

It was my voice. My much younger voice. And judging from the footsteps heading this way, my echo self was about to walk right in and catch me sniffing her leotards like a total freaking creeper. Hastily, I dropped the clothing and darted for the closet an instant before the door was pushed inward.

My younger self appeared wearing a blue bathrobe, her hair swathed in a towel. With the kind of absent gesture one makes when truly alone, she slid out of the robe, hung it on the hook on the back of the door, and bent to snag a clean pair of underwear out of the heap of them spilling from a crooked drawer. She moved easily with a fluid grace I had all but forgotten. A few bruises were normal from practice, but no signs of the bandages and carnage post-accident.

My first thought—I opined later—should have been *it worked!* Or maybe *I can't believe it*!

My actual first thought was *Alina was right, I* did *get fat.*

Because I had forgotten what it felt like to look like that. Lithe and strong and flexible. The muscles in my thighs and calves pronounced, my core strong and tighter than any drum. Once upon a time, I had been able to count on my body. It did what I commanded it to do. The supple muscle would move and respond the way it had been trained, never failing me when I was carrying dinner to the table or a stack of plates to the dishwasher. In that body, I could—and had—moved for hours nonstop, pain-free.

"Girl, you don't even know how good you've got it," I muttered

"Huh?" My PYT self slid a tank top over her perfect breasts and then turned to face the closet. One dark eyebrow rose. "Is someone there?"

Oh shit. Frigging fabulous, Joey. I knew myself well. Any minute she would yank the closet door open and shriek because a middle-aged woman in plaid pajamas had appeared in her bedroom.

Totally what I would have done.

Sucking in a deep lungful of air I closed my eyes and prayed for inspiration then marched out of the closet.

Well, *fell* is more accurate a description as, unbeknownst to me, my foot got tangled in the shoulder strap of my gym bag. Down I went like a ton of bricks. Instinct took over and my hands went out to brace myself before I face-planted on the hardwood. My bad wrist sang in protest but at least I didn't break my nose again.

"Who the hell are you?"

I looked up to see young Joey, hands on barely-there hips and a scowl on her face.

"Um…hi, Joey." The wretched strap had me good. My fingers dug and twisted to untangle the stupid piece of nylon, but it was like I'd been seized by a python that smelled of gym funk. The other me bent down and tugged on one end, helping free me from captivity. Finally, I shook it loose and then scrambled to my feet.

She resumed her stance, only her arms moved to cross over her chest. "How do you know my name? And why were you in my closet?"

My wrist was killing me from where I'd caught myself and the pain had blotted out the implausible story, I'd concocted about being a long lost relative on my father's side, which would explain how I knew certain things about her. But no relative would have been blundering about in her closet and wrestling with her gym bag. Stupid Robin Goodfellow and his stupid faery antics....

A lightbulb went on and I met her—my—eyes. "I'm your faery godmother."

Young Joey blinked. "Say what now?"

"Your faery godmother. Like in Cinderella? You know, be home by midnight before your ride turns into a pumpkin and all that."

She appeared skeptical. "Where's your magic wand?"

My hands were obviously empty. "I don't have a—"

A magic wand with a glittering silver star on top appeared in my hand.

"Awesome," my younger self's eyes were huge as she stared at the object. "So, like, are you here to help Bill Tucker fall in love with me or something?"

Bill Tucker was the guy who was destined to get in an accident that evening. "Oh no, this isn't about Bill. I'm here to help you with your gymnastics."

Her eyebrows pulled together. "Oh, I've got that covered. What I really need is a way to get Bill's attention."

"Trust me, you already have it," I sighed. This could backfire but.... "He's going to ask you out today."

"Ohmigod ohmigod ohmigod," young Joey squealed.

"When? Where are we going? Alina will totally blow a gasket if I skip practice but this is Bill Tucker. Ohmigod, I've got to call Darcy!"

Shit. "You can't go. No matter what he says or does. Joey, listen, this is very important."

She didn't even hear me. "Oh, no way. I wonder if he'll let me drive the Camaro. Where's he going to take me anyway?"

"To the hospital," I barked. "Which is why you can't go out with him today."

A little sunlight went out of her expression. "What are you talking about?"

"Josephine Louise Whitmore! Get your butt down here this instant!" Our mother hollered from the bottom of the stairs.

"Uh oh, she three named you. That means business." I swallowed and looked at the door. "Do me a solid and don't tell her I'm here, okay?"

"Why not?" She reached for her wide-legged jeans and yanked them up, then pulled on a black sweater with a blue horizontal stripe across the chest over the tank.

"Because she wouldn't understand. And I have a limited amount of time to do what I came here to do and having her grill me like a flank steak will only slow me down."

"Are you like, new or something?" Joey tilted her head and reached for her backpack. "You seem kind of nervous."

"This is my first gig." I offered a smile. "It's important that I get it right. Now go on, before she comes up here. I'll see you later."

"You're just going to hang out in my room all day?" Her tone was skeptical. "That doesn't seem very faery godmother like."

I waved the wand and nearly poked my eye out. "I'll head out as soon as you do."

Young Joey still looked unsure. Inspiration struck and I

added. "I'll do some recon on Bill for you but just promise me you won't go out with him!"

She grinned and then vanished out the door. My shoulders slumped and I sagged onto the bed and grumbled, "That was a disaster."

The mattress next to me dipped even though there was no one there. I started up and an invisible voice said, "On the contrary, lamb. You did rather well."

"Robin?" I blinked and he slowly appeared beside me. Long legs clad in black suit pants, and a matching jacket and a brilliant white dress shirt open at the collar exposing his tanned throat. "What are you wearing?"

He bounced up off the bed and spun around. "Do you like it? I got tired of the whole rugged outdoorsy look."

"I like your rugged outdoorsy look," I said and then clapped a hand over my mouth. "That just slipped out."

His eyes flashed and he leaned forward. Planting his fists on either side of my hips, he invaded my personal space with a predator's stealth and skill. "Do you now? And here I thought you were angry with me. Shall we kiss and make up?"

His scent wrapped around me, an enchanting blend of male spice and cedarwood. Temptation incarnate. His lips, so full and delicious looking and only an inch away. What would one kiss hurt?

Self-preservation reared its tardy head. I shoved him away and tried to ignore my thudding heart and gather my wits. "You can stop it now."

"Stop what?" he asked.

"Stop pretending that you're attracted to me. I've already cashed in the first trip so the bargain is officially underway."

One blond eyebrow rose. "You think I'm pretending to desire you simply to fulfill our bargain?"

"Why else?" I shook my head. "Don't answer that. Tell me what you're doing here?"

"Did you forget something?" He held up a hand and in it sat the hourglass. "It would be a one-way trip if you didn't have access to the sands of time. And as to your absurd notions...you're right. I don't need to seduce you into a bargain. You came to that all on your own."

He wasn't wrong. I had made the impulsive decision to travel back in time before having another row with my mother. Evidenced by the fact that I was still wearing my pajamas.

"It really worked?" I asked the fae. "I made it back to before the accident?"

"You saw your echo just now. Did she look fresh from a car wreck?"

"But what day is it? Damn it, I need a newspaper."

Robin held out a hand and a rolled-up paper appeared in it. "Your wish is my command."

I eyed the periodical dubiously. "And what will that cost me?"

"A kiss."

"No way." That way lay the dark path.

His lips turned up in a mischievous grin. "How about the peanut butter and jelly sandwich you promised me?"

"Deal."

He handed me the paper. My hands shook as I unrolled it. October 3, 1996.

"I can't believe it." I breathed. "It's really the day."

Outside there was the slam of a car door and then the churn of an engine. I went to the window and spied my mom and my younger self backing out of the driveway. "Okay, let's go."

"To get my sandwich?" he asked.

"And to get me some clothes I can wear out in public without attracting attention."

Fifteen minutes later, I stood garbed in my mother's mauve mock turtleneck with a button-down jumper that was baggy enough to hold my larger frame and slathered jelly onto the white bread. I set the knife down and pressed the jelly side to the peanut butter side, then laid the sandwich on a plate. Robin reached for it, but I picked up the knife again and cut the sandwich into two triangles. I picked up one half and pushed the plate to Robin. "Have at."

He picked it up and sniffed a mite dubiously. "You know the bargain still holds even if you poison me, lamb."

I rolled my eyes and swapped my half for his and took a bite. Chewed and swallowed. "There, you happy? No poison."

"I was merely teasing. You don't even have your own clothes." His nose wrinkled in distaste. "What is that garment you're wearing anyhow? It looks like grubby overalls and a really ugly dress had a baby."

"This was the height of middle-aged mom casual elegance in the 90s." I did a little spin. "I will blend in exactly how I need to. Plus, it has pockets."

"Here's hoping that won't have a comeback." Robin took a bite of his sandwich.

"So tell me, what's your plan?"

"Plan" was too generous a word for what I had. "I told me…the echo me…that I would spy on Bill Tucker for her."

He quirked a brow. "And how, precisely, are you going to do that, faery godmother?"

"Simple, I'm going to pretend to be the new librarian at school. Bill Tucker always had study hall first period and middle-aged women are all but invisible."

"And if your recon doesn't satisfy your echo?"

I shrugged and headed to the hallway where I snagged a pair

of my old combat boots. They were too narrow, which is why the other me was wearing the wider pair, but a few crushed toes were a small price to pay for fixing my whole adult life.

"How do I look?"

"Like a fashion disaster." Robin shook his head.

I raised a brow. "This from the guy who took me to lunch while I was dressed in men's sweats?"

"True enough. You are dressed just as dreadfully as usual. Come, lamb. 1996 awaits."

❄

No one stopped me or even gave me a second glance as I walked up the steps to Arnold Easton Jr/ Sr. High. A time before school shootings, metal detectors, and lockdown drills. One of the benefits of being a dead ringer for a middle-aged mom. I probably looked as though I was going to a parent-teacher meeting or had PTO business.

Robin had disappeared a few blocks back. Literally. One second, we were strolling arm in arm and the next he'd poofed away. I shrugged it off. He wasn't critical to my plan and was so handsome that he was sure to attract unwanted attention.

My too-tight boots squeaked a bit on the shiny blue and white blocky vinyl composition tile. It gave me a little pang to think that back in my own time, Dragon would be walking this same hallway. Guilt nibbled at me as I thought of her face the instant before the sands of time had snatched me away. What had she thought happened to me?

It was crazy to think she hadn't been born yet.

And then there was Clara the cat/puck. Trapped in a two and a half century old bargain with Robin, who had all but admitted that he sold thralls. I'd been thinking about her, too.

Even if she had gone bananas on me, I still wanted to help her.

First thing's first. I needed to keep my eye on the prize. Which was spying on Bill Tucker for my echo-self and convincing her to avoid going for a joyride with him at all costs.

I slipped through the library doors and into the first row of bookshelves before the librarian, Ham, looked up from his office where he possessed one of the few coveted computers in the building. The bell rang, the sound as familiar as the firehouse whistle at noon and the jangle of the bell over the door to the café.

The announcements came on and I listened to the senior class president rattle off the activities. Homecoming. I'd forgotten all about it. Next week was spirit week to be topped off on Homecoming weekend. Since I hadn't gone to the dance, the event had faded into the fog of memory.

Bill Tucker though…he was exactly how I remembered him. Tall, with broad shoulders and wavy golden-brown hair, the senior quarterback strode into the library like he owned the place. He was flanked by two of his buddies, laughing and being obnoxious like only teenage boys can be. Ham appeared to collect their passes. His fish-like lips pressed together in disapproval but he returned to his office without saying anything.

"Freak," Bill said and the cronies snickered. They thumped down into chairs and pulled out a deck of cards, not even pretending to do any work. They were seniors and football players after all. Stars of the school and the town. Who was going to stop them?

"So, you went out with Beth Yates last night?" Crony one —I couldn't recall his name so I mentally dubbed him Crab— turned to face Bill with a lecherous leer on his face.

"Did she put-out?" That from Goyle, aka crony number two.

Bill smirked. "What do you think?"

The cronies chortled. I wanted to go over there and smack the look off his arrogant face. And the other two for being such faithful minions. What had I ever seen in that…that…tool?

"Who's next on the list?" Crab asked.

In answer, Bill withdrew a folded piece of notebook paper from his pocket. I was too far away to see what was written on it but he said, "Joey Whitmore."

"Dude, she's only a sophomore." Goyle, the only one of the three who seemed to have anything resembling a conscience, looked concerned. "Is she even sixteen yet?"

"Dude, she's going to be a fucking Olympian," Bill said. "She's the cherry on top of my list."

"And I bet she's like, really bendy," Crab added. "All those mat routines."

More snickering.

My molars ground together. So, my life was ruined because Mr. Horny McHornytoad had targeted me to be "the cherry" on top of his fuck it-list.

No wonder he had never come to see me after the accident. It wasn't that he was embarrassed or ashamed for causing it. No, he just wanted to nail the future Olympian. And once any chance of me having a spot on the US team vanished, his interest had gone with it.

Damn it, I had never wanted a camera phone so much in my life to record what he was saying. There would be no way my echo self would go out with him if I played back his words. One problem, my tech hadn't traveled back in time with me.

So, how was I going to prove to young Joey that she wanted nothing to do with Bill the Thrill Tucker?

"I'm gonna catch her in between classes," Bill said to the cronies. "Set up something for tonight."

"Dude, you are a machine," Crab said.

"Her mom's on the town council." Goyle still appeared uneasy. "Do you really think—?"

Bill flicked a playing card at his friend's face. "Leave the thinking to me, dumbass."

No no *no*. I looked up at the plastic clock over the checkout desk.

Ten hours and sixteen minutes left to alter the course of destiny.

Someone tapped me on the shoulder. Ham had snuck up behind me and looked me up and down. "Can I help you find whatever it is you're looking for?"

His tone was the same flat and slightly disapproving one I remembered.

"Nope, I'm good." I hustled away from the stack and past the table of boys I'd been spying on and out into the hall. I strode down the corridor and around the bend and when I was out of sight of the office, plastered my back against the wall.

Another tap on the shoulder. This time, I jumped.

"Not very good at all the cloak and dagger stuff are you, lamb?" Robin asked.

"Where did you go?" I asked him.

"I had some shopping to do." He held a bag aloft.

"Shopping?" I eyed it dubiously. "Is that like a souvenir from our trip or something?"

"Hardly." After setting the bag down, he reached inside and withdrew two lightweight rain jackets. "Here, put this on."

Mystified I did as instructed even as I said, "That little rat bastard is gearing up to ask me, the other me, out. Apparently, I'm the cherry he's been after."

"Easy, Joey. You look about ready to burst a blood vessel."

He was right. My hands were clenched into fists and my whole body shook from rage. A lifetime of being cursed, taking dead-end jobs, and feeling like a failure all because I had attracted the attention of some ego-driven jock.

Robin had already zipped up his lightweight jacket and reached for the zipper on mine. "Do you want me to enthrall him?"

"You can do that?"

The corner of his mouth kicked up. "You know I can."

I actually considered it for a beat. If Robin put Bill in that trance-like state and walked him out of the building, there would be no way he could even ask the younger me out, never mind pick her up.

But that was wrong, wasn't it? Taking away Bill Tucker's free will, even if only for a little while.

I thought about his list, his words *cherry on top*, and blew out a breath. "You wouldn't like, keep him enthralled forever, would you?"

"Thralls only last for a year and a day," Robin said. "It's how people have been taken by the fae for millennia."

A year and a day of Bill Tucker's life in exchange for what?

I looked up into Robin's avid gaze. "And what will it cost me?"

His sapphire irises glittered with that predatory light. "How about that kiss?"

CHAPTER ELEVEN

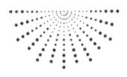

"The way to a man's heart is straight between the second and third rib."
-Notable quotable from Grammy B

My heart was battering my ribcage like a prisoner who desperately wanted out. There was no worming around this one. No peanut butter and jelly sandwich to save my bacon. If I wanted to get Bill temporarily out of the picture, long enough to get my butt to nationals and qualify for the US team, I'd have to do it.

"But what about Bill? He's the star quarterback. He can't just disappear in the middle of the football season. People would miss him."

"I can order him to resume his normal activities. The lights will be on, but nobody will be at home. Just like I did when I had you drive that gas-guzzling monstrosity. Remember?"

"And you could set him free, too right? The same way you did with me?"

He shook his head. "I won't give immunity to anyone else in this town. And you're stalling, Joey."

He was right. I was. My lips parted but before I could speak, the smart clicking of heels heading in our direction grabbed my attention.

Principal Mott, the whipcord lean woman who could rival my mother for her title as a tough-as-nails feminist approached the two of us. She wore plum colored slacks and a black silk shirt and her prematurely gray hair was spun up in an elegant twist. The look was timeless and classic. She'd stopped in for lunch at the café a week ago and other than a few more lines around her eyes and mouth, looked exactly the same.

She folded her arms, lifted her chin, and asked, "May I help you?"

For a moment I flashed back to how I always cringed beneath that piercing gray-eyed stare. Even when she was ordering a cobb salad. Then I recalled that I wasn't her pupil or even former pupil. As far as Principal Mott was concerned, I was some random woman.

Looping my arm through Robin's I pasted on a friendly smile. "Hi there. I'm Joey and this is my husband, Robin."

I felt him stiffen beside me but powered through with my BS. "We're thinking of buying a house in the area and wanted to check out the local schools before we commit. Isn't that right, honey?"

My fingers clawed into his arm with steady pressure. He didn't confirm my cover story, but at least he didn't deny it. In fact, he just stood mutely by my side, his theatrics nowhere in sight.

Her gaze was sharp as she assessed the two of us. Robin dressed well in his suit jacket and me in my classic mom get up. Him handsome and me, frumpy. Yes, we were a mismatched pair, but she was too much a professional to doubt my claim. "Well, I have a few moments if you would like a quick tour. I'm Principal Dana Mott."

She offered her hand and I let go of my half affectionate, half restraining hold on Robin to clasp her outstretched palm. After an uncomfortable moment similar to the one we'd had with Georgia, he took her hand and shook briskly.

"What grades are your children in?" She asked.

"Tenth and twelfth are the grades we're interested in." I gave the grades that my echo self and Bill Tucker were in automatically.

"Well, this is the main hall. If you will follow me, we'll start with the tenth grade and work our way up." Rounding on her stout heel, she turned and headed down the hall.

"What's wrong with you?" I tugged Robin along.

"You called me your husband." His tone sounded off.

"Well, I couldn't very well call you my boy-toy to my former principal," I snipped. "We needed some non-stalker reason to be loitering here. Come on."

The tour wound us through the building, past the computer lab, the gym, the art studio which was nowhere near as nice as my mother's. Everything looked precisely the way I remembered it. Even the smell of the industrial-strength cleaner was the same.

"What are some of your child's interests?"

I called to mind an image of Dragon. "Our daughter enjoys music and theater as well as reading. Mostly behind the scenes stuff."

"Excellent. The fall production is underway. *West Side Story*. She could probably join the set building crew, they always need an extra hand. And what about your son?"

The bell rang as we were passing the library. Through the open door, I saw Ham wandering about aimlessly looking stressed and confused within and watched as Billy got up from the table.

"He mostly likes to chase girls," I muttered.

Principal Mott paused by the door to home economics. "Where's your husband?"

It took me a moment to realize that Robin wasn't with us. For a moment I feared he had poofed out on me and I would be left to explain his disappearance. But then I spotted him in the hallway standing with Bill.

Oh no. Was he enthralling the guy? I hadn't committed to that course. How was it any better for Robin to take away Bill's free will and ability to choose for himself than for Bill to destroy my future?

"Robin, honey?" I called out.

Those intense blue eyes snapped up to lock with mine. A tremor of primal fear went through me. Something about him in that moment made him seem otherworldly. Alien. My mouth went dry and my hands started to sweat. Heart racing, I stepped back, wanting to put some serious distance between us.

My lizard brain was in overdrive, screaming warnings even louder than the sensible shrew. He was a predator. Dangerous.

And I was drawn to him. Wanted to throw myself into the chaos he represented. It was my reaction that startled me most of all.

"Billy? You better be getting to your next class." Principal Mott's words broke the spell. I thumped back down on my heels hard. What the hell had that been about?

Robin shoulder-checked Billy on his way past, which seemed kind of a dick move for an adult to pull on a teenager. Billy scowled back at him as he walked away with Crab and Goyle bobbing along in his wake.

"Shall we finish the tour?" Robin rejoined us without a word of explanation or apology. How come men could get away with that?

He's not a man, though. The sensible shrew shrieked so only I could hear. *He's a fae prince. And you just got a very potent look at what that entails.*

Principal Mott glanced at her watch. "I'm afraid I have a meeting starting in a moment. If you'll accompany me to the office, I'll get you the paperwork. You can take it with you and if you do decide to move forward with your home purchase you can fill it out and bring it back at your leisure."

We collected the paperwork and then headed down the steps and out through the front door.

"Well, that was utterly useless." I sagged. "Other than lying to my former principal and finding out that Bill Tucker is a giant creep, we didn't accomplish anything."

"Not entirely true." Robin extracted a piece of paper from his pocket and handed it to me.

"Is this what I think it is?" I snatched it out of his grip and unfolded the crumpled paper.

"Bill's hit-it list." Robin nodded. "I lifted it from him when he passed by."

"That's why you shoulder checked him," I realized. "But what was it you were saying to him?"

A glimmer of that dark thing that lived within Robin flickered in his eyes. "That he was slime and he had better stay away from Joey Whitmore."

A groan escaped. "No. You might as well have painted a big bull's eye on my echo self's back."

"I was trying to help," Robin muttered. "My inability to speak an untruth made me more of a hindrance than a help."

I blinked. "Wait, you can't lie?"

"I can't utter a statement that I know is false," he corrected. "That doesn't mean I can't adequately deceive most mortals. But that was why I couldn't confirm your statement that we were wed."

That was good to know. Food for thought. Later I would

pick apart all of our interactions and reexamine the things Robin had told me.

Turning my attention back to the paper, I scanned the names. "So, these are all of his conquests." Or his potential conquests. More than half the names had a line through them. A couple had stars. Frequent flyers?

Ick. Ick. Ick.

My gaze screeched to a stop. "Uh oh."

"What?" Robin glanced over my shoulder. "Find something useful to our cause

"There's someone on here…." I shook my head and then stared at the name that had a single line through it. *Ursula Green.*

But that couldn't be right. Could it? Ursula was even younger than I was, by several months. Her parents had been —or more accurately currently were—strict. They'd never let her date.

My mind raced with the possible implications of this discovery. Because of her crazy gymnastics rivalry, Ursula and I weren't close. She was stuck up and stand-offish but easy to ignore. I thought it was because people talked about me and she was sick of it. Or maybe jealous that the attention wasn't on her.

After my accident though, her patent dislike had gone from passive to active. Prank phone calls in the middle of the night coming from a blocked number, her tossing food at me in the cafeteria. Spreading rumors. One time she had even keyed my mother's car. I knew it was her, I'd seen her from my bedroom window. But I never told anyone about it. At the time it hadn't mattered.

But seeing her name on Billy's list shed a whole different light on Ursula's and my relationship. I just didn't know what to do with the information.

Robin still stood there, waiting for me to do something,

to make some sort of decision.

"I need a minute," I said to him and then turned my back and walked away.

"Lamb?" He called but didn't follow.

I walked up the street, past the senior parking lot where I spied Bill's Z-28 Camaro. It was shiny and black with rims that glinted in the October sunlight. A deep bubbling emotion, dark and sticky like tar threatened to fill all the hollow places in my chest. I had kept the feeling simmering on the back burner ever since I heard Bill tell his friends that I was next on his hit-it-then-quit-it list. Seeing the car though stoked the flames to a fever pitch. I walked through the lot until I stood in front of the vehicle.

The door was unlocked. I slid inside on the passenger's side. It smelled of Axe body spray, old French fries, and teenage hormones. White fuzzy dice hung from the rearview mirror, but I didn't see them.

In my mind's eye, I could still picture the view from within. The lurching panic as the tires spun, the sickening sound of metal as the passenger's side door crumpled in. The tinkling sound as glass shattered. The jerk of the seatbelt, which kept my body in place as the car was brought to a final stop by the telephone pole. The taste of blood as the vehicle that had felt so sturdy and powerful moments before crumpled into where I sat trapped. The pain, the fear....

Suddenly, I understood Ursula a whole lot better than I ever imagined possible. This much pent-up emotion needed an outlet. It needed someone to blame for causing such unrest. If there had been keys in my pocket, I would have seriously messed up his ride.

But I didn't have keys. And if I damaged the car in any way and got caught, I'd get tossed in jail.

So I did the only thing I could do.

I snagged his parking pass off the dashboard and stuffed

it in my pocket. Then I headed to the nearest payphone and called the impound lot.

※

Satisfaction filled me as I watched the tow truck haul Bill's ride out of the lot. It wasn't Georgia, obviously. She was still living as George in Tennessee. But it had felt good. The driver, Floyd Weatherby, hadn't questioned that I was an administrative assistant to Principal Mott. I had assured Floyd that no, the car absolutely didn't have a parking pass and therefore needed to be towed and impounded at the owner's expense.

And being a man of few words, Floyd got on with the job at hand.

Elation filled me. I had done it! I, Joey Whitmore, had changed the past. Even if my echo self wouldn't believe me about the list, there was no way Bill Tucker could scrape together enough cash to bail his ride before the impound lot closed at five on the button. Hell, I had been a working woman and I'd been saving up to bail my own ride for over a month.

"Proud of yourself?" Robin stepped up beside me as we watched the hoisted Z-28 disappear around the corner.

"Very," I told him. "I prevented the accident, exactly as I intended to do."

"Are you so sure about that?" Robin cocked a brow. "Your younger self seemed smitten with the boy."

I frowned up at him. "The car is out of the equation. No Camaro, no accident. And no jail time for me. Besides, the ride was half of the appeal."

He held his hand to his heart in an overly dramatic motion. "Why lamb, I had no idea you could be bought."

"Not now I can't," I told him. "Come on, we should get out of here before Billy discovers his car is gone."

One golden blond brow shot up. "And here I thought you'd like to see the look on his face."

I shook my head. "No, there's something else I'd rather see."

Feeling lighter than I had in recent memory, I headed back toward my neighborhood. Darcy's house, which in 1996 belonged to her parent's, sat at the foot of the hill. The big Victorian stood sentinel at the top. I bypassed our street and kept going. Robin trailed along beside me, hands in the pockets of his overpriced suit.

I stopped at the small white picket fence that overlooked the familiar ranch. Through the picture window, I could see a pair of slipper-clad feet held aloft by the footrest of the tatty recliner, too big to be Grammy B's.

"Lamb? You've gone paler than usual."

My hand flew to my lips. Sure, I'd seen the younger versions of Old Man Tate and Principal Mott and even myself. But those people were all still alive.

"It's my grandfather." I swallowed. "He died a few years ago."

"Well, why are you just standing outside. Why not go in and say hello?"

"What would I say?" The more I stared at those feet, the more I realized how impossible the situation was to explain. "Hi, I'm your granddaughter who traveled back in time. Sorry, I don't mean to snot rocket all over you, but you're dead in my time and I never thought I'd see you again? He'd have a heart attack twenty years before his time."

"Must you overthink everything?" Before I could stop him, Robin pushed his way through the gate and was striding up the concrete walkway to the front door.

"Robin, what are you doing?"

"What does it look like I'm doing? I'm knocking." The fae prince cast me a devilish wink and then rapped his knuckles against the door in rapid succession.

The feet disappeared from view and rather than stand at the gate gawking like a rube I hustled to Robin's side. The door creaked open and then there he stood. Grandpappy. He was tall and had broad shoulders that looked as though they could carry the weight of the world. Though his skin was wrinkled and his hair thinning, his blue eyes twinkled. His expression was of a man who loved life and had never met a stranger, open, and welcoming to all. He looked so much like the photo in my room, the one I had given to Grammy, that it stole my breath.

"Can I help you?" His voice was as craggy as the face of the mountain he lived on.

"Yes, hello. My significant other and I are in town on business." Robin put a hand on my arm. "We were wondering if we could speak to you for a few minutes. It concerns your granddaughter."

"Joey?" Grandpappy looked to me, and his eyebrows drew together. "Do I know you?"

"Distantly." I copied Robin's approach—tell the truth if not the whole truth. "We're interested in advancing her gymnastics career and want to get a little background information."

Grandpappy waved us into the living room. "'Fraid Betty is out for the moment, but can I fix you anything? There's some coffee left."

"Coffee would be wonderful." I took two steps toward the kitchen when Robin snagged me by the elbow.

My grandfather studied us for a moment before disappearing down the hall.

"You're supposed to be a stranger, remember?" Robin hissed before releasing me to wander over to the mantle where a photo of a gap-toothed toddler wearing a pink and purple leotard styled for the camera. "That you?"

I reached for the photo and he handed it to me. "Yeah, probably my first year in gymnastics. I would sleep in my leotard the night before because I was so excited to go there."

"So much dedication," Robin murmured.

"It was what I was born to do." At the sound of footsteps, I hastily replaced the photo.

Grandpappy appeared carrying two mugs of coffee in his big hands. He offered one to Robin, who declined and then returned to the kitchen for cream and sugar.

I couldn't stop staring at him. My grandfather. He was the one who had paid for my gymnastics classes all while I was growing up. He'd showed up to every competition, just like my mother and father and Grammy B.

"So, have you seen her perform?" Grandpappy asked Robin.

"My colleague here is familiar with her work, but I have yet to have the pleasure." Robin winked.

"Well, we can fix that right off." Grandpappy set his mug aside and reached for his trusty video camera. My teeth sank into my lower lip at the sight of his gnarled and arthritic fingers maneuvering cords so he could plug the thing into the television. How had I forgotten about his obsession with his video camera?

Probably because after my accident, he'd never brought it out again.

The screen flickered and then my image appeared. I was wearing a turquoise leotard with a golden sun on the right shoulder that sparkled under the gymnasium lights. It was a balance beam exercise, some sort of local competition at Alina's gym. The slate gray walls, the colorful mats, the music. I knew it wasn't a standard practice because I never wore the sparkly long-sleeved leotards during practice. The

Joey that launched from a springboard on to the balance beam didn't look much different than my echo self of earlier that morning.

I remembered that routine, had watched this tape at least a hundred times. Much like coaches watching game video to figure out where a team had a weakness, I had studied my technique, analyzing the precision of every flex of muscle and shift of balance. In this particular routine, I had wobbled on a cartwheel but stuck the roundoff landing.

Instead of watching the meet I had lived, memorized, and relived into infinity, I watched my grandfather. His expression surprised me. He always looked so proud of my performance. But now he appeared a little wistful. And was that… did I see a hint of regret? Why? The wobble wasn't for another twenty-two seconds.

Unable to understand the emotions on Grandpappy's face my gaze shifted to Robin. His attention remained locked on the Joey on the television screen but as though sensing my gaze, he turned to me and he quirked an eyebrow.

What did he think? Was he trying to reconcile the confident athlete on the television with the middle-aged train wreck he knew?

My shoulders bobbed up and down and I tore my gaze away.

The beam shifted to the floor mat routine. My choreography was solid as I did a roundoff directly into an aerial cartwheel and a stylized salute. Not as much height as I'd been aiming for on the saltos but still impressive.

God, I missed that feeling. Not just the movement and power, the skills I'd spend years developing, but knowing that I was in control. Willing and able to do anything, to handle whatever life threw at me, and know that I could stick the landing.

"We've heard your granddaughter is an Olympic hopeful," Robin murmured.

My grandfather shook his head. "She's incredible. I've never seen so much dedication in a child before." His brows drew down. "Sometimes I worry she's too dedicated though."

My throat went suddenly dry. "What do you mean?"

"She's not getting the chance to live. To be young. Her mother at that age was forever going out with friends to movies and dances. I spent many a night waiting up to make sure she made it home safely."

"And you want that for Josephine?" Robin asked.

I nudged him in the ribs. Hard.

"I want whatever will make Joey happy. It used to be gymnastics but something's changed in her." Grandpappy shook his head.

"Something like what?" My breath caught in my throat and if I could have withdrawn the question I would have.

But now it was out there...waiting.

Grandpappy shook his head. "She's just gotten so serious about it. Like every little mistake is the end of the world. That's no way to live."

My heart beat faster. "But...don't you want to see her make something of herself? I know her mother does."

He waved that off. "Prudence is a strong woman with high expectations. Joey could win a fist full of gold medals and Prudence would still say something to bring her down. Same way as Betty does to Prudence. I've been running interference between those two for years. Someone's got to. You know Betty's still on her case about marrying Paul? Land sakes, they've got a teenage daughter together so who cares if they tie the knot? But Betty won't budge. I think Prudence is almost ready to comply just to get her mama to hush up about it."

"You do?" I whispered.

He nodded. "It's the way it is with mothers and daughters. I've got the easy job, waiting up at night with the shotgun loaded for bear. Or boyfriends." He winked to take the sting out of his words.

"So, what will happen if Joey chooses not to continue to do gymnastics?" Robin asked.

I shot him a killing look but Grandpappy just shrugged. "I know my granddaughter. It may take her a while but eventually, she will find her way."

My head was spinning. Here I'd believed I'd let my entire family down as well as myself. But there sat my beloved grandfather telling me that I would find my way. His faith staggered me. The man who'd cheered me on at every competition had helped pay for a new leotard when I'd ripped my brand new one when money was tight and Prudence was on the warpath.

He believed I would succeed regardless of what I did. He just wanted me to be happy.

The sound of a diesel engine rumbling up the street snagged my attention at the same time as my grandfather looked up. "That will be Betty now. If you folks will excuse me, we have a lunch date. Unless you wanted to talk to Betty?"

I shook my head. And then, before I could stop myself, I hugged him with all my strength.

He paused for a moment, obviously startled that a strange woman would embrace him after such a brief acquaintance. But it was the last chance I would ever get to hug him. I wouldn't let it slip away.

No matter what price I had to pay Robin for this trip, it would be worth it. Just for that hug.

After a moment he settled one of those big gnarled hands on my back and patted me gently. "I'm sorry, I don't think I caught your name."

"It's Josephine, too actually." I sniffled and then stepped back. Robin put a hand on my shoulder. "And I'm very glad we had this talk."

The screen door opened and Grammy B appeared. Younger, feistier, and carrying a bag of groceries, which she plopped on Grandpappy's recliner. Her eyes flashed and she looked madder than a badger with a head cold. "Do you know what that busybody Elouise Kramer said to me? She said she saw Joey sneaking out of school with some boy. I told the old battleax she ought to have her eyes examined."

"Which boy?" I gripped her arm, startling her. "Did you get his name?"

Though I almost towered over her four-foot eleven-inch frame, Grammy could stare down a man twice her size. "And just what business is it of yours anyhow?"

"These people are athletic advisors interested in Joey," Grandpappy said.

"His name?" My heart was thundering against my ribs.

"Elouise didn't know his name, but he was wearing a jacket with school colors," Grammy said. "She thought he played football."

CHAPTER TWELVE

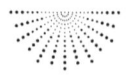

"A real friend knows when to talk and when to hold her tongue. A true friend knows when to listen. And when to cut a bitch."
-Notable quotable from Grammy B

My mind spring-boarded out of my body as I tried to come to grips with what Grammy had heard. Distantly, I heard Robin thanking my grandparents for their assistance, followed by the slap of the screen door. I'd left the house without a word of farewell.

No. There was no way my echo self would have skipped school if Bill Tucker asked. And anyway, I'd had his car impounded. It had to be some sort of mistake.

I stopped short and Robin had to twist so he didn't slam into my back. "I had his car impounded."

"What?"

I stared up at him. "Did you know this would happen?"

He shrugged. "You changed the course of events, effectively changing your own history. There's no way to predict what will happen from here."

"So this is my fault?" I asked. Oh god, it was. I'd had the car towed and then Bill had changed his plans for me.

He didn't have a car, but there was more than one way a teenage athlete could have her dreams derailed by the wrong boy. In trying to fix the past I'd gone and made it worse.

I started back up the street at a power walking pace, the windbreaker Robin had purchased flapping in the breeze.

Robin jogged after me. "Where are you going?"

"To find me. To stop me from doing…whatever that jackass Bill Tucker is trying to get me to do."

"But you don't even know it's true," Robin said. "It could be another girl."

I shook my head. "No, it's me. Elouise wouldn't have approached Grammy if she wasn't sure. Besides, I heard Bill say I was next on his little list. I thought he'd have the decency to wait until after school though. And what the hell am I even thinking?"

But I knew. My echo self was accustomed to winning. To beating the odds. Being stronger, faster, and utterly focused on her goal.

And this morning her goal had been Bill.

"We need to find her," I told Robin. "She's completely naive when it comes to boys like Bill. Any boys really. Forty hours a week of gymnastics does not make for savvy social skills."

"So where would he go?" Robin asked. "If you tell me a location I can transport us there."

"I don't know." The school was out, so was anywhere in town. "His house maybe? No, wait, his mom owned a catering business. She works from home. I doubt he'd take me there."

I stopped again and this time Robin did slam into my back.

"Ursula," I breathed.

"What?"

"Ursula would know where he takes girls to seduce them because he's already taken her there. We need to get back to school. To the baseball field behind it. Darcy has a class there. She can help us find Ursula."

"Hold on to me." Robin gripped my arm and then came that bizarre sensation of the world bending around us.

I staggered and this time Robin held a tight grip on me, pulling me into his chest. We had appeared behind the baseball field, just within a grove of trees.

"You all right?" Robin tucked a stray strand of hair behind my ear.

Though my knees felt weak, it had more to do with his proximity than the transition via faery prince. "You didn't tell me what that will cost."

His eyes glittered. "That one's a freebie. Is that her?"

I turned in the direction he was pointing and saw a petite blonde wielding a field hockey stick like a club. "Yup. Stay here."

Coach Calhoun, the old letch, was on the far end of the baseball diamond with his back turned on the benchwarming section. As was standard in his classes, the sports enthusiasts were playing while the slackers warmed the bench.

Darcy, while not athletically gifted, was a dirty player so she was sidelined more often than not. I saw a couple of the benchwarmers whispering and staring in her direction.

"What are you looking at?" she snarled.

The girls rolled their eyes. She gave them the finger as she waited for her chance to go out on the field.

"Darcy," I approached cautiously, careful to stay out of the reach of her hockey stick.

"Yeah?" She looked over at me and it took me a moment to recognize her. Not that she physically appeared much different. More that motherhood and life experience had mellowed the fire that burned so intensely in her. It was hard to reconcile this spitfire making doggy costumes and wrangling five children.

"Do you have any idea where Ursula Green is?"

"If she were up your butt you'd know it." Darcy's focus returned to the game. "Come on, Michelle. That was the shittiest pass since the coach tried to pick up my mom!"

Coach Calhoun turned beet red and then pointed down the hill back to the office. "Mercer, office. Now. And can I help you?"

It had been so long since I'd heard Darcy's maiden name that it took me a minute to realize he was talking to her. "Office is that way?" I chucked a thumb in the direction of the building and then raced after Darcy, whose temper helped her cover more ground than the length of her legs.

When we were out of sight of the field, I called her name again and added, "It's about Joey. I think she's in trouble."

Darcy slowed and gave me a quick up and down. "Are you one of Alina's stooges?"

I gestured to my overripe body. "Do I look like one of Alina's stooges?"

"No. You look normal. So what's your interest in Joey?"

My nerves were getting the best of me. "Look, I don't have time to explain."

Darcy folded her arms over her chest. "Then I guess I don't have time to help you."

I made a frustrated noise. "God, why are you always such a prickly pain in the ass?"

Her hands fell to her side. "Joey?"

I blinked. "You recognize me?"

She shook her head. "No. It can't be."

I remembered Robin's rules about how the human mind would work overtime to dismiss anything unusual. But Darcy was my BFF. My partner in crimes both foreign and domestic. I needed her to have my back. "Well, it is. I know you've been giving hand jobs to Mike Abrams behind his dad's barn."

Her jaw dropped and fire blazed in her eyes. "He *told* you? I'm so going to kick his ass—"

"You told me. Like two months from now."

"How is this possible?" She moved closer, scrutinizing me from head to toe.

"Look, it's a long story and by the time I explain it all, it might be too late. The Joey you know is in trouble. And I need to find Ursula because I think she knows where she—I—might be."

"This is so messed up," Darcy grumbled.

That was putting it mildly. "So, do you know where Ursula is?"

Darcy nodded. "She's got French this period."

I blew out a breath. "Let's roll."

I strode down the hill, ugly overall dress billowing in the breeze behind me. Darcy ran to catch up.

"So, like, you're from the future?"

When I nodded she asked, "Can you tell me something about my life then? In the future. I mean."

I hesitated. "Not sure if that's a good idea."

"Come on, I'm helping you, aren't I?" Darcy said. "I just want to know one teensy tiny little thing."

I blew out a breath. "Who you're going to marry? Where you live? How many kids you have?"

"Hell no. Did my dad ever get me the Lamborghini I wanted for my sixteenth birthday?"

I laughed. "No, he didn't."

"Damn. I guess my hints have been too subtle." Darcy flashed me her crooked grin. "You're still pretty cool, old Joey."

"Drop the old Joey part and I'll say the same thing about you." We entered the school building, ducking low so no one inside the glass-paneled front office could spot us.

Ursula's French class was on the third floor at the end of the hall.

"What are you going to say?" Darcy asked when I paused outside the door.

"That there's a call for her." One good thing about the nineties, only the uber-wealthy and people on television had cell phones. If a parent wanted to speak with a kid in the middle of the school day, they had to call into the front office.

Eventually, the web of lies I was weaving would catch up with me. But I intended to be back safely in my own time after I averted the disaster.

Raising my hand, I rapped smartly on the wood composite door. Mademoiselle Reiner appeared, her silver-streaked light brown hair cut and styled in what appeared to be a botched version of "the Rachel". She said something in French which, having taken Spanish for my language requirement, I didn't understand.

"There's a call in the office for Ursula Green," I spoke in my best professional secretary voice. "It's an urgent matter."

"Ursula," Mademoiselle Reiner called, not dropping the French accent at all as she made a rapid circular motion with her hand. *"Dépêchez-vous."*

Ursula collected her books and a mini backpack—it was more of a purse than something to hold schoolwork—and hastened out the door.

She looked exactly how I remembered her. Where Darcy

had always been petite, seeing Ursula looking so young floored me for a minute. She'd developed faster than we had and looked a few years older.

Her long red hair was loose down her back. She wore a black leather jacket over a black micro-mini and a ruffly white shirt that looked like she'd stolen it from a pirate. Her shoes were mock Mary Janes with two inch rectangular heels, putting her an inch over my five-foot-four self. No shlumpy sweaters and loose-fitting jeans ever covered up that incredible figure.

She glared at Darcy a moment before dismissing her to focus on me. "Is it my mom?"

"There's no phone call." I walked her a few feet away from the closed French class door. "I need to ask you about Bill Tucker."

Ursula paused in mid-step. "What? Why?"

It was a gamble, but then, so was traveling through time. Reaching into my pocket, I extracted the folded piece of paper that Robin had lifted off Bill earlier. "Your name is his list of girls he's…um…gone out with. Crossed off."

She shook her head back and forth, her lips pressed in a hard line.

I felt for her but I soldiered on. "Did you sleep with him?"

She shook her head back and forth, though if I was reading her right, it was more of a refusal to answer than denying the question.

"She's gonna freak out," Darcy said. "And the bell is about to ring."

"We need to get her out of the hallway." I didn't want her to escape into the packed crowd before I got the information I needed.

"The second-floor bathroom." Darcy pointed in its direction. "Drag her if you have to."

I didn't. Ursula came willingly with nothing more than an

easy grip on the sleeve of her coat. She appeared to be in shock. The girl's bathroom was right around the corner from the office. I tugged her into it and Darcy locked the door just as the bell sounded.

Ursula held her books over her chest like a shield. "I don't want to talk about this."

"Listen to me." I gripped Ursula by the shoulders. "We won't ever repeat a word of what you say to us to anyone else, okay? But damn it, you need to tell us about what happened with Bill. Did he...force himself on you?"

Wordlessly, she shook her head back and forth.

Darcy and I exchanged glances. Even with the gap of twenty plus years, we could still communicate silently. And we were both thinking that while it may not have been rape, there was something traumatic.

"But you did have sex with him?" Darcy pushed.

The skin on Ursula's forehead crinkled. "And if I say yes, what, are you going to call me a slut? Or a whore?"

Darcy opened her mouth, most likely to stick her foot in it, but I broke in. "No, we aren't. We're worried about you and all the other girls whose names are on this list."

"Who are you?" Ursula studied me up and down. "The new counselor or something?"

"I don't work for the school. So I won't tell your parents or repeat a single thing you say. I just want to help you." As the words left my lips, I knew they were true.

I did want to help Ursula. We had been friends once, when we were younger. Whatever had caused the animosity between us needed to end.

"Women ought to look out for each other," I told Ursula and Darcy. "Not tear each other down, but build each other up. Because when shit goes sideways, your friends are the ones who are there for you."

Darcy met my gaze and her lips twitched with a smile.

Ursula closed her eyes. "What is it you want to know?"

❄

"I SEE YOU'VE COLLECTED AN ENTOURAGE," Robin said as Ursula, Darcy, and I approached the spot where he was leaning against a tree. "You really are doing a number on your timeline, lamb."

I'd considered ditching them, but after what Ursula had revealed, Darcy wasn't just going to go back to class like nothing was up. And Ursula had insisted on coming along as well.

"I need to get to the Piney Gap Creek Reserve," I told him, not bothering to introduce the girls. "There's a campground there, closed for the season. Do you know where that is?"

"Yes." His eyes held that gleam that I knew all too well. Another bargain. I wasn't about to negotiate in front of the girls though. While technically they were my age, they hadn't lived through what I had, at least not yet. I didn't want them to see the negotiation that was about to take place so I turned to Darcy.

"I need you to do something for me."

She nodded, looking almost eager.

"Go to the town hall. The council meeting should be letting out soon. Tell…Prudence where I am. And what's happening."

"But—"

I held up a hand before Darcy could finish her protest. "We can't take you with us, not the way we're going."

"I can't rat out Joey to her mom." Darcy's gaze fell to the ground. "She'll hate me forever."

"No, but Ursula can." I stared up at my former nemesis who'd been through more than I could have imagined. "Can't you?"

Her lips parted and she nodded once. "I'll do it."

I watched them head down the hill and toward the parking lot, a lump in my throat. Seeing Darcy and Ursula united was not anything I had ever imagined.

How had I affected both of their lives? I hoped for the better.

Robin put his hand on my shoulder and I turned to face him head-on. "What's your price?"

His brilliant gaze dipped to my lips. "Tell me what's happening?"

I swallowed and looked up at him. "That's it? You want information? Not a kiss?" And why did that thought sting all of a sudden?

"I'll take the kiss freely given. But the trade is insight. What did Ursula tell you?"

My eyes narrowed on him. "Why this sudden interest in Ursula?"

Robin put his hands in his pockets. Something he did only when he was feeling defensive. "Who says I have an interest?"

My lips parted. "Oh my stars, she's next, isn't she? After you call in my bargain, you're going after her."

He hadn't come with me to the vet's office. Because he had been working Ursula on his own?

He didn't deny it. Which meant he couldn't. The fae prince couldn't lie, just like he'd said. It made sense. Ursula's husband had abandoned her. She was also middle-aged and unhappy. She worked for her brother because no one else in town would hire her. She had no friends, had driven almost everyone away.

And now I knew why. Or at least why she had started distancing herself from people. "God, you are just as bad as Bill, you know that? Line us up and knock us down. So no,

Robin, I won't kiss you and I won't tell you what Ursula told me in confidence."

He lifted his chin. "What does it matter, lamb?"

I poked him in the chest. "Don't call me that. And it matters because you are using us, toying with our emotions, our lives, for your own sick purpose. Clara wanted to save her child and you manipulated her to hold yourself in this world. You've traded women like me, sad, lonely middle-aged women, for favors from others of your ilk. Well, I'll tell you what, Robin Goodfellow, it stops right here, right now. With me."

"You don't know what you're talking about." His eyes flashed. "You can't just stop our bargain whenever you feel like it. You owe me for this trip."

"Maybe I do, but this trip isn't done yet." Tired of arguing with him, I jogged down the hill in the direction of my father's office.

"Where are you going?" Robin called, but I ignored him.

I had learned my lesson about trusting a fae prince. It was time I leaned on the people I knew I could count on.

Dad's black BMW was parked in the small lot behind his office. His keys would be in the little ceramic dish that held imprints from pinecones and acorns that I had made for him one year for Father's Day. If only I could get to them without arousing suspicion....

Luck was on my side. Through the plate-glass window, I spied Edith picking up her purse and heading toward the small restroom just off the kitchen. No sign of dear old dad. After inhaling a deep breath, I yanked open the door, snagged the keys, and whirled around before the bell even finished jingling.

I raced through the lot and unlocked the driver's side door. Inserted the key and cranked the engine to life. As I pulled out of the lot, I passed the startled face of my father as he carried a pizza back toward his office.

Not good. I wanted to call out that I would bring the car back but didn't want to risk being stopped. Instead, I headed out toward the abandoned campground at the Piney Gap Creek Reservation, where Ursula said Bill had brought her. Seduced her with kisses then cajoled her into going further and further.

She'd been a freshman. He was a junior. She'd wanted him to like her. So she went along with it, even though she didn't really want to.

It wasn't until later she discovered he had filmed their encounter. His list wasn't just a list of names, but of victims that he had filmed. Mortified, Ursula had agreed to keep quiet about the whole thing, terrified that Bill would reveal the sex tape to her uber-conservative parents. So he got to play his little seduction game again and again.

I even knew why my hormone-addled echo self had gone off with him in the middle of the day. Because better to skip school than gymnastics.

I'd taken the Camaro out of the equation but Bill must have borrowed one of his cronies' rides. But what was the hurry? Why had he pressed to get young Joey to the campground in the middle of the day when he had originally asked me out for that evening?

Then I recalled the way Robin had bumped into him and lifted the list. Damnit, I wasn't the only one who was changing the timeline. Bill must have decided to accelerate his plans for me when his list vanished.

My fingers drummed on the wheel as I made the turn off the main road and onto the dirt lane that headed up to the campground. The BMW bumped along on the pitted drive until my head smacked hard into the ceiling.

I cussed and then screamed when a familiar figure

appeared on the road in front of me. Both of my feet pounded on the brakes and I jerked the wheel so I wouldn't hit the faery bastard.

The seatbelt caught me. Forcing the air from my lungs even as it held my body in place as the vehicle skidded to a halt. I blinked, and the door was yanked open. I was unceremoniously pulled up out of the car.

"Are you hurt?" Robin's hands glided over me, presumably checking me for injury.

I knocked the questing appendages away and took a step back. "No thanks to you. What the hell were you thinking, popping in the middle of the road like that?"

He shrugged. "I'd never been here before. How was I supposed to know where the road is? And how did you get a car so quickly?"

"I sort of borrowed my dad's."

One eyebrow went up. "Sort of?"

I did a palms up gesture. "Okay, I took it. He saw me too, so the police shouldn't be too far behind."

He lifted my chin and searched my face. "Are you sure you are all right?"

No, I wasn't. Fury churned deep in my belly, most of it directed myself. Both the current me who had made such a mess of things and echo Joey who had blown off school for Billy.

"Joey, look. I'm sorry about the bargain."

I held up a hand. "Not now. I need to find Bill and my echo-self before it's too late."

The campground was made up of dozens of cabins that were little more than bunkhouses set in a semi-circle around a common green. The cleared space was dotted with battered picnic tables, tetherball poles, and a volleyball sandpit. There was no sign of another vehicle.

The first cabin we entered was empty. The mattresses on

the bunks had been zippered into what looked like giant body bags. Same in the next and the one after that. And the one after that.

"What if this isn't the place?" I fretted my bottom lip as we moved down the line. "What if he took me somewhere else?"

"Perhaps he did," Robin said. "Can you tell me what the big deal is at least?"

"The big deal is I am not supposed to lose my virginity today." I sat down on a stump. "Especially not to that tool."

"No, you were supposed to get in a career-ending accident today," Robin squatted before me.

"And I'm not even sure I prevented that." Another reason to get me away from Billy. "What if instead of preventing the accident, I've made it worse?"

"You always knew that was a possibility." He put a hand on the side of my face.

I leaned into the touch, desperately needing comfort. The sensible shrew shrieked without words, urging me not to lean on him. It didn't matter how good or right he felt. Robin Goodfellow was hazardous to my mental health.

I blew out a breath and then stood and marched down the slope toward the lake. The still surface reflected the brilliant blue of the October sky along with the fiery reds and oranges of the maples along the bank.

"He'd want privacy, somewhere out of sight of the main road," I murmured more to myself than to Robin. There. A glint of metal on the far side of the lake. I spied another wooden structure, this one larger than the cabins. "Somewhere like that."

It would take several more minutes to backtrack to the BMW and there was no guarantee the sedan would be able to handle the lake road leading to the structure. Part of it might be washed out.

Without asking, Robin snatched my hand in his and transported us across the water. We stood in front of a gleaming silver pick-up. I put my palm against the hood, feeling the warmth of the engine.

I looked up at Robin and nodded once.

He seemed content to stand back. Or maybe he was just trying to worm his way back into my good graces. "How are you going to play this?"

I huffed out a breath. "Epically. Like the pissed-off faery godmother I am."

I marched up the stairs and prepared to kick the door open when I heard the first scream.

CHAPTER THIRTEEN

"Hit 'em where it counts. Right in the wallet."
-Notable quotable from Grammy B

What was Billy doing to me in there? The scream emanated from a place of primal terror and the chord in it formed ice floes in my veins. I was going to put his nuts in a vice for frightening me that way.

Just as soon as I got in there.

For the record, kicking in a locked door is a lot harder than it looks on tv. Even with extra weight, I was still agile enough to plant my right foot on the wooden door while maintaining my balance on the left. Unfortunately, I had underestimated the amount of sheer force and power it would take to make the lock give way and the wood bow in. My borrowed boots didn't provide enough cushion and splintering pain reverberated along my calf from ankle to knee.

"Son of a motherless goat!" I yelped, hopping on one foot. My hands gripped the porch railing so I didn't topple onto my face.

"May I?" Robin asked.

I jerked my chin to the door and muttered, "Be my guest."

Robin didn't kick the door down. Instead, he reached for the handle and turned the knob. The door swung inward just as a second scream pierced the quiet fall afternoon.

I limped past him and into the darkened interior of the cabin. It was really more of a bunkhouse, much like the others with one long open room. Except instead of rows of bunk beds, there was one big bed, a couch draped in a sheet, and a fireplace filled with cobwebs. Probably the camp director's digs. The windows held no glass but had instead been covered with some sort of fabric that sent a diffused sort of light into the space, barely enough to illuminate the scene before us.

My echo self was on the bed, standing with a sheet covering her naked body. She was hopping up and down in a way that no one in their right mind would mistake for sexual. Especially when Billy stood on the floor, wielding what looked like a Bowie knife.

"What the hell are you doing?" I stormed toward him with all the fury of a woman scorned even as young Joey screeched, "Don't step on it!"

"Huh?" I looked down.

And shrieked at the sight of the copperhead snake curled beside the couch. It hissed and I scrambled back, nearly trampling Billy in my hurry to get away from the venomous reptile.

"Do something!" Joey shifted her weight, causing the bed to creak.

"Like what, ask him to stay for tea?" I snapped.

"Use your magic wand," she insisted. "Magic it away."

"What?" Bill looked between us like we had both lost our minds.

"I, uh, left it at your house." Besides it wasn't really a

magic wand, just a prop. My gaze slid to Robin, who shook his head back and forth. So there wasn't anything he could—or would—do to help.

My shoulders went up and down in a helpless shrug. "I must have forgotten it."

"You are the worst faery godmother ever," young Joey bitched.

"Maybe you should take it up with management." Gaze trained on the snake, I reached for Bill's hand. "Give me the knife."

The snake stared at us through its evil little eyes as though it knew what I intended. I looked at Robin again but his eyes were closed, his lips moving with silent words.

"Who the hell are you anyway?" Bill yanked his hand, still holding the knife out of my reach.

I glared at him. "I'm the woman who had your Camaro impounded."

His jaw dropped. "You *bitch*."

"Oh, that stung." I rolled my eyes and then snagged the knife from his hand before the idiot cut his junk off by accident. Not that there would be much to miss.

Not liking our exchange, the snake hissed a warning. I tensed, sure it was about to strike when a gray blur streaked through the still-open door. A mackerel tabby swiped out, claws extended, and beheaded the serpent as it uncoiled. The two segments fell to the ground.

"Puck?" I asked when I saw the familiar bent ear. "I mean, Clara?"

She blinked up at me but didn't speak. Probably because we had an audience. Robin bent down to scoop her up, but she arched her back with a hiss and he hastily stepped aside.

My hand covered my chest and I exhaled the breath I'd been holding, then looked at my echo self. "Get dressed. Your mother will be here in a minute."

"What?" Young Joey dove for her clothes. I was relieved to see she still had her underwear on. At least things hadn't gone too far.

Unless she'd been putting them back on….

"And you," I rounded on Bill. "What the hell were you thinking, bringing her out here? What if it had been a rabid raccoon, or a bear in here? Never mind a human predator. The two of you could have been killed!"

His mouth hung open, his gaze on the twitching segments of the snake.

I moved closer to him and lowered my voice. "Listen to me, now. You stay the hell away from her. And if you're smart, you'll destroy all the tapes you have of the other girls you brought here."

He swung his head to face me. "How do you know about that?"

I lifted my chin and fisted my hands on my hips. "I know all about your list, Tucker. And if you don't want to disappear for good, I would recommend reviewing how you've been treating these girls and adjust your course."

He took a step back, tripping on his pants. "You're crazy."

"I'm middle-aged. Same difference." I narrowed my eyes on him and in my best Grammy B voice barked, "Now git!"

He collected his clothes and without pausing to put them on, stumbled out of the cabin.

"Billy, wait!" My echo self cried as his bare ass disappeared through the open door. She hastened to put on her boots but the sound of an engine roaring to life was followed by a cloud of dust as the borrowed pick-up disappeared down the road before she could give chase.

"What did you do?" Joey cried. "He's going to hate me now!"

I ignored her. Instead, striding to the bed and plunking myself down. With my head on a swivel, I studied all the nooks and crannies of the space until I found what I was looking for.

Getting to my feet, I moved to the large chest of drawers that was draped with an old bedsheet. The top of it was littered with sticks and pinecones, but peeking out from in between two fir branches was the all-seeing eye of a video camera lens.

"He was recording you." I knocked the natural flotsam aside and picked up the camera to show her. "The same way he did with all the others."

Her lips parted and she shook her head. "No. I don't believe you."

"Then how do you explain this?" I held the camera aloft. "He targeted you from the beginning. He doesn't really like you. You were a trophy to him. Part of his collection."

"Easy, lamb." Robin put a hand on my shoulder. "She's been through a lot."

I glared at him. "I *know*. I also know what she'll have to go through in the future. And the sooner she learns not to trust predatory assholes like Bill Tucker, the better."

My heart pumped and my hands shook as the adrenaline worked its way out of my system. In the distance, sirens sounded. That would be my mom, calling in the cavalry.

I softened as I saw how defeated young Joey appeared. I turned back to Robin. "Wait for me outside?"

He hesitated a moment. "We best be gone before the authorities show up and start asking questions we can't answer."

"I just need a minute with her. Then we can go."

He blew out a breath and then nodded once.

I knelt in front of my younger self and braced for the worst. "How far did it go?"

She glared at me.

"Did you have sex with him?" I wouldn't relent.

Mutely, she shook her head.

I let out a breath, relieved that whenever her memories caught up to mine, I wouldn't have to carry the weight of that particular one. "That's good. You deserve better, Joey. Practice gymnastics and become an elite gymnast. Represent the US in Sydney. The sky's the limit as long as you are careful."

Outside, a car door slammed and I heard my mother's voice. "Josephine Louise Whitmore!"

"You better go out before she comes in," I said.

She was staring at me. "Why are you trying to destroy my life?"

I swallowed. "I'm not. I'm trying to fix it."

She stood up and held my gaze, hers burning with hatred. "How about you just go get your own life and stop screwing with mine."

I flinched and she pushed past me and exited the building. I stayed where I was, about a foot away from the dead snake. Clara sat beside me, bathing her tail as the flurry of activity outside reached a crescendo. For a moment I worried they would come storming into the cabin and demand to know who I was. But then car doors closed and the vehicles dispersed. No crime to investigate and Joey hadn't mentioned my presence.

"Thanks," I said to the cat. "You were great. Way better than me."

It was funny, I thought as I stepped out onto the porch. I'd hated and blamed myself for years but it was one thing to be disgusted by what I saw in the mirror, another thing entirely to meet my own gaze and recognize sheer hatred directed entirely at me.

And the day wasn't over yet.

❄

Robin stood on a small spit of beach a few hundred yards away from the cabin and stared at the flashing blue lights across the water.

"What's going on?" I moved to stand beside him.

"Cops are dusting for fingerprints." Robin looked down at me. "Good thing yours are legit."

"Yup. And since Dad had been teaching me to drive, they won't think a thing of it." I closed my eyes and leaned back against a tree. "I hate myself."

"And here I thought you hated me," the fae prince murmured.

I shook my head. "I don't hate you, Robin. But I'm not thrilled with you either. You hurt me."

"How?"

I cracked a lid, trying to decipher if he was being serious. His brows were drawn together as though he were truly trying to puzzle it out.

"Because you're going after Ursula. No woman wants to be with a guy who is constantly scanning the horizon for his next score."

"Ursula is business." He took a step closer. "You're more."

"How am I any different?" I shook my head. "She's a divorced middle-aged woman desperate to change her life. And so am I. We're both the type you target. And she's had enough shit to deal with. She doesn't need you, too."

"And now you worry for her, this woman who you have considered an enemy for most of your life." He shook his head. "Believe me, lamb. It may have started out as just another bargain but something is different. I can't explain it, but I feel it here." He thumped his heart over his chest.

"I'm not buying it, pal." I was so over men and their bevy of lies. Bill, saying I was special to him. George promising to love me forever. Now Robin.

But the fae trickster didn't back down. "You know I can't

utter a falsehood. There is something about you, Joey. Something unique and so rare it's precious. In all my centuries I have never seen anyone as brave or as determined to do what is right. You are…pure goodness."

I snorted. "Would pure goodness have considered having you enthrall Bill?"

He waved a hand as though erasing my argument. "You considered it because I offered. But you didn't go through with it. Even if it is the easiest solution to your problem."

"Taking someone's free will away is wrong. Completely and totally wrong." I pinched the bridge of my nose. "How messed up is it that I have to explain that to you?"

He flinched and backed away.

A distant rumble of thunder foretold of the coming storm. I blew out a breath. "Take me back to my house. I need to keep watch over myself. At least until after the accident."

He was silent as he offered me his arm. I took it and we slid across town before I could ask what the price was.

Did it even matter? I was already in it up to my sagging boobs.

We appeared in the front parlor. The grandfather clock in the hall chimed three deep bongs. I staggered over to the fainting couch and put my head in my hands. Just a little over four more hours and then I could go back to my own time, having changed the future.

Why wasn't I more excited about it?

"Are you sure this is wise?" Robin asked. "Waiting here? Won't your mother and echo self be on the way back here directly?"

I shook my head. "Gymnastics practice is from three until six. Mom will wait there and then chew me out on the way home."

Robin nodded, though his brows were pulled together in deep concentration.

"What?" I asked him. "What is it?"

He shook his head and then pasted on a fake smile. "Nothing for you to trouble yourself over? Do you have a plan?"

I swallowed. "Yeah."

He didn't pry. "Good, I will return at seven."

Without another word, he vanished.

"Can't wait." I blew out a breath. His sudden avoidance reminded me of George's behavior in the weeks leading up to his confession. Eager to be away from me, nervous and twitchy when we were together. I knew all the signs of a guilty conscience. The question was, what else was Robin hiding from me?

My stomach growled, loudly. Diet would start as soon as I got back to my own time. Although maybe my new self would be in better shape. Having wheatgrass smoothies and drinking green tea instead of gorging on ice cream-enhanced coffee. Either way, the new diet would start as soon as I returned to the future. For now, I decided to raid the fridge.

I struck gold when I discovered half an apple crumb pie on the top shelf. I popped it in the microwave to warm and had just settled down with it at the small table in the kitchen when the back door opened.

"Thought I would find you here. Did it work?" Darcy asked as she dropped her backpack down beside the table. "Did you get there in time?"

"According to me, yes. The other me, I mean." I tucked into the pie and around a mouthful asked, "Where's Ursula?"

"She had to get home, though she said she would come by later. Which is weird as hell, because, are we really going to start hanging out with Ursula Green?"

"She's been through a lot." And there was more to come. I

debated telling Darcy about the fae prince who had both me and Ursula in his sights, but decided she'd had her world upended more than enough for one day.

"Yeah, she has." Darcy headed for the silverware drawer and snagged a fork for herself. "I know you're going to share that since you couldn't have made it happen without me."

I grinned at her. "Darc, promise me you'll never change."

She made an x over her chest. "Cross my heart and hope to die. Stick a big, rubber dildo in my eye. Slightly used, natch."

We laughed and then finished the pie.

Outside, a car door slammed.

I frowned and glanced at the microwave display. "It's only three-thirty."

Darcy got up and headed to the door. "It's the other you and your mom. And she looks massively pissed."

Crap. "Which one? Me or Mom?"

She shrugged. "Take your pick."

I glanced around and then made an executive decision and headed for the cellar door. "Mom doesn't know about me."

Darcy nodded. "Secret's safe with me, babe."

The dank oppressiveness of the root cellar swallowed me just as I heard the back door open and my mother said, "Darcy, what are you doing here?"

My bestie was fast on her feet and said, "I brought over my chem notes for Joey. Since she missed class."

I winced. Probably better not to bring that up.

"That's very considerate," Mom's voice sounded tight. "I'm just going to change before Paul gets here and then we need a little family time."

"Uh, sure," Darcy said.

The sound of my mother's heels clicking on the hardwoods echoed as she headed down the hall to her bedroom.

I debated emerging from my hiding spot, but then Joey said, "I can't believe you helped her."

"Me?" Darcy's tone was incredulous. "I can't believe you went off with that tool Bill Tucker to some shag shack without telling me."

"He's not a tool," young Joey said with more heat than I would have anticipated. "And where do you get off being mad at me? You're the one who ratted me out to my mother."

"'Scuse me for being worried about you." Darcy's voice dripped with scorn.

"Did you know Mom pulled me out of gymnastics for a week? And I'm grounded through Halloween."

I sucked in a sharp breath at her words. *No.* If I didn't qualify for elite status this year, I'd never make it to the Olympics. I needed to do those 40 hours a week with dedication and focus. A week out of the gym would put me at a serious disadvantage.

"Well, maybe you should have thought of that before you ran off with the tool." There was a scuffing sound, followed by the slam of the door, telegraphing Darcy's enraged exit.

Pounding footsteps thundered upstairs, followed by another slam, this time of my bedroom door.

Slowly I crept out of the cellar and moved into the kitchen where the pie plate sat. Empty and waiting to be scrubbed clean so it stood ready to do what it was meant to do.

Kinda like me without gymnastics.

There was only one more course of action. One thing I really didn't want to do. I needed to talk to my mother. Tell her who I was and why I'd come back. I knew she would help me fulfill my dream. The thing with Bill had shaken her. After she had a little bit of time to reflect, she'd see that I was just growing up and assist me in making my own choices.

Besides, there I stood, the cautionary tale of what would

happen to her daughter if she didn't have gymnastics in her life.

If she believed me.

Big fat if.

The back door opened before I realized anyone was there. I froze like a deer in the headlights as Paul Blackthorn strode inside. No time to hide, to get out of his field of view.

His eyes went wide when he saw me. "You. You're the woman who took my car aren't you?"

"I can explain." The words of anyone who has ever been busted for doing something wrong. My mind groped for a suitable reason why I, to his knowledge a total stranger, would have taken his car. Would he believe I was his daughter from the future?

With my mother, I stood a small chance. But dad was a man of facts and science. He enjoyed science fiction but didn't believe it was anything more than a product of artistic invention. I remember watching the movie *Back to the Future* with him when I was about eight and having him explain to me why time travel was impossible all throughout dinner.

"What's going on here?" Mom, clad now in a dress almost identical to the ugly one I'd borrowed reemerged into the kitchen. It was the first up-close look I'd had of her in this timeline. She was about my age though much like the dress, she wore the years better. "Who's this?"

"The woman who stole my car." Dad crossed his arms over his chest and stared down at me. "And broke into your house apparently. I'm still waiting for an explanation of why."

Mom reached for the phone hanging on the wall. "I'm going to call the police."

"No, wait." I lunged for the phone and yanked the jack out of the wall. "I'm sorry I took your car, but I needed to help Joey."

"What does Joey have to do with any of this?" My dad asked.

"Everything. You need to listen to me, for the sake of your daughter's future." I sucked in a big breath and then said the words. "You see, I'm Joey. I'm from over two decades in the future. And I'm here to tell you that what you decide to do now will affect my entire existence."

My parents exchanged a, *she's out of her mind* look. I couldn't blame them, but I needed to get them to believe me somehow.

"Look, I know you two have been spending a lot of time together and that you, Mom, are actually wondering if maybe you should marry him after all these years of casual dating."

My mother's lips parted.

"In my version of the future, that doesn't happen. Because in about two hours, the Joey you know gets in a horrible car accident." I held up my wrist, pointing out the surgical scars which had faded to pale white streaks.

"My wrist was pulverized and there was no way I could have recovered enough to make it as an elite gymnast in time for the next round of Nationals. My career was over before it began. And I have been completely miserable ever since. You," I pointed to my father. "You told me that your biggest regret in life was not standing up to mom and pulling me out of school this year, before I got involved with Bill Tucker. He was the one who was driving when I got hurt."

My mother gasped but my father was frowning. "How did you get here?"

I held his gaze. "You wouldn't believe me if I told you. What I can tell you is that the three of us have been existing in a sort of half-life for more than two decades. You have no grandchildren. You're still living the same way you are right now. I'm a joke around town because I can't hold a job for more than six months. I still live at home, and I married a man who turned out to be a woman. Is that what you want for your only daughter?"

Horror filled my mother's big blue eyes and she looked to my dad. He still appeared skeptical but I could tell my words spooked him because he lowered himself into a nearby chair.

Mom stepped forward and reached out to touch me. Her gaze searched my face and she murmured, "It really is you, isn't it?"

I nodded. It was harder to hold her gaze than ever. Mom didn't hide what she felt. Not ever. It was all there on her face, every second of every day. An open book just waiting to be read. I'd grown used to the constant frustration in the lines around her eyes and disappointment that flickered over her mouth when she heard about my latest foible. But now she studied me with an intensity I hadn't seen since my accident.

Dad being dad, wanted proof. "Tell me one thing that only Joey would know."

My teeth sank into my lower lip as I sorted through possibilities. "You caught me stealing fifty bucks from your wallet when we were at the hotel in Atlanta. I cried and begged you not to tell mom and you agreed. Said I could clerk in your office on the weekends to make up for it."

And I could see from the stunned look on my mom's transparent features that he'd upheld his end of the deal.

"What did you need money for?" Mom asked.

"Your birthday gift. I'd spent all the cash I had on Olympic souvenirs and forgot your birthday until the day of. I ended up getting you this cheesy glass dolphin from the hotel lobby."

She wrapped her arms around me suddenly and held me close. "Oh Joey," she sobbed.

Dad rose and then wrapped his arms around me too. We

stood there in a little circle of family love and support. Something I hadn't even realized I'd been missing even more than the feel of chalk on my palms or the rush of executing a perfect routine.

I soaked it up, glad that I had decided to be honest with them and that they believed me. Not just that, but they believed *in* me.

"Listen," I said and pulled away. "We don't have much time. I've already changed some things but I won't know if I prevented the accident until 7:19. Don't let the other me out of your sights."

"I'll go get her. Er...you," my mother said, leaving the two of us alone.

He brushed some hair out of my eyes. "You're so beautiful, you know that?"

Heat stole over my face. "You have to say that, you're my dad."

But he shook his head. "No. You look like your mother. I see her in your eyes, her bravery. And your grandmother's stubbornness."

I had never thought of myself as particularly stubborn before. That was pretty cool though, thinking that there existed some resemblance to the two most magnificent women I'd ever known. The pleasure at the thought vanished when my mother's cry echoed off the walls. Dad raced for the stairs with me hot on his heels.

Mom stood at the doorway to my room, staring at the curtains that billowed in the gusting wind from the coming storm.

Young Joey had disappeared.

CHAPTER FOURTEEN

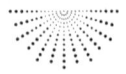

"They call it the change of life because the woman who goes in isn't the same as the one who comes out on the other side."
-Notable quotable from Grammy B.

"Robin," I hissed into the darkening night. "Are you there?"

It was ten to seven. The fae prince said he would return precisely at seven. My parents were out combing the streets, looking for young Joey. I could do nothing but pace from the front door to the back again and again, frustrated that I didn't know myself better.

I hadn't gone to Grammy B's. That was the first place my mother had called. Nor had I showed up at Darcy's doorstep or gone to the gym. The packed gym bag was still in the back of mom's car. Alina hadn't seen me. I had no other friends that I would turn to. Mom and my dad had taken to driving around town, looking for me.

Much as I hated to admit it, I needed the fae prince's help.

Desperately. And I was afraid I was going to have to do something I didn't want to in order to secure it.

Correction: I would probably have to do something I desperately *did* want to do but was afraid to do to get his help.

But I was out of options. And almost out of time.

The rain had started up in earnest, the wind plucking several of the newly turned leaves to the ground. I'd called the impound lot and found out that Bill had somehow sprung his ride. He was out there on the streets tonight, unaware of what would happen. Was my echo self with him?

The hourglass was still in my pocket. For a moment I considered using another trip to go back a few hours and hogtie my teenage self until the crisis passed. But that would mean one less trip for me to right a great wrong.

"Meow."

I looked down to see Puck sauntering up the steps. She rubbed up against my ankles, tail sticking straight up, back arched. "Have you seen young Joey, Clara?"

"She can't answer you, lamb." Robin appeared as though pulled from the darkness itself. "This version of her can only speak with me. And I have stronger control over her actions. Her autonomy grows by leaps and bounds after the turn of the century. She can understand you though."

I recalled the way he'd closed his eyes, the way the cat had come streaking into the cabin to fight the copperhead. "You summoned her earlier, didn't you?"

He nodded. "The same way you just summoned me. The bargains we make bind us to each other mystically. What's wrong?"

I petted the cat, unable to look him in the eye. "Everything. I've gone missing again. My echo self I mean. And I haven't a clue where I would be."

Robin leaned against the porch railing. "Don't you?"

I let out a breath. "Maybe. I just don't want to admit that my, the other me, is so desperate that she would go after Bill Tucker even after what happened earlier."

"Humans always think they know themselves better than they actually do. You pushed and now she's pushing back." For once he didn't sound condescending, more resigned.

I was silent for a moment, letting that sink in.

"What can I do?" He prompted.

A slow breath escaped. "I need your help to find me."

"You know the price for my help." Sapphire eyes glowed in the darkness. "Ask and we'll strike a bargain."

I swallowed. "I don't want to bargain."

At his raised brow I added. "I want to kiss you because I want to. And I want you to help me because you want to. No tricks, no trade, no price. Just basic caring and human decency."

"An oxymoron if ever I heard one," he scoffed.

A growl escaped my lips and I muttered, "Don't be a jerk. I have had my fill of them today."

"So, you admit you want to kiss me then?"

I didn't see any point in denying it. "Yes."

He unfurled from his casual pose and stalked closer. "And what makes you think I want to help you?"

"Because you could have been curb-boosting me all day. You gave me little trips around town and stayed with me, even when I lashed out at you. And you defended young Joey when I would have made verbal mincemeat out of her. I think you are invested in the outcome of my journey. I think you want me to succeed."

He shook his head. "Lamb, you are delusional. I live only for the bargain, whether it succeeds or fails."

"Then why do you want me to kiss you so badly?" I held my breath, waiting for his answer.

His eyes glowed in the dim light. "I couldn't say."

I wondered if that meant he didn't know. At first, I thought he just wanted to push my buttons, to make me squirm since that was the fae prince's MO. But I was beginning to believe that Robin was hanging around with me, not because I was one of his bargain biddies, but because he actually liked me.

As much as I liked him. While I'd paced and fretted and thought over all that had occurred, I'd come to the conclusion that yes, I did harbor feelings for Robin. Friendship and the first tinge of heat that came with sexual interest. He was beautiful and interesting and he made me laugh, made me feel desired.

Those budding emotions had gotten hurt when I found out that he was planning to move on to Ursula. That I would be cast aside like dirty laundry when all this was over. The understanding didn't change the fact that I craved his kiss, hungered for a taste of him, even if he was evil and manipulative and I was only a temporary fascination in his immortal existence.

But life had taught me that nothing lasted. Youth and beauty faded. Physical strength diminished as wisdom flourished. Love changed. The world spun on and time passed whether I lived my life or didn't. Whether I took risks or played it safe.

I was done playing it safe.

So I pushed off the steps. A breeze stirred the hair on the back of my neck. Water dripped from the still wet leaves as I moved across the concrete path toward him. He waited, that hot green gaze boring into me. His hands clenched into fists at his sides as though he had just stopped himself from reaching for me.

My hands smoothed up his chest. Beneath the windbreaker that matched my own, he had changed back into the flannel shirt tucked into jeans. Because I said I preferred this look? I did. It made him seem infinitely more accessible to me than the power suit. No changing the fact that Joey Whitmore was a small-town girl at heart.

The sweet scent of autumn leaves mingled with the spicy musk that was his unique fragrance. My inhale reached all the way to my toes, determined to savor the moment.

"You're making me crazy," he muttered.

I shook my head. "That was never my intent."

"I know. That's why it works. No games or guile, no power plays. You have no idea how appealing you are to me, lamb."

He dipped his head and waited. Through the screen door, the first bong of the hour sounded on the grandfather clock. Seven PM. We were almost out of time.

My hands slid up to grip his shoulders. I had to stand on my tiptoes to reach his lips. Soft, so incredibly soft as I brushed my mouth against his. It was a light, sweet kiss, one filled with affection and gentleness, admiration, and a spark of magic.

Another bong. A third. I brushed my lips across his and held my heat and need in check. I was no randy teenager to lose myself in a kiss. And yet, when his hands drifted to my hips and he pulled me even closer, my toes curled. I lapped at the seam of his mouth tentatively and a harsh groan escaped. He tasted like sin, like the very essence of life itself. A wild thought flitted through my mind. *This is what I've been missing.*

At some point, my fingers tangled in the soft strands of his hair. I gripped him as though I never wanted to let him go.

A sexual fire burned in me. A flame I had all but forgotten I possessed. Kissing Robin fed it, made it burn brighter… hotter…until it threatened to consume me.

The seventh and final gong sounded and though I didn't want to, I withdrew.

"Please help me find her." The words were exhaled from my mouth even as I gulped for air. "We're almost out of time."

He too seemed out of breath. His eyes were hot as they fixed on my lips as though he'd gotten only a small taste of a dish he craved. Then he stepped back from me and shook his head. "Come on, I know where to look."

He held out a hand and I took it. The connection felt different this time. My awareness of him was open. In fact, everything seemed sharper, more compelling. It was as though when lost in the throes of that kiss I had developed another sense that fed me new information about the world.

Would it fade? If not, could I close it back down? Would I want to?

Judging from the way he wouldn't meet my gaze something had changed for Robin too.

But there was no time to talk about it.

Robin shifted us from the wet walkway in front of my house to a gravel path that stood before a rickety-looking barn.

I spun in a circle, not recognizing the location. A farm for sure. What looked like a hillside dotted with Christmas trees rolled down the hill. Bill Tucker's grandparents had a Christmas tree farm. This must be their property. Without the streetlights that stretched along the walkways in town, I only had the light of the moon to go by but it didn't appear there were any other structures nearby. "Are you sure this is where I am?"

He nodded wordlessly and pointed to a circular turn around with an old chestnut tree in the center. A dilapidated tire swing hung from its branches and beside it….

The frigging Camaro.

No. Damn it, what was my echo-self doing? Though I had made some boneheaded choices, I never considered myself stupid. But here was the proof that I very well might be a complete moron. After the disaster of the afternoon, my sixteen-year-old echo self had sought out Bill Tucker again. Inadvertently, my gaze slid to where the fae prince stood.

I must have a thing for bad boys. And my dad was right, Grammy B's stubborn streak. Everyone had told me Bill was using me. I'd shown myself the video camera, heard about the list. I knew my parents would be out of their heads with worry. And I was still in there.

Josephine Louise Whitmore, you are a dumbass.

If our lives hadn't been tied together I would have left her to it. Even if I managed to prevent the accident, Bill might knock me up. Or give me an STD.

But our lives were bound together. I had to help myself. Even when I wanted to strangle myself.

The large doors to the barn were sealed up tight but there had to be a standard size door around there somewhere. I lurched ahead, stumbling on the uneven and soggy ground. Robin caught me by the arm before I went careening into a drainage ditch. "Lamb, think this through. If you bust in on them again and they take off in that car, you'll have engineered the very situation you've been striving to avoid."

A sound of frustration bubbled from the pit of my stomach. "So, what should I do? Sit out here and wait for them to finish? I can't do that."

Misting rainwater dropped off his hood and onto my hand. "Maybe we should use some magic."

"Like what?" I asked.

"You had the right idea with the car." He chucked his chin toward the Camera.

"I forgot my—" I held out my hand and the magic wand

appeared into it the same way it had that morning. "Never mind. How do I do it?"

"It's just like with the time travel spell. Imagine the outcome you want and focus that will through the wand. It's a tool that will manifest what you envision."

I envisioned. Straightening my arm, I pointed the wand at the car and pictured a massive orange gourd.

Nothing happened.

"It's not working," I grumbled.

"Try again." Robin placed his hand over mine. "You can do this, Joey."

I closed my eyes and took strength from the heat of his hands. The warmth coursed through me and shook something loose.

"That's it," Robin crooned in my ear. Every hair on my body stood at attention. A prickle of raw power, like that of electricity proceeding a lightning storm, surged through me. The world faded away until it was just the two of us, the wand and the car. Against the shell of my ear, the fae's lips whispered a rhyme. "If you can see, it can be."

I repeated the words to myself, picturing, seeing it.

My lids lifted and my lips parted. There before me stood a four-foot-tall pumpkin, complete with trailing vines and crooked stem.

A thrill coursed through me. I had done it. "It worked!"

"Not exactly." Robin circled my chin with one finger and adjusted it so I looked to the spot beside the pumpkin.

Where the Camaro still sat.

"Damn it," I snarled. I'd done magic, a real honest to goodness transformation spell like a real faery godmother. And I'd frigging missed. Morphed the Chestnut tree not the stupid car.

"Try again," Robin urged, but as he spoke, the barn door

was dragged open. The inside looked like a gaping maw of an angler fish as two flashlight beams flicked on.

"Joey," I called and ran toward my echo self. "Come with me, now. You've got everyone worried sick about you."

"What are you doing here?" Young Joey shone the light into her own face, probably to add a solid visual to how irritated she was by my arrival.

Her hair was mussed and pieces of straw clung to it and her sweater. She had that just gone for a roll in the hay look. I glared at her and at Billy. Had the idiots even practiced safe sex?

"That's my question exactly. Did you not pick up on the fact that he's total scum? What about the list? The videos?" I made a grab for her arm but she capered away.

"You mean the video camera you obviously planted?"

Billy dropped an arm around her shoulders. "I told you she's got some sort of sick crush on me. She's been following me around town for weeks."

"You little bastard," I lunged for him, sorry I hadn't taken Robin up on enthralling the tool. Look what he did with free will. Lied to get his way.

"Get lost." Young Joey said as she headed to the car. "You're the shittiest faery godmother ever."

"You don't understand." I couldn't let her get in that car, no matter what. I knew how that would end. "Damn it, Josephine Louise Whitmore, you will ruin the rest of your life if you leave with him now."

"It's my life." She yanked open the door with a huff and then shut and locked it behind herself. Billy scrambled to the driver's side. Headlights cut through the darkness, blowing my night vision. I hissed like a cat, but circled around to the front of the car and put my hands on the hood. Billy just flung his arm over the back seat and shifted into reverse.

Tires spat gravel at me as he did a broken K turn and then headed down the hill back to town.

"No," I cried and took a few staggering steps down the hill after them. My wand was still in my hand but if I turned the car into a pumpkin now, what would happen to Joey and Billy? Would they become mice? Pumpkin seeds?

Robin was at my side in an instant. "Where does it happen?"

"Oak Summit Drive." I glanced at my watch. 7:12. "In exactly six minutes."

"We can still beat them there." He held out a hand and I took it.

Again with the sideways lurching sensation. "I'd say I'm getting used to that but I'd be lying." My stomach turned over and for a moment I was sure that apple pie would make a comeback.

Robin wasn't paying attention. Instead, he was looking around at the sharp blind curve that led uphill. There were streetlights on the left side of the road, along the sidewalk. Oak Summit connected directly to the heart of town. "You said you struck a phone pole, right?"

I nodded. "After skidding on wet leaves."

His gaze fell to the discarded yellow, red, orange, and brown detritus, littering the road. "Okay. Use your magic wand and get rid of them."

"Like a leaf blower?" Maybe a gust of wind could whisk them all out of the path of fate.

"Put them back on the trees, brush them off to the side, incinerate them. Just do something," Robin urged. "Quickly, lamb."

I huffed out a breath and then extended the wand. My lids lowered as I tried to picture the scene. My pulse was hammering hard, thrumming in my ears. Each beat seemed to be thumping out a message in morse code. Out. Of. Time. Out. Of. Time. One chance to get this right. Magic curled around the wand clutched tightly in my fist as I thought **no more leaves**.

Robin swore. "What did you do?"

"What?" I opened my eyes and gasped in horror. The trees above had dropped all of the remaining leaves like they were hot.

"Oh no. I thought no more leaves, but the magic thought I meant *on* the trees." Was that even possible? Was magic sentient? Bare branches stretched to the dark sky as though asking the cosmos why they were naked already.

"Try again," the faery urged.

I had to get it right. Had to work a spell. Maybe I could move the phone pole?

"Headlights," Robin pointed. His pallor had turned white as chalk and his eyes appeared haunted as they turned to me. "Joey, I think, I think this moment might be…fated. There's no avoiding the crash."

"No no no! It can't be." Frustration bubbled up and I stamped my foot. "Damn it, I'm no good at this magic thing. Can't you do anything?"

Robin stared at me for a long minute, his expression unreadable. "No. But there's one thing you can do. But I don't think—"

"What?" I was not above begging. I had already driven my younger self directly into Billy Tucker's clutches, revealed time travel and their stagnate futures to my parents, and potentially destroyed my relationship with Darcy. If I didn't manage to avoid this accident…. I gripped him by the front of his shirt, ready to shake him silly. "Whatever it is, whatever the cost, I'll pay it."

I could hear the engine rev as the Camaro accelerated up the hill. Too fast. It was happening too fast, just like before.

"Please Robin." I licked my lips. "Tell me, what can I do?"

He reached for my cheek, brushed his thumb over it. "Switch places with your echo self."

"What?"

"Joey Whitmore is destined to get in that accident. But you can replace her in the car."

Relive that crash. Fix my future. I hesitated only a moment and then dug the small hourglass out of my pocket and handed it to him. "As soon as I do, I want to go forward. Back to my own time. Will you promise to get me there?"

He took the hourglass from me and nodded.

I took a deep breath and turned. The engine roared as the car came up the hill.

Robin gripped me and turned me to face him. His expression was haunted, his tone bleak. "I don't want you to do this, lamb. What if the accident is worse than before? What if it kills you?"

"Just get me back to my time," I said. "I'm trusting you to do it."

He let out a ragged breath and then stepped away.

The headlights crested the hill. Seconds remained. I only had one final chance to get this right. *Switch me for her. Her place for mine.*

The wand vibrated in my hand. Power built and built. One second, I was standing at the side of the road looking into my own wide blue eyes....

And then I blinked and found myself in the car. The scent of air freshener filled my nose as the Goo Goo Dolls blared from the radio. My echo self stood alongside the road. Her expression utterly stunned.

"What the hell?" Billy's head whipped toward me.

"Look out!" I shrieked as he hit the wet leaves. Tires skidded. He jerked the wheel. Brakes screamed. The car skidded. Billy let out a strangled yell as the vehicle spun out. The phone pole was closing in. Fear flooded my body as we spun and spun, careening out of control.

Impact.

Glass crunched. Metal groaned. My body jerked forward though the seatbelt held firm as the airbag deployed, hitting me in the face. Instinctively, I clutched my bad wrist, preventing it from being trapped by the crumpling metal. The taste of blood filled my mouth and I knew that my nose had been rebroken.

But not my wrist. Not young Joey's wrist. I'd spared her the trauma of the accident. She could go on to Olympic glory.

I did it. Triumph that I hadn't felt in forever blotted out the pain and I started to laugh. After a lifetime of losses, finally one for the win column. Fate wanted an accident with Joey Whitmore? Well, I'd survived it, not once, but twice.

Fate could bite me.

A groan sounded from the other side of the car. My laughter cut off abruptly. Billy Tucker's head lolled, his eyes fluttered. A stray piece of glass had cut a jagged scar into the side of his temple and blood spilled down.

"You okay?" I asked him.

He groaned again just as the driver's side door was wrenched open.

"Billy!" My echo self screamed and dragged him out of the car.

"No need to thank me." I spat blood and reached for the seatbelt. "Honestly. Don't gush, it's embarrassing."

Dizziness washed over me, I closed my eyes, knowing I should struggle my way out of the car. I would after I shut my eyes for a moment. And then a familiar voice muttered, "I've got you, lamb."

The cool autumn air of October 3, 1996, tunneled and faded into history.

CHAPTER FIFTEEN

The familiar warm feel of flannel sheets on a winter morning caressing my body coaxed me out of my stupor. This wasn't a normal morning though. For one thing, every part of me hurt, like my body was one massive bruise, though the pain was more acute around my face. Damn, what had I been doing yesterday? I would have to take a whole bottle of Advil to dull this throb.

To get more comfortable and snag a few extra zzzs I shifted from my left side to my back. A groan escaped as the soreness spread. That was no good either as not only did my nose hurt like hell, it was damn near impossible for me to breathe through.

It came back in a rush. Swapping places with my echo self to save my gymnastics career. Time travel with a fae prince.

My eyes snapped open to an unfamiliar ceiling. No settlement cracks, or ornate molding. Just smooth, white sheetrock gleaming in the winter light as though it had been freshly painted. Not my bedroom in the Victorian. Not the dingy apartment George and I had shared.

Where was I?

Slowly, trying to avoid any quick movement that would increase my pain, I pushed my body upright. There were two windows where the bay should have been and no bench seat. Instead, a cushy looking floral armchair with a matching ottoman sat in the far corner. There were a pair of pants draped over it.

Specifically, male pants. The matching suit jacket peeked out from beneath.

A soft snore alerted me that I wasn't alone.

Heart hammering, I turned my head to face the other side of the bed. It was occupied. The covers were drawn up to my bed companion's waist and I could see a well developed and naked male back that rose and fell in the steady rhythm of a sleeping person.

"Robin?" I whispered but immediately dismissed it. My bedmate's hair was a medium brown, not the faery's golden locks.

Okay, Joey. Do not panic, The sensible shrew urged.

She was right. I couldn't scream just because I'd awoken with a strange man in my bed. I needed to find out who he was. Then I could scream.

Doing my level best not to jostle the mattress, I slipped out from beneath the covers. And nearly shrieked when the cold air slapped my skin. Instead of my cozy long pajamas, I wore a skimpy black lace nighty. What was I, insane? No one wore this sort of garb in the mountains in the winter, not even as underwear.

I scanned the room for a bathrobe but didn't see one. There was a burgundy throw on the ottoman so I snatched that up and wrapped it around myself. A quick scan of the room revealed a long white antique dresser with bottles of lotion and various perfumes spread out over it. A flat-screen television was mounted in the corner and beyond that— thank you, universe—a bathroom.

I tiptoed inside and shut the door. The aches and pains were forgotten as I spun to face my reflection in the mirror.

The first thing I noticed was the mess of bandages covering my face. Only my eyes and lips were visible beneath the gauzy swaddling. Um, the hell?

My gaze drifted down and my breath caught. The blanket fell to the ground, forgotten.

I was thin!

Well, thinner. Nowhere near my sixteen-year-old gymnast self but still a far cry from the plush version of me that Alina had called fat. No wonder I was parading around in a skimpy nightgown. A body this fit needed to be showed off, like all the freaking time.

I tried to smile but it hurt and once more I glanced at the bandages covering my face. What was up with that? And as thrilled as I was to be thin, it seemed odd that I would bother with the skimpy lingerie while sporting mummy wrap over my face. I raised a shaking hand to touch my nose, then paused, studying my wrist. No surgical scars marred the smooth tan flesh.

And how was I tan in the winter anyway? Maybe I'd traveled to some Caribbean island for a few weeks. I'd always wanted to do that, a booze and cruise, maybe with Darcy.

Out in the bedroom, an alarm clock blared to life. I yelped and then stuffed a fist in my mouth to belatedly muffle the sound.

"Jo?" A man's voice called.

Should I answer him? I didn't even know who he was. Damn it, where was Robin when I needed him?

The bathroom door opened and I squeaked as the man appeared, wearing only a pair of black boxer briefs. *No.* My jaw dropped. *It can't be.*

But it was.

"There you are. You forgot to shut your alarm off." Pete

Green stretched, showing off his well-defined abs and pecs. My gaze drifted lower as I saw he had the quintessential morning boner.

My hand flew to my mouth, checking for drool. Pete Green stood there, in the bathroom, with me. And he had a freaking hard-on.

He was still looking at me, obviously waiting for an answer.

"Sorry," Through sheer force of will, I dragged my gaze back to his face. "I was just…." The words stalled out and I waved as though I could conjure the appropriate end to the sentence out of thin air.

"Is it hurting?" He moved closer as though to inspect.

I slammed my ass up against the counter, leaning as far away from him as I could. "A little." Maybe he knew what happened to me.

He shook his head. "I don't know why you do that shit to yourself."

I gasped, having never heard Pete curse before. Not that I didn't think he was fully capable of it, but it just seemed so out of character.

Wait, to myself? What did he mean?

Before I could ask, he turned his back on me, obviously heading for the toilet even as he continued, "There's nothing wrong with aging naturally."

Oh my stars, he was intending to *use* the porcelain throne in front of me. While we were having a conversation.

I pushed off the counter and bolted for the bedroom, ignoring his call of, "Where's the fire?"

"Gotta go!" I raced out of the bathroom and the bedroom still clad in blanket, bandages, and baby-doll nighty. The morning erection had almost stopped my heart. No way could I handle seeing Pete Green pee in front of me.

Who did that? I stopped, trying to come to terms with

what had just happened. George had never done that but from what Darcy said, that was standard behavior of men. Specifically, married men.

I had been so focused on my right wrist that I hadn't thought to check my left hand. I lifted it up to my face and stared. There sat a diamond and sapphire studded gold band. It had to be a wedding ring.

I was married to Pete Green! I did a little caper, right there in the hallway. Oh, happy happy day, it had worked! I, Joey Whitmore, had changed my entire destiny.

The hallway was brighter than the bedroom. I was on the second story of an open-air foyer that overlooked a massive great room below. The triangle windows were covered with heavy shades, giving no hint to what lay outside the house. Everything was white, brilliant, and clean. My own house! With my own husband that was really a man! And I was thin!

Life couldn't get any better.

A glint of sunlight reflecting off glass caught my eye and I stopped dead in front of a transparent display case. Tears welled as I looked at the sight of an Olympic gold medal.

First place in floor routine. Beside it sat a silver with a small card underneath. Second for uneven bars. Bronze for the vault. My hand covered my trembling lips. Not just one Olympic medal, *three*. I couldn't believe it. It had all been worth it. So what if I had lost my virginity to that tool Billy Tucker in a frigging barn? I was an Olympic champion.

I closed my eyes and pressed my bandaged forehead to the case. Everything I had longed for so desperately had become mine. I wanted to shout to the heavens. I knew that if I had just dodged that accident everything would work itself out.

My stomach growled. Loudly. Reluctantly, I turned away from the glorious sight of those medals and headed to the spiral stairs that led to the main floor.

The kitchen was at the back section of the house and on my way, I looked for more clues to what new forty-something Joey's life was like. Did Pete and I have any kids? That thought drew me up short. What would it be like to meet my own children for the first time? Were they young? Or maybe teenagers. Boys or girls? If I had been at the Olympics in 2000, when I was twenty, I could have adult children by now! How long had Pete and I been married? Frustration gnawed at me. I had so many questions and no one to ask.

Hopefully, any potential offspring were nothing like I had been as a headstrong teenage gymnast. Until I'd been forced to deal with myself directly, I didn't realize what a bratty pain in the butt I'd been. *Note to self: cut mom some slack.*

The side by side stainless steel refrigerator stood to the far end of the room. I moved to stand before it and then opened the doors, revealing its contents. Vegetables, vegetables and more vegetables littered every shelf. No eggs, only a cardboard container proclaiming to be egg whites. Almond milk, fat-free salad dressing. No orange juice or yummy looking leftovers to nosh.

I opened the freezer side. Regimented stacks of blue Tupperware stood in a row. A whole cellophane-wrapped salmon stared up at me with an accusing dead eye. Stifling a shudder, I shut the fridge and tried my luck with the glass-fronted cabinets.

Lots of fiber-rich whole grains and beans in identical glass containers with obvious labels. It looked like Jamie Lee Curtis's house. I remember reading an interview about her super filing system one time in a doctor's office and thinking that looked like a monkey-butt ton of work.

Everything in the cabinets would require soaking and preparation. No peanut butter or worthless white bread. Not a damn thing ready to eat or drink that had an iota of flavor. Plus all those vegetables would require immense amounts of chewing, which I doubted my sore face could handle. Was this really how I ate every single day?

I'd just settled on some tasteless whole-grain crackers and a glass of water when a vibrating sound caught my attention. A very fancy cell phone stood in a charging port, the display lighting up with an unknown number.

To answer or not to answer? That was the question. Dealing with an automated message about my car's extended warranty or worse, election spam, was not high on my to-do list. But what if I did have kids out there in the world somewhere? They might need me.

I couldn't figure out how to release the phone from its charging stand so I just held the whole thing up to my face and pressed the green icon. "Hello?"

"Is he there?" A terse female voice asked.

"Um...who are you looking for?"

An audible and clearly exasperated sigh and then, "Damn it, Joey, I don't have time for your BS. Put my brother on the phone."

I blinked. "Ursula?"

"Now," she barked.

I set the phone charger down just as the sound of shoes echoed over the kitchen tiles. Pete stood there dressed in a suit and tie, though he paused when he saw the activated phone screen. "You answered my phone?"

Uh oh. Not that he had his name bedazzled all over it or anything. "Sorry. It's Ursula and she sounds impatient."

Avoiding my gaze, he reached for the charging station and then depressed a button and sprung his tech from its prison. He held it up to his ear and then muttered, "Hang on a second."

Ursula said something snippy on the other end of the line, but I couldn't hear exactly what.

"No coffee?" Pete scowled at the empty pot on the counter.

"I couldn't find any beans." Plus the thing looked so high tech it could probably launch the space shuttle.

He stared at me as though I lost my mind. "They're in the freezer."

"Oh. I forgot." Jeez, I hope they didn't smell like fish.

"I'm late for a shareholder's meeting." Pete turned away without a word.

"Oh, okay. See you later then?" I was relieved that he was heading out. I needed some time not under scrutiny to search for answers. Like what was he a shareholder of? How long had we been married? And were there mini Joeys and Petes out there in the world?

"I have a late surgery." He said shrugging into his coat, still not looking at me. "You'll probably be asleep by the time I get back."

"Oh, okay." Maybe it was the fact that I wanted him gone, but it seemed almost as if Pete was as eager to be out of my presence as I was to be out of his.

His footsteps faded and before the front door shut I heard him say, "No, I haven't told her yet."

Was he talking about me? What was he going to tell me?

"I thought he'd never leave." A familiar male voice said from behind me.

"Robin." Relief filled me and I whirled to face him. "Where have you been? I'm groping around here like a couple of virgins in the dark."

"I was at your house. Or rather, your former abode, since that was the point where you traveled back. You however have taken up residence in your echo self's body. Is that because of the accident?" He reached toward my face, though he hesitated before making contact.

"I'm not sure." I was just about to take the bandages off

because wearing them was completely unnerving. "Will you help me?"

He nodded and made a spinning motion with his finger. After presenting him with my back I stood perfectly still and waited. Robin tugged and I felt the top layer of bandage give way. "Thank you, by the way."

He paused. "For what?"

"Getting me out of the wreck. And bringing me back here." I'd had enough of the 90s for one lifetime.

The unwinding continued. "And is it everything you wanted?"

"Other than the weird mummy wrapping on my face, yes. I won Olympic medals. Three of them!"

"Congratulations," he murmured and then added, "That should do it."

Pieces of gauze were stuck to my tender face. Slowly, I tugged them free and then turned back to face him. "Well?"

He shuddered visibly.

"What? What's wrong?" I whirled and faced the gleaming metal of the double wall ovens. My face was red and puffy, the skin looking like a cross between sunburn and anaphylaxis. Plus bruising consistent with the first car crash. I reached up to touch my face and then winced.

My nose was clearly broken, just as I thought. But what was with the redness and wrapping? "I'm a mess."

"My guess is your echo self just had a chemical peel," Robin said. "That would explain the burns. The rest is from the accident."

"Can you heal me? Like you did when I cut myself?"

In answer he held his hand up to my face. "I'll do what I can, though if you heal from the elective surgery too quickly people might notice."

"No wonder Pete wouldn't look at me." And he didn't even know about the accident.

"Ah yes, the fair-weather veterinarian. You've seen him already then?" There was a sharp note in his voice.

Slowly, the aches and pains began to ebb. I sighed in relief and held up the hand with the ring for him to inspect. "I think we're married. He was here earlier but he left."

"That's all I can do." Robin's hand fell to his side. "It seems as though you got everything you wanted."

"I can't wait to tell Darcy about all this." But first I needed to find my own cell phone and maybe put on something other than the blanket-nighty combo. No way would I go out in public looking like I'd gone three rounds with Rocky but Darcy's house would have real food full of carbs and best of all, coffee that hadn't been fraternizing with dead fish.

I headed back up to the bedroom, dropped the blanket before the walk-in closet. A small segment on the left-hand side held men's clothing. The rest….

A squeal escaped and I spun in place while taking in the rows and rows of beautiful garments. Silk blouses that matched the shade of my eyes exactly. Tailored slacks. Dry clean only little black dresses. Thousands and thousands of dollars' worth of luxurious choices.

I selected a ruby red twinset and a houndstooth skirt along with some wicked looking calf-high boots that were meant more for foreplay than cold weather. Whatever took the attention off my face. On that note, I snagged a black fedora and oversized sunglasses to hide the worst of the mess.

I snooped through the nightstand—was it snooping if it was your own stuff? —and found my phone plugged into a charging port that was built into the top drawer. It had a thumbprint lock on it. Weird, I'd never used that sort of security before. Maybe it was standard on that model. Anyway, it wasn't a problem. I pressed my thumb to it and the screen came to life.

The image there brought tears to my eyes. Twenty-year-old me, standing on the podium with Olympic gold around my neck. I got a little lost in imagining the moments. Damn, I wished echo Joey would hurry up and merge with me. I wanted the memory of that life-changing win. Plus, all the others from the last twenty odd years.

It took a bit of hunting, I really wasn't a tech person, but I finally found the contacts list. Or at least where it should have been. There were no contacts, only Pete's cell preprogrammed in. Maybe the device was new.

After running a brush through my hair—which was much shorter and well-styled compared to pre time travel Joey—I donned the garb along with a sleek black ankle-length coat, stuffed the cell in a pocket, and then headed down the stairs. Robin stood by the case holding my Olympic medals. His expression was inscrutable. He looked up at my approach.

"What do you think?" I spun in place, knowing that, chemical burns and bruises aside, I looked better than I had in years.

"Ready?" Robin held out his arm.

My hands fell to my side. "You don't like it?"

"I didn't say that."

I snapped a finger and pointed at him. "Exactly. That tells me that you don't like it. What's wrong with it? Other than the face, I mean."

"Nothing's wrong. Not exactly." He sighed. "If you want the truth, I liked you better before."

My lips parted but I couldn't think of a response. He'd liked me fat and shlumpy and living hand to mouth? Or maybe because I wasn't as needy as I had been. That must be his type. Thinking of him as the villain didn't make his rejection sting any less though. It surprised me how I'd grown used to his flirting and the little compliments. Not to mention the heated looks.

What I needed was some girl-time to ground myself in my new reality. "Take me to Darcy's."

He cocked a brow. "What's the magic word?"

I huffed out a breath. "Why are you being so difficult?"

"I'm not." He folded his arms across his chest. "But neither am I your personal taxi service. I would appreciate a modicum of courtesy."

And here I thought we'd moved beyond his need to wheedle and cajole. Did he want me to propose another bargain? Screw it, I didn't need to put up with his moods. "You know what? I bet there's a car around here somewhere. I can drive myself."

"Suit yourself." He vanished between heartbeats.

It was only after he was gone that I realized he hadn't once called me lamb.

※

There wasn't a car in the garage attached to the house. There were three. My jaw dropped as I took in the sleek silver convertible, the shiny red SUV, and the mammoth black pick-up truck. Never mind that Pete had driven off in something. Four vehicles.

Since it was still mountain winter and the truck put out the wrong vibe for my sexy boots, I selected the SUV. An illicit thrill went through me when I discovered the leather seats were heated. The thing still held that new car smell which thankfully didn't come from an air freshener tree.

A garage door opener hung from the sun visor and I depressed the button, revealing the snowy expanse of nature and majestic mountain views. I backed out of the garage carefully. The driveway was long and windy but there was a spot just outside the garage which I used to turn and face forward.

I'd never been to this precise hilltop before and took a moment to get my bearings. The house, a stone and glass edifice, sat on a cleared hilltop. I'd been so overwhelmed by the situation that I hadn't stopped to take in the setting. Large pines, birches, and oaks cocooned the steep downhill paved and freshly plowed driveway. Piles of snow were carefully pushed off the sides. No other houses were visible from the lot. In the distance, the blue ridge mountains surrounded me on all sides, royal blue jewels in a magnificent crown.

I steered the SUV downward, going slow in case of black ice. It wouldn't do to wreck my comfortably heated SUV on my first foray out. The drive stretched on for more than a mile when I spotted the lone mailbox at the end. Good thing I hardly ever got mail. Trekking down there to retrieve it in the winter sounded like a special hell.

Beyond the mailbox the trees cleared and widened into a road I didn't recognize. Where the hell was my house situated, on the moon? Good thing I'd found my phone. After opening the GPS, I punched in my father's law office address. It was in the center of town and from there, I could easily get to Darcy's or anywhere else.

Address unknown, the thing flashed back.

What? That couldn't be right. Maybe I'd fat-fingered the numbers. I tried it again.

Address unknown.

Anxiety bubbled up in me. I took a deep breath and tried Darcy's address, sighing a little in relief when the directions flashed up on the screen. Though the distance shocked me. Thirty-seven miles? That couldn't be right. It would be over an hour round trip to visit my mom or Darcy or Grammy B every day.

Again, I pictured the stunning view and all the empty rooms inside the estate. I hadn't done much exploring yet, though it was clear that if Pete and I did have kids, they were grown up and living elsewhere. No toys or gaming consoles, no messy rooms. The house was neat as a pin. I bet Darcy overnighted sometimes, like the place was a spa. Mom and Grammy probably came to stay with me some nights too, maybe with cookies or a lasagna, giving me and Pete a break from the quinoa and egg-white lifestyle.

Okay, so maybe living in the middle of freaking nowhere had its plusses.

I turned toward Darcy's, enjoying the luxury of being behind the wheel of a car that I was sure would start when I got back into it and didn't fart clouds of smoke every half a mile like Earl did.

On my way into town, I passed Firefly Lane. The urge came over me to turn the vehicle up the hill. I didn't like how Robin and I had left things. I really had begun to accept him as a friend. A sly, devious, and lecherous friend that was looking out for number one, but if I could befriend Ursula, then I could deal with Robin's antics.

My hands clenched the steering wheel tightly. Darcy would help me figure out what to say to smooth it over. And then I would stop by and see Grammy and my mother, maybe have them up for dinner.

Darcy was just coming down the steps to her house when I pulled up to the curb. Not wanting to leave the warmth of the SUV, I rolled down the window and called out. "Need a ride, little girl?"

Her head snapped up from where she'd been rooting through her purse. "Joey?"

"In the flesh." I grinned.

She stared at me sans reciprocating smile. "What are you doing here?"

"I wanted to see you." Why was she being so standoffish? That wasn't Darcy's style at all.

"I have somewhere to be." She turned her back and headed towards her Subaru.

My jaw dropped. What was going on? An emergency maybe. I rolled up the window and then slid out of the SUV. "Is it the kids? I'll come with you."

She sighed. "If you must know, I have a job interview."

"Job interview? What about your doggy costume business?"

She shook her head. "I don't know what you're talking about. Look, I don't want to be late. Mike and I need this. I'm sure you've heard that he lost his job. Or maybe you didn't. When was the last time you left your fortress on the hill?"

What was with all the animosity? First Robin and now Darcy? "Look, if you need money I can—"

"Do *not* finish that sentence." Her eyes flashed with a warning.

I held out my hands helplessly. "Darcy, we're best friends. If I can help you out of a jam, I want to."

"Best friends?" She laughed but it held no humor. "Since when? We haven't spoken in years."

"Years?" Horror filled me at the thought.

"Twenty four years to be exact. Right around the time, you decided that screwing Billy Tate was more important to you than I was."

"No." That couldn't be. I needed Darcy.

"You know I tried. After the accident that ended Billy's football career and he moved away, I tried to talk to you. But then you were too busy being an elite gymnast. You didn't have time for me or anyone."

"That's not true." She was my rock, the person who made me laugh and see the bright side even when I didn't believe there was one. I always made time for Darcy.

"Believe what you want." She yanked open her car door and inserted the key, giving the engine time to warm up. I rushed around the front of the car and to the driver's side before she could drive away. The wind tugged stray blonde hairs out of her untidy bun.

I curled my fingers over the top of the car door so she couldn't shut it. "Please wait. I just want to talk. There are things you don't know about and I really need someone to talk to."

"That's it? One day you just drive up and park in front of my house and I'm supposed to drop everything and be your sounding board?" She shook her head in obvious disgust. "Grow up, Joey. We aren't kids anymore."

She yanked the door out of my grip and slammed it in my face.

I watched helplessly as she drove off without a backward glance.

CHAPTER SIXTEEN

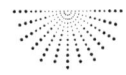

On wooden legs, I returned to the SUV and then sat there, stunned. Damn it. I knew that fight young Joey had had with Darcy was new to this timeline but I didn't think it would have caused such a rift between us.

My head reeled from all the information she'd dumped on me. I didn't have time for her because of the Olympics. That sounded bitter as hell. Like she was jealous of my success.

The more I thought about it, the more sense it made. Sure, I'd made a mistake with Bill Tucker and I had been a bitch to her about it. I'd heard the conversation firsthand. But to blame my elite training for the downfall of our friendship? My career had lasted maybe four years after high school at the very most. She could have tried harder in the intervening years.

I was so busy rationalizing what had just occurred that I didn't realize the buzzing sound wasn't part of my chaotic thoughts but instead, the vibrations from my cell.

I fumbled with the thing until the screen faced me. It was a local number, but not one I recognized. "Hello?"

"Hey hot stuff, you need to get down here. Pronto," an unfamiliar male voice said. "I know you're taking some much deserved me time but—"

"Who is this?" I asked.

"Trevor." There was a pause and when I didn't answer he added, "Your fabulous assistant."

I had an assistant? How cool was that? The question was, what was it he assisted me in doing?

"Okay, Trevor. Slow down and tell me where you are."

Another moment of silence. "Um hello? At your new gym of course."

My new gym? Implication, that I had at least one other older gym? Holy shitake, Batman! Of course, it made sense that I devoted my professional life to gymnastics. "Oh, right. And…what seems to be the problem?"

His voice dropped to a whisper, "There's an uber bitchy woman demanding to see you. She's been quite forceful about it."

In the background, I heard the drunk slurring in a heavy Romanian accent, "It was me. I was teaching her everything she is knowing."

My jaw dropped. "Does that woman have short-cropped blond hair, strongly built, and a glare that makes you want to wet your pants?"

Trevor lowered his voice. "I wouldn't call her strongly built but the hair/glare combo is spot on. Should I call the police?"

I blew out a breath and tried to envision it. Alina on what sounded suspiciously like a bender. So much for her body being a temple. I needed to talk with her in person. "This is going to sound strange but what's the address for the gym?"

Another pregnant pause. "Are you sure you are okay to drive? You must be on some pretty heavy medication."

"Yes. I'm just...programming my new phone's GPS and it's taking all my concentration." Good thing I didn't have Robin's lying impediment.

"2803B Skyhawk Court," Trevor rattled it off, still sounding unsure.

"I'll be there as soon as I can." I hung up and then tapped the address into the GPS. The location was remote, about halfway between the town limit and my house on the hill. And it took me right down the main street and past my father's office. But since I was so close, I decided to drive up the hill to the Victorian and see if mom was home. A friendly face was a must after the knock-down-drag-out with Darcy.

I pulled to a stop in front of the house, relieved to see that it looked just as it should have. A great swell of longing filled my chest as I saw the walkway between the front gate and the porch hadn't been shoveled. No lights were on and my mother's car was gone. If Robin had brought us back the same day as the one I'd traveled back from, Dragon would presumably be at school already. Shoot, and I had promised to drive her.

Well, in the other timeline.

I was starting to see why Robin had cautioned me about jumping forward again. The gaps in my knowledge were more like bottomless moon craters. I pulled the car to a stop and then tromped across the unshoveled walkway and carefully up the sagging porch steps. I raised my hand to the doorknob and then paused.

Trevor had sounded like a nice guy. It wasn't fair for me to leave him to deal with Alina all on her own. Pivoting on my heel, I traipsed back to the SUV. I'd try my family again later.

I took the turn and headed into town, my anxiety growing

with every mile. I didn't like the fallout with Darcy. And Pete hadn't even given me a goodbye kiss, though he'd been ready to pee in front of me. So, life wasn't perfect. Judging by the pain on my face this version of me had obviously made a few mistakes. But I was sure I could fix it, given time.

My lips parted. Time. I had one trip left. Maybe I could go back to an earlier version of myself and make peace with Darcy.

But then I would be back in my plus-sized body with no way forward again. No, Darcy was an anomaly. The rest of my life was everything I had ever dreamed of having. The beautiful house, the cars, running my own business. Being married to Pete Green. An Olympic gold medal.

The smile died on my face as I turned onto Main. Where my father's tidy little two-story brick office building/apartment complex had once stood was now a three-level parking structure across the street from a ski shop. Both of my feet hit the brakes and the SUV fishtailed before coming to a stop. The pick-up behind me zoomed around my still vehicle, honking his displeasure.

The garage attendant, a young man with shaggy dark hair came running up to the car. I depressed the button to roll down the window. He blanched when he saw my face but then forced a professional smile. "Can I help you with something, ma'am?"

A shaking finger indicated the lot as I breathed, "How long has this been here?"

He followed my finger with his gaze. "The parking deck? Oh, about three years."

"What happened to the building that was here before? The lawyer's office?" I braced myself for the answer.

He frowned at me. "Dunno. It was an empty lot for most of my life."

He looked about twenty.

"Are you sure you're okay, lady? Need me to call someone?"

"No. Thanks." I rolled the window back up before he could say anything else.

I carefully blanked my mind and continued on my way out of town. Okay, so that had been a shock. But it could be a good thing. Maybe my parents had gotten married and my father had moved his law office to another building. I was sorry I hadn't gone into the Victorian and gotten the answers.

Needing reassurance, I pulled over into the Presbyterian church parking lot and dialed my mother's number from memory. She picked up on the third ring. "Joey, I really can't talk right now."

"Are you married?" I blurted.

I could practically hear my mother scowling. "Of course I'm married. What sort of question is that?"

Relief filled me to the brim. Yes, I had gotten that part right. Mom and dad were happily married. I was about to ask her if I could speak to dad when she said, "Now I've got to go. I'll call you back later."

Click.

Robin had been right about one thing. The changes without the memories to explain them were jarring. I'd better get used to the changes though. Another twenty odd years of random shocks were in my future.

One came not even five minutes later. My new gym was a sight to behold. An elegant new structure with cathedral ceilings and two-story tinted windows that would allow the inhabitants to see out but no one driving by to peer inside. The sign in the lot was all black and white elegance with the name Joey's Gymnastics and Fitness Center. A silhouetted female figure doing a handstand and split on a balance beam drove the point home.

The lot held two other vehicles. A blue battered Toyota and a silver Lexus. The sun was out, the temperature swinging above the freezing point and melting the snow on the blacktop. I parked to the rear of the lot, not wanting to take space away from any patrons who might show up, and then picked my way carefully over the patches of slush between me and the front door. Finally, my hand wrapped around the cool metal and I yanked it open.

Warmth and light filled the space. My lips parted as I took it all in. A tall unmanned receptionist's desk sat to the immediate right of the doors. Beyond it was a gorgeous work-out space. Mats in primary colors, foam block pits, beams of different heights. Mirrors on the back wall reflected both the outside light from the glass windows and the dimmable recessed lighting above. It was utterly incredible, taking the best of every gym I'd ever seen and melding them into the perfect space for gymnastics.

And this was just one of my gyms!

"Oh, I am so glad you're here," a male voice called from up above. Craning my neck, I looked up to the catwalk over the uneven bars to see a man with skin the color of fresh coffee and the darkest hair and eyes I'd ever seen. He was short but well-muscled, as evident by his skin-tight blue and black tiger-striped leotard that left absolutely nothing to the imagination.

"Trevor?" I cleared my throat to disguise the fact that it had come out as a question.

"Ssshh, I think she may have passed out." He did a quick up and down motion with both hands and then checked over his shoulder before heading for the stairs. "Not surprising. I think she drank enough vodka to sink a Broadway matinee. Are you sure you don't want me to call the cops?"

I shook my head. The last thing I needed was nosy investigators eyeballing my face and asking me questions I had no clue how to answer. Instead, I asked Trevor, "When did she show up?"

"She was here when I arrived. It looked as though she camped out in the doorway with a bottle in a bag. I tried to sneak past her but she sort of barreled through the door and demanded to speak with you. She got belligerent when I said you wouldn't be in today. That's when I called you."

That didn't sound promising. "Where is she now?"

He gestured back the way he'd come. "Passed out on the couch in the consulting room."

My face hurt too much to offer him a reassuring smile so I said, "Okay, I'll take it from here. You just do…your thing."

I headed for the stairs, trying to look as self-confident as I ought to be in my place of business. I wasn't. Alina scared the crap out of me when she was sober. No way did I want to deal with her drunk and disorderly. But what other choice did I have?

The consulting room looked like a cross between a therapist's office and a conference room. Dove gray walls, a white tile floor, big leafy green plants. Framed black and white photos of gymnasts were compiled along the back wall. A glass-topped desk that held no books papers or even a computer. There were two rolling chairs on either side. Two couches that looked too new to be truly comfortable.

Passed out on one was a woman I didn't recognize.

My mouth fell open. No way. There was no way in hell that this doughy figure with the beet-red face and dirty sweatpants could be Alina. Sure, the hair was the same shade of blond with the rough cut that had been twenty years out of date when she'd coached me, but there could be plenty of people with that retro style. Or women who let their toddlers do their hair with safety scissors. There were broken capillaries all over her nose and her skin looked windburned.

But I'd heard her voice on the phone. Yes, she'd been drunk and slurring, but it had been her sharp tones, her clipped accent. I stared at the snoring figure for a full minute trying to reconcile the woman who had inspired terror and awe with this not-so-hot mess.

My gaze slid to the door. Maybe I ought to just leave before she woke up. But that wouldn't be fair to poor Trevor. Besides, I owed it to Alina to hear her out.

So I sat down at the conference table to wait.

❋

The beeping startled me awake. I blinked my eyes open and took stock of my surroundings. My face was pressed against a cool hard surface and I'd been drooling in my sleep. Snazzy.

I sat up, wincing at the crick in my neck, and reached a hand back to rub the aching muscle. Another beep and I realized the sound came from my jacket pocket. Probably an alert on my cell phone.

I fumbled for the device just as a loud groan came from the couch. Alina's lids snapped open and she stared at me through bloodshot blue eyes.

My mouth went dry and every muscle in my body seemed to seize up. There was something in her gaze that I'd never seen before. A level of hatred that radiated out from the core of her being.

"You." Her dismount from the couch was far from graceful. She basically rolled off of it and then staggered to her feet. It was hard to tell if she was still drunk or hungover but either way, the energy coming off of her was pure menace.

"Hi, Alina. How are you? You look…good." I shoved the

chair back from the glass and iron table. Instinct told me to keep the piece of furniture between the two of us.

She spat on the floor. Then her lips curled up in a grimace as she raged, "It's all your fault!"

I shook my head from side to side, denying whatever it was she was trying to blame me for. "I don't know what you are talking about."

"The drugs," she spat.

That stopped me short. "Drugs? What drugs?"

"Ephedrine. The compound you took to secure your place on the Olympic team."

She might as well have struck me. "I never—"

"You told the media that I gave it to you unknowingly when we are both knowing the truth." She made a grab for me.

I spun away and my back slammed against the wall. "What? No. I would never have taken something illegal."

"You *begged* me to get you concentrated doses. I told you no, told you over and over. But you got them somewhere and used them. And dragged my name through the mud to save your own sorry reputation." She lunged again and again I dodged.

"This has to be some sort of mistake." The words spilled out more for me to reassure myself that the crazy drunk lady was full of it than to diffuse Alina's wrath.

"No mistake. Your television interview was clear enough," she spat. "Keeping those medals mattered more to you than anyone or anything. Even the people who helped you obtain them." She advanced, still wobbly but the determination that was such an innate part of her makeup shone.

My heart pounded as though I had been dosed with something. Just like she accused me. She lurched like Frankenstein's monster and I went down to my hands and knees and then crawled beneath the glass top desk and made a b-line for the door.

Downstairs Trevor was taking a preschool group through some stretching exercises. He blinked when he saw me stumble down the stairs. "What's wrong?"

From the upstairs, I heard a crash. Apparently, Alina was hulk smashing the hell out of the consulting room. There was little doubt in my mind that she would be hot on my heels in a minute.

"Call the police," I shouted and rushed past him out to the safety of my car, groping for my keys. My impractical boots skidded on a patch of ice and my feet went out from under me. The keys skidded across the slippery concrete walkway and ended up under a minivan. I dropped to my hands and knees even as the door behind me burst open.

"Come back here, Joey Whitmore!" Alina shrieked. "Come back here and face me!"

I gave up on the keys and slithered beneath the minivan just as she made a grab for my hair. I ducked and rolled, ruining my expensive outfit in the process.

She grabbed but there was no way she would fit beneath the car. That didn't stop her from reaching underneath and trying to drag me out by my ankles.

"Let's talk about this," I shouted.

"The time for talk is gone," she snarled. "You've ruined my life!"

The next several minutes consisted of her flailing around all sides of the car endeavoring to snag me and me curling up like a shrimp, only to have her claw after me again and again. I ducked and rolled, and shrieked as she snagged my hair. She yanked a fistful free. My head throbbed painfully. My clothing was sopping wet from rolling in the slush and I shivered as great gusts of wind seemed to delight in trying to turn me into a human popsicle.

After what felt like an eternity, a siren pierced the air, and the sight of blue flashing lights crested up the hill to the gym. Alina shrieked like a fury as the police brought her down to the ground, her eyes promising retribution. Then she was hauled away.

A man's face appeared—his brilliant blue eyes mirthful. "You all right, ma'am?"

Robin, dressed as a patrolman, was enjoying the situation way too much. He reached a hand under and I grasped it, letting him haul me back onto my feet.

"What are you doing?" I asked as he took out a notebook and pencil.

"Questioning the witness."

"You're not a cop," I hissed between chattering teeth.

"Well you know that and I know that but no one else here knows that. They all think I'm a transfer from Charlotte."

He walked me over to a police cruiser and popped the trunk. After extracting a blanket, he wrapped it around my shoulders and rubbed with vigor. Then he moved back to the minivan, knelt down, and emerged holding my keys.

Gratitude filled me at the sight. If I'd had to bend back down, I probably wouldn't have made it up again. "I thought you were angry with me."

"You're the one who sent me away," he pointed out. "I simply requested that you ask for favors nicely."

"You're right." I ducked my head, unable to meet his gaze. "It was lousy of me to assume you would just drop everything to magically chauffeur me around town."

He curled a finger beneath my chin. "It's downright decent of you to admit that, lamb. How are you liking your new life?"

I just shook my head, unable to talk about what Alina had accused me of. No children, no Darcy, and my gold medal might not even belong to me. Plus my body was a mass of bruises, I was sopping wet and half-frozen.

"Want me to take you somewhere?" Robin asked.

I studied him from under my lashes. "What's the price?"

"No price for a friend." He smiled softly. "How about your mother's house?"

I thought of her always full coffee pot and big chenille blankets. "That sounds perfect."

Robin opened the passenger's side door to my SUV and I scrambled up.

"Aren't you going to tell anyone where you're going?" I asked.

"They won't notice." Robin turned the engine over, slung his arm over the back seat, and reversed the vehicle.

I didn't say anything until we passed by the parking garage that had once been my father's office. "Everything is so different. I can't believe how much."

Robin cast me a sideways glance. "You sound surprised. Don't you know how integral your life is to those around you?"

"Yes, but this is just more than I expected." A hell of a lot more. I was starting to discover something about Olympic Gold Joey. I didn't like her very much. What sort of person tosses away her best friend over a loser guy and blames her former coach for her drug use?

A shitty person.

Robin made a sound that could have been either agreement or indigestion. He pulled to a stop in front of the Victorian.

I reached for the door handle but paused when I realized he wasn't doing the same. "Aren't you coming in?"

He shook his head. "Clara is probably in there. The last thing you need right now is the two of us getting into it." He pressed something into my hand. The hourglass. Purple grains of sand sparkled in the bright winter sunshine.

"You're a good friend," I said to him. "Apparently, my only friend."

His lips twitched just a little. "No one else has ever called me a friend and meant it."

I shrugged and pocketed the hourglass. Then, not knowing how else to escape the awkward moment, slid out of the car and slogged up the walkway to the front porch.

I turned the handle and frowned when I discovered it was locked. Weird. We never locked the house midday. Maybe Dragon had locked up on her way to school?

There was a fake rock that had a hide-a-key spot beneath the swing. I bent down to retrieve it and used it to unlock the door.

The door swung inward with an ominous groan that sounded like a horror movie special effect. "Mom?" I called out.

"Joey?" I heard her call from the conservatory. "What are you doing here?"

I toed off my wet boots and then padded on stocking feet toward the door. "You hung up on me earlier. And I've had a hell of a day and I just needed to come home for a bit."

My mother pushed through the swinging door that separated the kitchen from her office. She was busy fumbling with the belt tie on her bathrobe. It brought me a modicum of relief to see the shiny gold band on the fourth finger of her left hand. At least one thing was going right in the rewritten timeline.

"Oh Joey, your face," she breathed.

"It looks worse than it is." I waved it off.

"This really isn't a good time for a visit." Mom grabbed me by the arm and began towing me toward the front door.

"What?" She was evicting me?

She made an exasperated noise and tugged more forcefully. "How about if we do lunch at the café later in the week. On me."

"Mom? What's going on?" Then I really looked at her. Middle of the day, bed head and wearing a robe. "Oh my god, you were having sex, weren't you!"

"It's not a crime," she huffed.

I blushed a little. The thought of my parents having sex was still uncomfortable, no matter that I was supposed to be mature. "Of course it isn't. How about I go upstairs and wait for you to finish?"

"Prudence?" A male voice called out.

I froze. That was not my father's voice.

"Are you coming back?" The swinging door opened again and there stood Randy. The head mechanic. In his boxer shorts.

Horror filled me as I spun to face my mother. My voice shook as I asked, "How could you do this? You're a married woman!"

She blinked. "What are you talking about?"

My whole body shook, not with cold, but with absolute fury. "What about Dad? Did you even think of him?"

My mother's baffled expression morphed into one of concern. "Joey, are you feeling all right?"

"How could you cheat on dad?" I raged.

"Cheat on Paul?" My mother shook her head, her silver and brown bob swinging. "Joey, he's the one who left me."

CHAPTER SEVENTEEN

My body had gone numb. Distantly, I heard Randy tell my mother he had to get back to the garage. I sat at the kitchen table and stared into the untouched mug of coffee before me.

My father was gone. He'd skipped town. Never in a million timelines would I have believed that he would do such a thing. He'd been chasing my mother for his entire adult life. What would make him give up?

"Meow," I looked down to see Puck rubbing up along my ankle.

"You were right." I had no idea if she knew anything about the other timeline. I picked her up and held her in my lap. She didn't speak. I wasn't sure if that was because she couldn't speak or because she didn't feel the need to rub it in.

"Is this what happened to you?" I asked. "You wanted something so badly that you turned your entire world upside down only to find out that you didn't fit into your life anymore?"

She stared at me with big unblinking eyes, then head-butted my hand so I would scratch her.

My mother pushed through the swinging door, now fully dressed and looking miffed. "Honestly Joey, I don't know what to do with you. Most of the time you can't be bothered to respond to a simple text message. And then you come barging in here acting like it's some sort of crime for a woman to sleep with her own husband."

I looked up at her. "I don't understand why you would marry Randy. You, who is so anti-marriage."

She shook her head. "I've never been anti-marriage. I just didn't want to marry Paul."

"Why not?" I asked. "You raised a child together for crying out loud. What is so wrong with being married to my dad?"

"Do you really need to ask me that?"

"Yes!" My tone had passed hysterical and was zooming into a range only dogs could hear. "I don't get it. You loved him and he thought you hung the moon. Tell me why that isn't enough?"

"Because! I lost myself with Paul. I became Mrs. Blackthorn, not Prudence Whitmore. We were a couple, we had to do everything together. I never wanted my identity to hinge on a man. I always knew it would be that way, but he just kept pushing until I knew he would leave unless I gave in." She turned away to stare out the window. "But then he left anyway."

My mouth was open. "And you just let him go?"

She made a face. "What should I have done, hogtie him to the boiler?" She smiled though it was a little sad. "That's what my mother would have done."

Something about the way she said that made my skin prickle. "What do you mean, would have?"

But mom wasn't paying attention. "I think I agreed to marry Paul because I was lonely after Grammy B's passing.

You were always busy and I just…I wasn't used to being alone."

No. Not Grammy. She couldn't be gone. I reached across the table and clamped my hand down on my mother's. "What happened to Grammy?"

She tried to tug her arm free but I wouldn't let go.

"Mom, tell me. What happened?"

She stared at me, her blue eyes lined with silver. "After your grandfather died, she decided to sell the house. It was too much for her to deal with. I offered to move her in here, but she didn't want to be a burden. So she went into that retirement home. That was six months before the electrical fire. It was right down the hall from her room. The smoke inhalation killed her before the fire department could respond."

A single tear rolled down my cheek. No no *no*. This was all wrong. Grammy was supposed to be sitting in her chair, finagling cookies out of me.

My lips parted as dawning realization gave way to horror. But I hadn't been around to help take care of her. To make meals and make sure she ate, to visit, and ask for her advice or play cards or look at pictures. She'd been left alone with her memories of a better life. There was only so much my mother could have done. Hadn't grandpappy summed it up perfectly? Someone needed to run interference between Grammy B and mom. And I hadn't been there to do it.

Mom took my cold coffee over to the sink and dumped it out. Then she braced her hands on either side of the basin. "Look, Joey. I know it's hard for you to see me with Randy, but he's my husband now. He's good to me. I am asking you to respect that."

"Do you love him more than dad?" I don't know what possessed me to ask that question. It was foolish and I really didn't want to hear her say yes because that would break my heart.

Mom turned and I saw a fresh line of moisture running down her cheek. "I'll never love anyone the way I loved your father. But he chose to leave so I'm doing the best that I can."

"But—"

"No," she stabbed a finger in my face. "No more. You always took your father's side in everything. He's been gone for years and still, you take his side. He isn't this great infallible being, he is just a man. So for once, please, see him as the flawed human being he is instead of blaming everything on me!"

With that, she stormed out of the kitchen without a backward glance.

I set Puck on the floor and then just sat there. Stunned and filled with total disbelief. Grammy dead. Dad was gone. Me a druggie and a crappy friend and daughter and granddaughter because I'd let all this happen.

My phone rang and I closed my eyes, unable to deal with any more. Let voicemail eat that one.

Instead, I headed outside. I'd borrowed a pair of leggings and dry socks from my mother along with a heavy sweater. The beautiful clothes I'd donned that morning were unsalvageable. Stupid Alina. I wasn't sure if I was more upset with her or myself.

Probably myself.

Puck followed me as I walked the short distance to Grammy's house. There was a for sale sign in front of it. A lump formed in my throat as I recalled seeing Grandpappy sitting in the chair, feet up, and taking his leisure as he waited for Grammy B to come home. I recalled the disturbed look on his face as he watched my gymnastics video, how he said I was changing.

But no Grandpappy or Grammy B waited inside the

house. In fact, it looked empty of all the furniture and mementos of two lives well lived. Someone else would move in eventually and make it theirs. All because I hadn't been available for her.

I'd spared myself the accident. And it had turned me into someone I didn't like and wasn't proud to be. So what if I had a gold medal if I didn't truly deserve it ?All the things that it had stood for in my mind, hard work and integrity, weren't a part of my life.

"Excuse me?" A male voice called out from behind me.

I turned around and my mouth dropped open in shock as I saw the one man I never thought to see again. "George?"

It was him all right. The shaggy dark brown hair and kind brown eyes. No sign of Georgia's elegant coiffure or long nails. Just an average man in coveralls.

He flinched when he saw my face but asked, "Have we met?"

I shook my head and then added lamely, "It's on your nametag."

His head bobbed up and down as though that made sense. "Right. Do you know where Tyson Ridge Road is?"

I moved closer to the tow truck, still staring in amazement. "George, not Georgia?"

He frowned at me. "What?"

"You. You're really Georgia." At some point, I'd moved past the worry that other people would realize I didn't fit in with this timeline. I didn't want my echo self to catch up. I didn't want the memories of me being a complete tool.

"How—?" George was staring at me, mouth open.

"That's who you are," I confirmed. An alternate timeline or not, some things were universal. It made me incredibly sad to see that Georgia hadn't emerged from her George shaped chrysalis. Why not?

Because he wasn't married to you. The sensible shrew whispered.

Could she be correct? All this time I'd believed my marriage to George had been a farce. I'd been so worried about how everyone else in town saw me, their judgment over what happened between us that I hadn't seen the good it had done in George's life.

The support he'd needed and the courage it had given him to take the final step.

"You are Georgia," I said, holding his gaze. "You can drive a tow truck and look fricking fabulous and date big hairy truckers like nobody's business."

"Who are you?" George asked.

I blew out a sigh. "Your faery Godmother."

With that, I turned around and headed back to the Victorian.

※

I didn't call out to my mother, just headed up the stairs to my bedroom and sat on the window seat. Same view, different world. After a moment, Puck entered. My stomach growled. I'd been hungry since I woke up in bed beside Pete. No wonder I was such a bitch. I went through life hangry.

My phone buzzed again. I cursed and then fumbled with the thing.

There was a string of unanswered text messages from Pete. The first one read *Joey, we need to talk. Call me.* The next, *I am leaving you. Joey, the creditors are calling, you are way overdue on the mortgage payments. Every CC is maxed out. Where is all the $?!?* A quick follow up. *You need to vacate the house. We need to liquidate.* Followed by, *I met someone else.* The most recent, *Don't pretend you didn't see this coming. We don't want the same things anymore.*

I laughed and it was a distinctly unhinged sound. What sort of chickenshit ended his marriage via text? Robin had called it. Pete Green wanted whatever he didn't have waiting at home. I'd take on the blame for losing Darcy, for Grammy B and my parents. But to hell with Pete.

Sometimes an ass was just an ass.

"It sucks, doesn't it," Puck said. "The realization that you had it better before the bargain?"

"Clara?" I asked.

She prowled across the floor and then lept onto a spot by my feet. "Yep. And I have to say, I agree with the dickhead. I liked you better before."

"You remember before?"

"I journey with him, keeping him anchored between timelines."

"Dragon?" I was almost afraid to ask.

"I heard your mother on the phone with someone named Hannah earlier. She said she was sending Diedre to a boarding school overseas."

I closed my eyes. "Of course she is." So Dragon was being sent off again because her mother didn't want to deal with her. Maybe that would be better for her in the long run.

"Prudence was also extremely worked up about some loan for a place on Skyhawk Court if that means anything to you. Apparently, the bank is going to foreclose on it."

"And the hits just keep on coming." My eyes burned with a dry grittiness. I had no tears left to shed. Not for self-pity, or even for my family that was in fact a hot mess.

"Are you going to attack me again?" I asked the cat, half hoping she would.

She scratched at her bent ear with a hind paw. "I think you've been punished enough, at least judging by your face."

I stared at her. "You're so calm. You were going to scratch my eyes out before."

"That's when I thought we stood a chance of defeating him." She began to bathe her tail. "But you're in it hip deep and sinking fast. He's got you exactly where he wants you. One more trip and you're all his."

My hand drifted to the pocket where I'd stashed the hourglass. "So, all I need to do is go back and stop myself from interfering with the timeline in the first place and it will set everything to rights?"

The cat swiveled her neck to stare out the window. "Everything except you will still owe him. No matter when you travel to, past or future, it is your final trip and then Robin Goodfellow is free to collect his debt."

So I could go back, stop me from interfering with Joey. Maybe knock my adult echo self unconscious before she interfered. Or kidnap her. All so that my journey would end and Robin would move on to bargaining with Ursula while cashing in my end of the bargain.

"This sucks." I set the hourglass down on the bench seat and stared at it.

"Tell me about it," Clara murmured and settled down between my legs, tail twitching. "Family curse."

"What do you mean?"

Clara sighed. "It's not important."

"Somehow I doubt that."

Her big cat eyes stared up at me. "You know that child I told you Robin saved? His last name was Whitmore."

My lips parted. "Are you saying…?"

She bobbed her head. "We are related. I think that's why he targeted you. There's something in our genetic lineage that he is after. I don't know what or why. I don't even know if he knows. But this was bound to happen. I'm just sorry it's happening to you, too."

I turned and stared out the window as the late afternoon

sun faded to a purple twilight. I barely even flinched when the repo truck came for my SUV.

"I have to stop the bargain," I muttered to Clara. "One last trip and then I'm stuck wherever I go. So this is my last chance to right the big wrong that's been done."

The cat's tail twitched but she said nothing as I reached for the hourglass. Unscrewed the top and plucked out a single grain of sand. I didn't know what to picture, so I pictured the words even as I spoke aloud.

"Take me back to the day before Clara made her bargain."

The cat's eyes rounded and an instant later, Robin appeared, "Joey, you can't!"

But it was too late. My lids lowered and swirls of sucking color appeared. The grain of sand in my hand disappeared and I was lost to the current of time.

CHAPTER EIGHTEEN

NORTH CAROLINA COLONY, WINTER 1769

Either I was getting used to traveling through time or there was something about journeying outside of my own timeline that helped keep me conscious. One second, I was sitting in my window seat and the next I was bumping along in the back of a horse-drawn cart. The first sense that registered was the smell. It was truly foul, a combination of a port-a-john and fresh manure with a healthy dose of the hay I was lying in. I sat up as the conveyance pulled to a stop in front of a dingy-looking building with even dingier people milling about in front of it.

"What in tarnation you doing back there?"

I turned to see a rumpled old creature all knobby knees and elbows with a long unkempt beard staring at me through squinted eyes. He did a slow up and down perusal of my body, his bushy eyebrows disappeared beneath the brim of his battered hat.

I glanced down and made a face at my wardrobe gaff. I was still wearing the leggings and sweater of my mother's only now I'd reverted back to my pre-time travel weight.

Where before the sweater fit almost like a dress, it hugged my hips and breasts in a way decent for the twenty-first century but decidedly less so for the eighteenth.

Plus, it was cold as hell and I wasn't wearing a coat.

"I'm looking for Clara," I said.

"Clara who?"

I made a face. Why hadn't I bothered to get her last name before I'd embarked on this journey? Or a description of where she'd lived or what she looked like? I knew she was an ancestor, but which side, Grammy's or Grandpappy's? Panic filled me as I realized I might have wasted my final trip through time. I hadn't left myself a ton of excess to accomplish my task and I was totally not prepared.

A hand gripped my shoulder. "I've got her, Joseph. Probably just another prostitute from down the mountain looking for work."

I sputtered and then gawked up into brilliant sapphire eyes. The bastard caught me already. Unlike me, Robin wore period-appropriate clothing of a lace-up shirt tucked into buckskin pants with a heavy woolen coat over the top.

"If you say so, Sherriff." The man with the cart gave me a quick up and down and a gleam of interest sparked in his eye. "Let me know if she starts working over at the tavern. I'll throw a few pennies her way."

"A few pennies?" I spluttered but Robin steered me out of the snow and mud-filled street and toward a sagging wooden building.

"Come with me, you foolish little lamb," he growls.

"Where are you taking me?" I tried to tug my arm free but his grip was like that of a vice.

"Away from the slaughter." He pushed through a door then slammed it shut behind him, blocking the chill winter air. Not that the air inside was much warmer. The light was dim and I scanned the dank space. We were inside an actual jailhouse. The two barred cells in the back of the one-room building were a dead giveaway.

"What were you thinking, coming back here?" Robin removed his coat and draped it over the chair next to a battered desk.

I moved to the pot-bellied stove which radiated a decent amount of heat, at least enough to warm my frozen backside. It was a challenge to glare at a man while rubbing feeling into one's posterior but somehow, I managed. "It's my trip, I can do what I want with it."

"So you come back to pre-revolution North Carolina? Do you have any idea how dangerous this place is?"

"Probably more so with you telling everyone that I'm a prostitute." I snapped.

He removed the hat and then ran a hand through his hair as though he was agitated. "You don't get it. You'll be lucky if they don't burn you as a witch."

"A witch?" That caused me to draw up short.

"You bet your sweet ass. At least a prostitute has some level of protection as far as society goes. But a lone middle-aged woman that no one knows?" He shook his head as if unable to contemplate it.

I lifted my chin to glare at him. "You're just mad because I'm here to stop Clara from becoming your eternal anchor."

"Is that really what you believe?" He laughed. "Oh, of course, it is. You think me to be nothing more than a selfish bastard, like all the other men in your life."

"What do you mean?"

He held up a hand. "The boy at school who took your virginity as some sort of souvenir. Your father who left, your grandfather died, your first husband is a woman and your second ran off with another woman. Hell, even the manager at the diner let you down. Haven't they all aggrieved you in some way?"

I shook my head. "I'm not some kind of untrusting shrew. I am just—"

"Cursed with bad luck?" Robin raised an eyebrow. "That's what you were going to say isn't it?"

It was. I had to press my lips together to keep the words from tumbling out. But could I really continue to blame luck? I'd made choices in both timelines. Smart choices, terrible choices. Some had turned out well, others, not so much. But they'd been mine. So could I really keep blaming bad luck for everything that went wrong?

Robin took a step closer. "And now you're here, in 1769 to right a wrong on your family."

My chin went up. "That's right I am."

Robin sighed and scrubbed a hand over his face. "You can't undo it, lamb. Clara must make that bargain with me. If she doesn't her son will die, as will your whole family line."

I shook my head, unable to believe what he was saying. "There has to be some way."

"I wish there was." His expression was pure regret as he added, "I truly do. But this is one of the knots you cannot untie. Not without unweaving the fabric of the universe."

My arms came around my body. It was all for nothing? One last trip, me blowing my wad for no good reason? "No, there must be a way. You told me that this couldn't happen."

"Not if you were journeying within your own lifetime. I had no idea you would go and do something like this." He shook his head. "But that's just you all over. Unpredictable, rash, driven. Stubborn. It's not enough for you to fix your old life, you needed to rescue the puck who bargained herself into her role."

"You're using her wrongly." I step forward and poke him

in the chest. "She wanted to help me as well as free herself. But what she really wanted was to live out her life where she belongs. I messed up my life and it had nothing to do with that car accident. At least one of us can have a normal life."

"So you came here? What, did you have a hankering for diphtheria?"

I raised my chin. "Finding out she's part of my family only makes me more determined to help her."

"Clara's son marries a girl and they have five children. The first Whitmore generation born in the independent United States. No bargain and those children aren't born. No Grandpappy. No Prudence Whitmore." His eyes are more solemn than I'd ever seen as he adds, "No you. You will erase yourself from existence."

I clung to the thread of possibility. He didn't know everything. "Well, what if I didn't? Maybe her son will live. You don't know that."

"Even if he does, your interference will create a paradox too big for the space-time continuum to right. No Clara the puck means you will never come back here to stop her from entering the bargain with me. And if you don't come back here, Clara will become my anchor. It is inevitable."

I blew out a sigh and paced the dusty floorboards of the small room. There had to be some way out. Some way I could save Clara two and a half centuries of servitude without putting my family tree through the wood chipper.

The shadow of an idea crept into my mind. Maybe…just maybe…

I stopped and turned to face Robin. "I want to meet her."

He scrutinized my face. "Why?"

"Why? Because I have never even seen what she looks like as a person. You say she's a distant relative. So I want to see her face to face."

He put his hands in his pockets. "Only if you swear you won't try to talk her out of bargaining with me."

I stuck out a hand. "Agreed."

Robin clasped my hand in his and then pulled me flush against him. His other hand rose to stroke my cheek. "You foolish little lamb. What am I going to do with you?"

My heart thundered against my rib cage. "What is it you want to do?"

"Oh, all manner of wicked things." He sighed and stepped back. "For now, I suppose I'll need to find you some era-appropriate clothing. Wait here."

I lowered myself into the lone chair and held out my hands to soak up the warmth from the pot-bellied stove while running my plan through my brain again and again. It was risky. It might not work. But it was the best I had.

Robin returned with a sparrow brown woolen dress, a heavy gray wool cloak, and a checked brown bonnet. "So you aren't mistaken as a whore again."

"You're the one who said I was a whore!"

"Wishful thinking on my part. I know my lamb can't be bought." He chucked me under the chin.

"Do I want to ask where you lifted these from?" It was too cold to remove my leggings so I decided to leave them on beneath the bulky dress. I ducked behind the stove to remove my sweater, turning my back on Robin as I did.

"I have my sources." His voice sounded strained.

I chanced a look over my shoulder and was unsurprised to find him staring at me. "You could be a gentleman and turn your back."

"Where's the fun in that?" He winked.

The dress was heavy and scratchy but much warmer as the bulky fabric enveloped my cold flesh. I stepped out from behind the wood stove and reached for the cloak and bonnet.

"Ready?" Robin tucked a stray lock of hair behind my ear, his expression almost tender.

At my nod, he led me out the door and across the battered planks of wood that were the closest thing to a sidewalk the era had to offer.

We passed a church, a tavern, the post office, and a small country store that sold everything from bags of oats to fence posts to bolts of cloth. On the far side of the street, there stood a smithy, a row of stables, and the original town hall. Every building was made from the same log-style construction and only the church and the store had glass windows.

"It's so strange," I murmured as I followed in Robin's wake. "It's my town but at the same time it is nothing like my town."

"What a difference a few centuries can make. Personally, I am a fan of indoor plumbing." He held his nose as we passed an outhouse. And I thought the manure smelled rank.

A stray snow shower sprinkled down on our heads and I was absurdly grateful for the ugly bonnet as we left the center of town, heading down the street toward a few lone cottages. I had to lift my skirt to keep it from dragging in the muck and displaying my not era-appropriate shoes.

"I have a question." My breath huffed out in a cloud of smoke as I struggled to keep up with Robin. At least his clothing aided movement instead of restricting it.

"What's that, lamb?"

I snagged his arm and pulled him to a stop. "How come you haven't called in your favor yet?"

He stared down at me, his blue gaze intense. "I haven't decided what I want that favor to be."

"Why not? I thought you picked women based on your need as well as theirs. What were you originally intending for me?"

His gaze darted away and he began walking again. "It doesn't matter now."

Stop feeling sorry for him, the sensible shrew muttered. *He's sold women, enthralled them, and traded them for favors.*

She was right. I knew it and yet I also knew that Robin was lonely. His own mother banished him from her presence. His bargains and playful attitude hid the reality that he was condemned to live a long life with no one to share it. Other than Clara who hated and resented him.

"You wanted me to be your anchor, didn't you." I asked. "To take Clara's place."

His lips parted. He licked them and then looked away. "How did you guess?"

I shrugged. "Because it's what I would want. A friend to be a companion instead of someone who was constantly trying to undermine me. Who hated the sight of me."

He swallowed. "But I can't have that."

"Why not?" My heart pounded.

"Because you would be just as indignant over my bargains as she is. Probably more so. You'd grow to hate me." He continued walking and muttered, "It's my destiny, to be forever alone."

I knew how that felt. Two timelines, no true partner. But at least I had a family to lean on.

Speaking of which. Robin stopped and pointed. Up ahead a cottage sat beside a babbling stream. Though it appeared much different than in my own time I recognized the spot instantly.

"This is where Grammy B's house sits. Will sit, I mean." I hadn't realized how long my family had owned that piece of property.

Robin paused and stared at the place. "It's been over two hundred years and it looks exactly as it does in my memories."

The light from within flickered and a woman's figure moved past the window. "Is that her?" I asked Robin.

When he nodded, I took a step forward and then another.

"Where are you going?" His tone was filled with panic.

"To talk to her of course."

"But you said you wouldn't."

I turned to face him. The waxing moonlight caught in his sapphire irises. "You don't want me to warn her? Then make that my favor."

Robin blinked. "What?"

"My end of the bargain is that I won't talk Clara out of bargaining with your echo self."

"You won't." Robin shook his head as though unable to believe I would be so reckless. "You have too much to lose."

I shrugged. "Robin, I'm a middle-aged woman. I am used to losing. What doesn't kill you makes you stronger. Do you really want to find out if I'm bluffing?"

He prowled closer. "I could take you away from here. Sell you to one of my kind."

"Is that what you want to do?" I searched his face.

Slowly he shook his head.

I paused the same way I did before doing a rigorous move during a floor routine. "Then make the favor that I won't talk Clara out of bargaining with you."

"You don't know what you're asking," he pleaded. "The next one—"

"Her name is Ursula," I snapped. "Not the next domino you have set to fall. That's right, she's not in a bargain with you. So this is it. Either you let me wreck the timeline or you go back to where you came from, bargain less."

"I thought we were friends." His tone was quiet and filled with a note I couldn't read.

A lump formed in my throat but I still managed to get the

lie out. "We can never be friends, Robin. Friends look out for each other, not just themselves."

Heartbeat. Heartbeat. Heartbeat. An eternity seemed to pass between the two of us, gazes locked, wills battling silently. Everything rode on his next move. On his choice.

Robin exhaled audibly. "Joey Whitmore, as a favor to me to finalize our bargain, I ask that you do not try to dissuade Clara from taking on her own bargain." He held out his hand.

I took it and gripped it hard. "Accepted."

Purple, blue, and gold swirls twined around our hands, sealing the magical pact. A world of emotion registered in his eyes. Fear, sadness, and what I thought was a glimmer of respect.

Robin vanished.

My hand fell to my side and I closed my eyes. That was harder than I'd imagined. Even with all he'd done, Robin had come to matter to me.

I moved down the hill. There was a split log bench beside Clara's front door. I tucked my feet up and wrapped my cloak around myself to conserve body heat. Then, there was nothing to do but wait.

I had made a promise. And Joey Whitmore kept them. But one thing that Robin had taught me very well. It's not what you vow, but what you don't vow that counts.

※

Hours passed. Inside the family had gone to bed. I could hear a child's occasional cough and the sound of a woman weeping. I wanted to knock, to go in and comfort her but I didn't dare leave my post. The house blocked the worst of the wind but my body was half-frozen when he arrived. A stranger in fine clothing with piercing blue eyes. He emerged out of nothing and nowhere. There was a soft shimmer, an ethereal wind and then he stood before me.

He looked so like my Robin that I felt a pang. But there was no spark of recognition in his gaze.

"I want to make a bargain," I said before he could speak a word. "With you."

He blinked and his full lips turned up in a predatory smile. "Do you now? What for?"

"The same as you came here to offer Clara." I shook out my skirts and got to my feet. "The life of her son for a favor."

He tipped his head to the side as though he were trying to puzzle me out. "Why would you do this?"

"Clara has a son to look after and protect. I don't have anyone." The people that would truly miss me were part of a timeline I could no longer reach.

Inside the house came another pitiful cough. It was now or never.

I took a step forward and put my hand on his chest. "I know that you need an anchor to stay here. She doesn't. I also know that part of you is decent. You don't really want to separate a loving mother from her only son, do you? Not when I can willingly serve the same purpose."

Again his gaze roved my face as though hunting for the trap. This earlier version of Robin was much warier than the one I knew. Was that because he had just come from the fae realm?

At long last, he offered his hand. "The bargain is struck, then."

I reached forward and shook. "The bargain is struck."

The clock in the center of town tolled midnight as the colorful swirls of the bargain broke free. But instead of the lulling swirls, I'd known from before, these were like razor blades cutting through me.

"What's happening?" Robin shouted. His gaze was wild

and he glared down at me with malice and fear. More so than when he'd been recalled. "Who are you?"

His genuine terror scared me more than anything else. My arms burned, and my heart pounded. I tried to withdraw my hand from his grip but they were sealed fast.

Colors swirled around me, pulling my feet from the ground. We spun in a circle, faster and faster. My gorge rose and I barely kept from retching.

Then the colors exploded and left me floating in the void. My sight dimmed to a pinprick and I knew no more.

CHAPTER NINETEEN

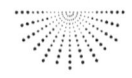

"All's well that ends well. Hogwash. Nothing ever really ends except in faery tales."
-Notable quotable from Grammy B.

Yellow light danced just beyond my eyelids. I groaned and rolled over, burrowing down deeper into the warm embrace of my comforter. The tick of the radiator, the sound of the water in the pipes from my bathroom. Familiar morning sounds.

Then a young female voice accompanied by a tap on a door. "Joey?"

I opened my eyes just as Dragon walked into the room. "Hey, I thought you were going to drive me to school. Did your alarm not go off?"

Disoriented, I pushed myself upright and took in my surroundings. Same room as always. From downstairs the smell of coffee and the sound of Patsy Cline belting out the lyrics to *Walkin' After Midnight*.

Dragon scowled at me. "Is everything all right?"

"What day is it?" My throat was dry and full of frogs.

"Um, Wednesday. My first day of school, remember?" She squinted at me as though trying to locate my damage.

I let out the longest breath of my life. I was back where I belonged. Fat ass, broken nose, throbbing wrist, the entire Joey Whitmore package. I was even wearing my fuzzy flannel pajamas, not some slinky nightgown. Back in my room. In my life.

I bounded from the bed and rushed to my cousin. Plucking her up like a daisy, I spun her around in a circle, laughing with giddy relief. No dysentery or whoring in the seventeenth century for this chick!

"Are you all right?" Dragon asked as I set her down.

"Better than all right. And yes, I'll drive you. Just let me find something decent to wear."

"All right. I'll just wait downstairs." Dragon ducked out of the room her brows still pulled down as though wondering if I was on the verge of mental collapse.

I pirouetted to my dresser and yanked opened my top drawer, sighing in relief when I spied the cheap yoga pants and tank tops. Not a single piece of designer clothing. I dressed in plain cotton underwear and bra, a black pair of pants, and pulled a white long-sleeved v neck tunic over the top then layered a red wooly vest on top of that. I twisted my hair up and snapped a clip over the top of it to hold it in place. A pair of chunky socks followed by a quick glance in the mirror. My reflection was grinning like a fool. I was back, baby.

I thundered down the stairs and almost ran smack dab into my mother. She wore a smock to protect her clothes and I breathed yet another sigh of relief when I saw that her left hand was blessedly ring-free. "Oh, Joey. I wanted to talk to you about yesterday."

"Later," I said. I was about to rush past her when a thought dawned on me. "Mom, are you going out with Paul later?"

Her delicate eyebrows drew together. "Yes, we were going to see a movie."

"Sounds good," I breathed. "Just do me a favor and don't get married."

"I wasn't planning on it." She sniffed in indignation. "And don't forget to put gas in the car!"

After snagging my coat, purse, and snow boots I headed outside to where Dragon already had the car idling. Smart kid.

"You want to drive?" I bent over the door to ask.

"I don't have my permit," she looked interested though.

I winked at her. "I won't tell if you won't. And the roads are plenty dry."

She thought about it for a beat then shook her head. "But maybe I can go get my permit later this week?"

"Sounds good to me." It would motivate me to spring my VW just so that Dragon had something cooler than mom's unreliable POS to drive around town.

We headed over to the school, Dragon worrying a hangnail and me so wound up it wouldn't have been too surprising if I jumped out of my skin.

My cell rang just as we were pulling into the parking lot. I fished it out of my pocket and was relieved to see Darcy's drunken countenance appear. "Hey, I am so glad to hear from you!"

"Okay, weirdo. I just talked to you last night," Darcy said. "You want to come over for coffee?"

"Meet me at Grammy B's. I'm bringing Dragon to school then I have a stop to make." I needed to see my grandmother and Darcy desperately. It's absolutely true what they say, you don't know what you've got until it's gone.

With a grin in place, I walked my cousin into her first day of school. Principal Mott stood at the door, looking only a little bit grayer than she had in 1996. "Ms. Whitmore."

"This is my cousin, Dragon." I put my hand on the girl's shoulder. "It's her first day."

"Is that so. Well welcome, Dragon. The first thing we need to do is go to the office and get your schedule."

"You okay?" I nudged her in the ribs. She looked at me and then nodded once.

"Good to see you, Joey." Principal Mott nodded at me. "You're looking well."

"I've never been better." With a final wave and a promise to pick Dragon up at three-thirty, I headed back to my car.

I drove into town and parked in a space in front of dad's office. No parking deck, just the small stately building. I spied him through the window, phone pressed to his ear. I exited the car, blew him a kiss, and then marched to my destination.

Alina stood, hands on nonexistent hips, and scowled at the team of workers that were installing some mirrors. "Not there. Where is your head, up a goat's ass?"

I tapped her on the shoulder and she slowly turned her attention on me.

"I got fat," I told her.

She stared at me, both eyebrows raised as though my admission surprised her. Of course with Alina, it was hard to tell until she had you trapped beneath a car.

I pushed on. "No more back handsprings or saltos for me. But I know I can be healthy again if you help me. And I can help you run this place. Make it a little more inviting and a lot more profitable. So you can do what you were born to do and train champions while I help everyone else."

She rounded on me, all-powerful compact muscle. "And

this is the Joey Whitmore I am remembering. To do or die in the trying. You will work here, yes."

"Yes. Gymnastics is what I was born to do," I told her. That was the only part skinny Joey seemed to have gotten right. The piece that was missing from my existence. My bad luck hadn't come from an accident or because I'd missed out on making the Olympic team. It came about because I'd turned my back on my purpose. As Alina had said, to do or die trying. I didn't need a gold medal. I just needed to love the sport and immerse myself in it as much as I possibly could.

Alina raised her chin, her blue eyes flashing and, thankfully, bloodshot free. "You start tomorrow, yes? Help me unpackage the equipment."

I pressed my lips together to keep from remarking on how that sounded. "I'll be here at eight."

❄

"Unpackage the equipment," Darcy wheezed and wiped tears from her eyes. "Holy hell, I wish I had heard her say that. And she has no idea that it sounded like a free-for-all event at a marital aide party?"

"None whatsoever." We stood on the front steps to Grammy's house. On the same spot where Clara's house had once been. Where a member of our family should always reside.

I used the key to let myself in. Immediately comforted by the sweet scent of cinnamon potpourri. Grammy B shuffled out wearing her customary tracksuit and pink slippers. It took all of my willpower not to pick her up and squeeze the stuffing out of her.

"Joey. And Darcy too. What are you girls doing here?"

"We came to have coffee with you. I brought a crumb cake." Darcy held the box aloft.

Grammy's gaze lit up. "Well don't just stand there. Come on in."

We shucked coats and dumped purses before I headed into the kitchen to brew a pot of java.

"So, what's new with you, Darcy? Been a dog's age since I've seen ya." Grammy B asked my friend when we were all settled around the table with a mug of coffee and a slice of cake.

"Between the business and my kids, I've been swamped," Darcy said. "I decided I needed a mental health day before the storm rolls in tonight."

"Storm?" I raised a brow.

"Haven't you been paying attention to the news? We're going to get two to three feet starting at midnight. The kids will be out of school for the rest of the week. And here you are about to get a new job and leave me in the lurch." Darcy looked a little crazed by the thought.

"You can always ask Dragon. If school is canceled, she might be willing to help."

"Only if she's a masochist," Darcy grumbled good-naturedly.

I reached across the table and grabbed Grammy's knobby hand. "I found out something interesting. Did you know that Grandpappy's great great great great grandmother Clara originally lived on this property before the Revolutionary War?"

Grammy B squinted at me. "Well, I'll be. I knew his family owned this land for a good spell of time, but I had no idea how long."

"It was a one-room log cabin," I added.

Darcy shuddered. "I can not imagine how people survived in such close quarters, especially in the winter. Most of the time it feels like the kids are hanging all over me. I'm lucky when I can shower without someone busting in to use the toilet."

We chatted for another hour before Grammy said she needed a rest.

Darcy and I snagged our coats but then I turned to my friend and said, "Go on, I'll be right behind you."

I settled Grammy in her chair with a blanket and the remote as well as her cell phone.

"Where's your kitty today?" Grammy asked.

"Home. Her real home. I found out where she belongs."

She smiled. "You're a good girl, Joey."

"Grammy," I said. "Do me a favor and try to be nicer to Mom when she comes by later. You're the most important person in her whole world, you know."

"Think you got that backward. You are her world. Mine too." She patted my cheek and pretended not to see the tears that lined my eyes.

"Where did you hear about all that?" Darcy asked me as we stood by her car. "Your great however many times grandma Clara, I mean?"

"Straight from the cat's mouth."

"Huh?"

I shook my head. "Never mind."

Darcy asked, "We on for Wine Wednesday later?"

"Hell yes." I pulled her into a great big bear hug and held on tightly. "My life just isn't the same without you. And maybe we should invite Ursula. Oh, and Georgia, too. Make it a real girls night."

"I'm cool with Georgia…but Ursula? Are you cracked or just smoking it?" She shuddered at the thought.

"She's been through a lot. And I think she could use a few friends."

"She'll probably tell us to go to hell." Darcy cautioned.

"Probably." I agreed. "But we still ought to ask. It sucks to feel alone all the time, to know you don't have any real friends to turn to when shit hits the fan."

Darcy studied my face. "What's gotten into you?"

"I promise, I will explain it all later. Over wine." I climbed behind the wheel and headed out to Firefly Lane.

The car bounced and bumped along the road the same way as it had every time I'd visited. I stopped well before the slope of the hill, engaged the parking brake, and headed up the rest of the way on foot. My heartbeat hammered against my chest as I made the ascent, not sure what to hope for.

The tree stood there, but it was only a tree. No magic house, no swirls of gold or purple, or anything remotely magical.

I walked around it, letting my fingers trail over and over the solid trunk. Questions filled my mind. What had happened to Robin? Had he made peace with his mother? And more importantly, had he ever really existed at all?

In the bright light of a winter afternoon, it was easier to imagine that it had all been a chaotic and involved dream. I mean magic hairbrushes and trips through time didn't happen to women like me.

Yet I felt different. Changed.

Whether Robin Goodfellow was real or imagined, he'd come into my life at the absolute lowest point. He'd given me confidence and helped me find my path. Whatever his intentions had been, if he was some figment that had represented all the men who had ever let me down, at the end of the day he'd helped me. He'd been kind to me, flirted with me, and helped me figure out who I wanted to be when I grew up. He'd shown me what truly mattered.

"Thank you for everything," I touched the tree and pictured his sapphire eyes and luscious lips.

"Oh, you're very welcome, lamb." A familiar male voice

said from behind me. "And don't forget, I will be collecting that debt."

I whirled around, my heart pounding against my ribs. There he stood. Back in the same denim and flannel outfit, he'd worn the first time I'd seen him. Devastatingly handsome with the mischievous gleam in his eyes.

"Robin!" I threw myself at him and held him tight. "I was so worried about you."

His tone was flat. "Somehow, I find that hard to believe."

After an awkward moment, I realized that he wasn't hugging me back.

"What's wrong?" I stepped away, chilled by more than the wind cutting through my coat. "Are you upset with me?"

"Upset? Why would I be upset?"

Was that a trick question. "Um, because I weaseled out of our bargain?"

"I'm actually very proud of you. But like you said, we were never friends. You tricked me and found a loophole to nullify not just Clara's bargain, but every other one I've made for more than two and a half centuries. It's sort of difficult for me to stay on the mortal plane when my anchor *hadn't been born*." His voice rose in volume until the final words echoed off the mountains.

I lifted my chin. "If you expect me to apologize—"

That wicked gleam appeared in his eyes. "Of course not. What I expect is for you to uphold your end of the bargain. To be my anchor and to do me a favor."

My teeth sank into my lower lip. "You figured something else out that you wanted from me then?"

He moved closer, his step an odd combination of seduction and menace. "Lamb, I have had two hundred and fifty years to consider the possibilities. I have literally had nothing but time and when my own echo self from 1769 caught up and I realized what you had done, well, let's just say I am *beyond* ready to cash in a favor."

I swallowed. That didn't sound promising at all. "So, what exactly does this favor entail? Enslavement? Torture?"

"Of the most acute kind." His lips turned up and my heart flipped over in my chest. "Because in one month's time, Joey Whitmore, you will become my wife."

He vanished without another word.

My jaw dropped. His wife? Was he nuts? He was a fae prince!

And I was…well, I was pretty frigging awesome. I was a time-traveling faery godmother. And if I didn't want to marry Robin Goodfellow, then I wouldn't. He could just pick another favor or go kick rocks. *Ever hear of free will buddy?* The sensible shrew snarked.

My feet took me back to the car. There was a spring in my step and a smile on my face. Robin was all right. Pissy, sure, but hale and healthy. And I was relieved. Even excited because he would be back in a month. *Sounds like a date to me.*

I was back to competing in life. The judges were ornery and biased. All I had to lean on was myself.

And whatever the personal cost, I was prepared to stick the landing.
~The End!

Feeling the need for more faery shenanigans? Buy The Fae Side of Forty, *book 2 in the Magical Midlife Misadventures series now!*

IT'S NOT MY WORDS THAT COUNT. IT'S YOURS!

Please consider leaving an honest review for this book. Reviews help readers like you select the kind of books they like and help authors like me sell books to the right readers. I found one of my favorite series from a two star review.

Thank you for reading!

Jennifer L. Hart

ABOUT THE AUTHOR

USA Today bestselling author Jennifer L. Hart writes about characters that cuss, get naked, and often make poor but hilarious life choices. A native New Yorker, Jenn now lives in the mountains of North Carolina with her imaginary friends. Her works to date include the Damaged Goods mystery series and the Magical Midlife Misadventures.

Subscribe to Jenn's author newsletter, Hart's Hitlist.

Printed in Great Britain
by Amazon